Stolen at First Sight

Renee Wilde

Literary Wanderlust | Denver, Colorado

Published in the United States by Literary Wanderlust LLC, Denver, Colorado. www.LiteraryWanderlust.com

ISBN print: 978-1-956615-48-7
ISBN digital: 978-1-956615-50-0

Printed in the United States of America

Dedication

To Grandma

Chapter 1

"Oh, my—" Millie could feel her eyes rolling back as the man's tongue caressed her nub in a way that most men had to be taught. "God!" she shouted when he slid two fingers inside her, and she felt herself quiver around him. He laid a trail of small kisses on her belly as he traveled back up to nuzzle his face into her neck.

"Mildred," he whispered, and Millie felt her lip wrinkle as she recoiled from both the sentimental tone of his voice and the use of her full name.

"That was lovely, er, Peter, is it?" she said as she rolled over and grabbed her dressing gown from the chair near the bed. She wrapped herself in it and went to throw another log on the fire. "Now, if you don't mind, it's been a bit chilly these nights, and..."

Peter, if that was in fact his name, stood and began fastening the laces on his breeches. "Chilly indeed," she heard him mutter. She pretended to busy herself with her toilette, running a brush through her hair with her back to him, while he finished getting dressed. She could still feel the languorous warmth in her belly from their activities, but now she was sleepy more than anything.

Peter had been quite amusing, and quite talented, so she decided she would keep his card, but the nuzzle had frightened her a bit. Millie enjoyed men, had many lovers, but she was appalled by sentimentality. It wasn't that she didn't believe in love. Her closest friend in the whole world was blissfully happy, and with a Duke no less, but Millie just didn't see it for herself. Entanglements hampered one's freedom, and she was quite enjoying her freedom. Living modestly in Bloomsbury on the income from her former employer Annelise Heatherington's career as an actress, singer, and courtesan, in the house Annelise's daughter had given her afforded Millie the kind of lifestyle most women could scarcely imagine. She was free to sing, free to paint, free to plan her future, and free to take anyone she liked into her bed.

The thing was, she liked that relationship to *stay* in the bed. She sighed as she heard Peter's footsteps approaching behind her. She set the brush down on its mirrored tray and turned, pasting a very fake smile on her face, trying to remember to be kind.

"Peter," she said, taking his hands. "It was a lovely evening. I'd be happy to repeat it sometime."

She watched as Peter's lips flattened into an almost-frown. "Sure," he said. He looked past her at the mirror behind her on the dressing table and picked up her brush, running it through his disheveled blond hair. She put a hand on his shoulder and gave him a pat. He looked down at her and the frown was fully visible now.

"They told me about you, Millie," he said, shaking his head. "The Ice Maid of Bloomsbury, they called you."

She laughed. "A personality carefully cultivated, I assure you."

He narrowed his eyes a bit. "We could be friends," he said, lifting his voice toward a question at the end.

Now she let her smile become patronizing. "I have plenty of

friends," she replied. "I don't bed them."

"Don't you want something more?" he said, gesturing around him. "Don't you get lonely?"

"Oh, Peter," she said, "If only you knew. I've never been happier to be alone." She stood and helped him with his coat before coaxing him to the door. "I did mean what I said, though...you have certain skills that should not go to waste."

He snorted. "You know I'll be back, Ice Queen."

She smiled and closed the door behind him, returning to her dressing table near the fire. She sat, picked up the silver-backed brush again and began absently running it through her hair. She stopped as she saw her reflection in the mirror. She looked like she'd just had a delicious orgasm. Her cheeks were flushed; her curls, tight and black as night, stuck straight out from her head where they'd come loose from their pins. She looked and felt thoroughly satisfied. Something Peter had said did echo in her mind, though. Not the "aren't you lonely" part. That was preposterous. She had many friends and relished the solitude and obscurity of the house that had been her home for so long. No, it was the "don't you want something more" that niggled at her, forcing her to admit that she *had* been stagnating here. It had been two years since Anne had married the Duke of Sutcliffe and given Millie the house in Bloomsbury. Two years she had been living a life of leisure and, well, if she were honest, some dissipation. She deserved it after a childhood in the streets of Venice, half-starved and always chasing her mother's dreams of love, before watching her waste away and finally succumb to the whore's disease that the chase had left her with.

Coming to Bloomsbury with her mother's colleague, Annelise Heatherington, had been a huge step, even though she had come first as a lady's maid. Annelise had been willing to raise her along with her own daughter, Anne, but Millie had no desire to live that life. A life in the shadows, living in the servants' quarters, comfortable, fed, and out of the spotlight, had appealed to her more than anything then. And even still, neither Anne nor her mother had ever treated her like a servant. Now, since Anne's marriage, Millie had moved into the family rooms of the house, but it was the same home it had always been. She, though, wasn't quite the same woman. She was starting to face the fact that she was growing, and the comfort of the Bloombsbury house was starting to feel a bit stifling.

She stood and wrapped her dressing gown more tightly about her, tying it at the waist. She pulled her wild curls back on top of her head and secured them with a comb. As she wandered the room, picking up articles of clothing, she found Peter's cravat. Drat. Had he left that on purpose, so he'd have to come back for it? She knew many women who'd used that trick successfully on any number of occasions, but she'd had yet to find a man who'd try it. She raised an eyebrow with a new grudging respect for this Peter of the magic tongue, but she threw the cravat in with the rest of the washing. She went to the door and called for her maid, Yvette.

"*Oui, oui,*" Yvette huffed, coming up the stairs quite out of breath. Her beautiful blonde hair hung about her shoulders, one of which was bare from the way her night dress had been hastily thrown on without tying the laces.

Millie laughed. "I believe I interrupted something," she said knowingly.

Yvette rolled her eyes. "I guess I didn't," she said, poking her head cautiously into the room before coming in.

"Just another Saturday night in Bloomsbury, I suppose," Millie sighed. "Will you take this washing out?" She paused, then narrowed her eyes shrewdly at Yvette. "Then feel free to get back to your, ahem, *lady.*"

Yvette laughed saucily. "You don't have to tell me twice," she said, picking up the basket with the laundry and then backing out of the door.

Millie went to the little cabinet next to the bed and withdrew a bottle of claret and a cut crystal glass. She watched the burgundy liquid swirl around and catch the light from the fire, then downed the glass in one gulp before pouring another. She had wished Yvette might stay and have a chat. They usually did chat in the evening before bed, but obviously Yvette had more important things to attend to this evening, and Millie didn't begrudge her that one bit. Still, Peter's voice echoed as the night closed in.

Don't you get lonely?

When Millie awakened, it was from a deep and troubled sleep. The empty crystal glass had fallen from her hand and rolled across the carpet. That must have been the crash that woke her, she thought, her head throbbing and groggy from the claret. She sat up, one hand pressed against her forehead, and tried to peer at the clock above her fireplace. In the dimness she couldn't quite see the position of the hands, but the embers in the fireplace had died almost all the way down, so she knew it must be the wee hours. Maybe four? Around half past four, one could start to hear the carts making kitchen deliveries, and everything was silent.

There it was again. It wasn't a crash—it was more of a rattle. Not very loud now that she could hear it more clearly. Perhaps Yvette had come back upstairs for something? Millie was still wearing her dressing gown, so she stood and gathered it more tightly around her waist. It was quite chilly now that the fire had burned down, and it was extremely dark. She crept her way across the room and put another log on the dying fire, then turned to go back to bed when she heard the rattling again. She realized it was coming from the room next to hers, Anne's old room. She frowned quizzically and called out, "Yvette?"

She stayed still, almost breathless, waiting for Yvette to respond, and when she didn't, Millie became slightly concerned for the first time. A little shiver went up her spine, and she pulled the light fabric of the dressing gown about her again, as if to armor herself against the fear she had begun to feel.

She shook her head and straightened her back, striding confidently toward the door, her bare feet making no sound on the thick carpet as she moved. She told herself it was silly to be alarmed. The noise could be any number of things. It could be a mouse in the wardrobe in Anne's old room, or Yvette sleepwalking, or even a woodpecker. It really could be anything.

She reached her hand to the doorknob and hesitated just for a moment before pulling the door all the way open and stepping into the broad, thick chest of a man.

"Good God," she cried at the same moment that the man muttered a low, harsh curse. She tried to back up, but he had taken her by her shoulders. She was so close to him that she had to crane her neck to look up at him, though he was not that much taller than she, and she soon discovered it did little good since the top half of his face was covered by a black silk kerchief with holes for the eyes. Still, she could feel his piercing glare inspecting her.

"I was told this house was empty," he growled.

"Well," Millie said, and she couldn't help the wry annoyance in her voice, despite the danger she imagined she might be in, "You were obviously misinformed."

The man laughed and then leaned down until his lips almost grazed her ear. "You don't sound afraid," he said in a whisper.

Millie inhaled sharply at his nearness. The scent of him, musky but also a little sweet, like vanilla. Why *wasn't* she afraid?

"No, not afraid," she whispered. "Annoyed." She took a step back. "What are you doing in my house? We don't get a lot of cat burglars in Bloomsbury." She crossed her arms over her chest and cocked her head at him, eyebrows raised.

"I do apologize," he said, and he had the absolute nerve to give her a gallant little bow. "I was told there was no one in residence here."

"As you said," she bit off in response. "But you see, you were mistaken." She gestured to herself, a little up and down wave of her hand.

He sighed. "Yes, that's quite a quandary for me."

She snorted. "Me, too," she said. "You see, you have the advantage. You are fully dressed, and totally incognito, yet here I stand, in dishabille, and you obviously must know who I am."

He shook his head, pressing his lips together in a slight frown. "Well, there you have me. I do not have any idea who you are. I don't know who hired me, either." He shrugged. "The fewer questions, the better. I was sent for..." his lips pressed closed, seeming to think better of continuing that thought.

Millie narrowed her eyes and looked at him sidelong. "What could anyone want with anything here?" she said. It was a comfortable, cozy, and lovely house in a nice artistic neighborhood, but there was certainly nothing here of any great value, save the sentimental sort.

The man shrugged again. "Like I said, the less I know, the better."

"Well, then, can I kindly ask you to get the hell out of my house now?" Millie asked.

He laughed and stepped back, lifting his hands almost as if surrendering to her. "Naturally," he said, giving her that little mock-gallant bow again. Now that he was a little further away and her eyes had become used to the darkness, she could more fully see his powerful form in the dim starlight. He wasn't tall or particularly broad, but she could see his shape clearly. His frame narrowed to a lean waist, neatly wrapped in a band of the same black silk as his mask. He wore the usual breeches and shirt, again all black, but no waistcoat or coat, and instead of the usual polished Hessians she was used to seeing on men, he wore soft, almost slipper-like shoes, also black. His entire look was designed to evade detection, and Millie found herself fascinated despite herself, especially since he had made it so clear that he had no intention of harming her. She wondered if he was even in the right house, but she wasn't about to ask and give up any of her own information.

"You certainly look the part of the cutpurse," she said, the corners of her mouth quirking.

The man flinched as if she'd smacked him. "Burglar, my lady, if you please. A cutpurse is a filthy cur, preying on people's sense of safety and their obliviousness."

Millie raised her eyes. "You don't think I felt safe in my own home? Only to discover a *burglar* preying on that sense of safety?"

He smiled and nodded, acquiescing to her point. "Quite right, and I do apologize for that, as I've said repeatedly—I am not in the habit of entering occupied homes."

She set her lips in a grim line. "Fair enough," she said, narrowing her eyes, "But you never did tell me what you were looking for. Or am I not allowed to ask?"

He laughed. "You most certainly are not. You see, my stock in trade is discretion." He touched two fingers to his forehead as if tipping a hat to her. "And with that, my dear lady, I must make my leave."

She laughed and stood aside, motioning him past her. "You may go out the front entrance this time," she said. As he brushed past her in the hallway, she could smell him again, that same sweet, earthy smell. She must still be feeling the claret, she thought wryly. She almost felt attracted to this *burglar*. When he had just passed her, he turned, and she could see his eyes, though it was too dark to make out the color shining behind that mask. He held her gaze for a long moment before he winked and then disappeared down the stairs.

Millie felt herself slump back against the wall, as if all the air had been sucked from the room. She took a deep breath in, then straightened and tried to walk as steadily as she could back to her bedroom. The fire was roaring now, and there was a warm glow in her bedchamber, but as she loosened the belt around her dressing gown and turned to her bed, it seemed as cold and unwelcoming as it ever had. She sighed and removed the dressing gown, climbed under her coverlet, and finally drifted into a restless sleep.

~*~

Jack rounded the corner to the alley before slumping back against the cold gray stone of the house. He felt as if his breath had been completely knocked from him. There were plenty of nights he'd almost wished for some burly guard to find him— he'd been itching for a fight lately if he were being honest. But being caught by a woman threw him. She was certainly not a girl, though she was small, several inches shorter than he. No, she was a woman, through and through. In contrast to her petite stature, she had a touch of the wild about her, from the untamed curls piled loosely on her head and falling out of the comb she'd tried to master them with, to the remnants of what appeared to be a love bite on her neck. He wondered who she was. She was clearly the mistress of the house, but he had been told the house was vacant since the new Duchess of Sutcliffe had left. And, though the woman he'd just met appeared to be supremely confident and unruffled, there was something about her that made him immediately understand she was also no duchess.

Jack shook his head as if to clear his thoughts, and stood straight once more, pushing off from the wall with his slippered foot. No, certainly no duchess, he thought, and that was precisely what he liked about her. He heard a clattering of a cart coming up the street out front and realized it must be almost time to meet VanHinkel. He cursed to himself and set off at a light run through the shadowy alleyways to find a hack that could take him to Vauxhall.

As he rode through the streets, dawn started to break, and the city became alive. He absolutely loved this time of day. He used to love seeing it upon waking earlier than anyone in his house, when he'd creep downstairs and then run through the fields, sometimes in summer just in his breeches, training his body to go faster and faster, further and further. He'd be home, washed, and at the breakfast table before anyone else in the house was awake. He'd relished those times when he could be the most free. Now, the only way to be free was to completely run away from everything he'd known in his former life, and that included seeing the dawn from the proper side. He saw the soft light of sunrise only after a long sleepless night of sneaking and hiding, and frankly, he wasn't sure which he preferred more. At least he had no one to answer to, no one to explain his whereabouts to, no one poking around looking for him. His valet and his cook were the only humans he ever saw more than once, and they, like him, were the pictures of discretion. He'd made sure of that. He'd also made sure that even they didn't know who he really was.

The hack pulled up short in Vauxhall, right near the pleasure gardens. Jack threw a coin up to the driver, then rapped on the side to signal he could leave. He walked past the entrance to the gardens, where brightly dressed men and women were still spilling out into the street after a night of fun. Some walked, but most stumbled. Jack turned away from them, disgusted. He'd never been able to abide anyone who couldn't hold their drink. These people were shells of themselves, really, and he had no sympathy for them at all. He rounded the corner and saw VanHinkel sitting on a short barrel, tapping his foot and checking his watch fob, waiting for him.

He came forward and nodded to the man. He'd worked for several different clients since becoming a burglar, and he'd liked very few of them, and trusted even fewer. Even so, VanHinkel gave him more pause than most. The man was...distasteful, to say the least. He wore a greasy brown shirt, unbuttoned at the top, with no waistcoat. Jack squinted. He couldn't be sure the shirt was brown—it could have once been white. He stopped himself short of openly sneering.

"VanHinkel," he said. He took the little velvet purse from the bag connected to the sash he wore around his waist.

VanHinkel came forward, his eyes greedy.

Jack shook his head. "Not so fast. There's the matter of

payment?"

VanHinkel snorted. "You'll get your money, Jack Covert. I always pay my men."

Jack stepped back and held both his hands up, the velvet purse still dangling from his left. "I'll be the judge of that," he said curtly, then turned his right palm over, waiting.

VanHinkel sighed. "Very well." He reached into his pocket and pulled out ten shining gold guineas.

Jack nodded with approval. "I'll take these now, and the other forty, when you verify the goods."

"Aye, aye," VanHinkel said, his voice terse with impatience, "Now show it."

Jack pocketed the guineas and then pulled the little opening on the velvet purse before turning it over and emptying the contents onto his palm. In the light of day, the little locket, just a simple piece of worked tin with decorative scrolls scratched into its surface, seemed even more worthless than he'd thought. He didn't allow that thought to pass to his face, though. "Here it is. Is this what you were looking for?"

VanHinkel betrayed himself with a sharp intake of breath. "Yes, yes," he said, as he picked up the locket and turned it over in his hands. "Yes, it is indeed." The man stank of sweat and stale brandy, but Jack did not back away as he watched VanHinkel pop the little clasp on the side and open it up. In the locket lay only a few short locks of curled hair, rolled carefully in upon themselves so as to fit in the small space. VanHinkel laughed out loud then, "Yes, indeed it is, my boy." Almost absently, he reached into his pocket again and pulled out four ten-pound notes. He handed them over to Jack without so much as another glance in his direction, and Jack could feel the hairs on the back of his neck stand up. Why was this man so eager for a worthless locket with only hair inside? Jack narrowed his eyes, then stood up straight as he put the bank notes away.

"Pleasure doing business with you, VanHinkel," he said.

"Oh, of course," VanHinkel replied, and Jack was aware that VanHinkel barely registered his existence now, so intent was he on staring at that locket.

Jack made a big show of striding away and hailing a hack, but he only hopped in for one block, then got back out and circled his way back around Vauxhall Garden, leaping up to the roof of the storage shed near the alley, and creeping on his hands and knees until he could see VanHinkel from above. He waited, breathless and silent, for what seemed like hours, but the sun told him it was only about twenty minutes, until the sound of approaching footsteps caused him to sneak backward on the ledge to be sure he wasn't seen. His ears strained to hear everything going on below, but the sounds of the city waking made it difficult. He could tell right away that these men weren't VanHinkel's sort. They were clean, stealthy, and deadly looking. And they wore black silk masks just as he did.

The black-clad men talked in low voices that Jack couldn't quite make out, but he heard VanHinkel's voice loud and clear and sinister when he pulled out the locket. "We found her, all right," he said.

Jack felt the hair on the back of his neck stand on end. All along he believed the locket he'd been asked to procure was some trifle of the new Duchess's. He'd had no compunction stealing her, just as he had no compunction from stealing from any of their ilk. Now that he'd left their life and made his way on his own, he had no patience or sympathy for the *ton* and their endless balls and parties. But these men couldn't be talking about the new Duchess of Sutcliffe. Everyone knew where she was, happily ensconced with her new baby in Sutcliffe House in Mayfair. They must be talking about the lady he'd met this evening. He surprised himself that he felt protective of the little thing. Though he'd been sure never to harm anyone in his pursuits, he also wasn't usually terribly concerned about their welfare otherwise. He flattened himself against the roof and crept toward the edge so he could hear what they were saying.

VanHinkel nodded. "As soon as possible," he said, nodding with a dark and knowing look.

"Aye," one of the men in black responded with a curt nod. "We can do it quick."

One of the other men held out a black-gloved hand, and VanHinkel placed a bank note in it. "This now, the rest when I read about it in the papers."

Jack recoiled, his stomach dropping. He'd known the men were up to something dark, but he hadn't quite believed VanHinkel to be capable of planning a *murder*. His thoughts turned immediately from what was happening below to the woman from Bloomsbury. He had to warn her. The men crept silently from the alley, and VanHinkel waited a few minutes before leaving himself, whistling as if he were a tradesman about his work. As soon as Jack watched the other man round the corner, he swung himself down from the roof, hanging deftly from the gutter, then dropped to the cobblestones below. He tore off his mask and the sash at his waist, then smoothed and combed his hair with his fingers before stepping into the street in front of Vauxhall Gardens. He hailed a hack and gave it the Bloomsbury address. He just hoped he wasn't too late.

Chapter 2

Jack realized just how tired he was when he found himself dozing off during what seemed the interminable ride back to Bloomsbury. Once the hack pulled up, though, his senses returned, sharp and alert. He hopped down and crept to the side of the house and back to the alley. There, he found the kitchen door wide open. He peered in. A tall, buxom blonde woman stood at the stove, humming to herself. Jack smiled as he recognized the bawdy tune she was singing. He straightened and knocked on the frame of the doorway.

The woman nearly dropped the coffee pot she'd just picked up from the stove, and Jack tensed as he saw the coffee threatening to spill over the side of the pot as she turned quickly. Though he'd clearly startled her, her expression was more annoyed than alarmed.

"*Oui?*" she asked.

Jack cleared his throat. Now that he was here, he wasn't sure what to say. *Can you tell your mistress the burglar needs a word?* That would never do. "Is your mistress awake yet?"

The maid snorted. "Highly unlikely," she said, her French accent light, but unmistakable. "That is who the coffee is for."

Jack took a deep breath. "It's imperative that I speak with her," he said, realizing how ridiculous he must sound.

The maid narrowed her eyes. "May I say who is calling? Most callers come in through the front door," she said, gesturing with her head toward the front of the house, as if speaking to a child.

Jack smiled in spite of himself. "Yes, I am fully aware that this is...unconventional. But I believe her life may be in danger."

The maid's spine straightened and her brow furrowed.

Jack continued, "It might be best if you brought her here, to the kitchen, that I might speak with her." The maid looked at him with narrowed eyes again, so he hastily added, "You are free to stay if you do not trust me." She nodded, satisfied with that, and wiped her hands on her apron as she left the room.

It seemed like long minutes before he heard footsteps on the stairs leading down to the kitchen, and every muscle tensed while he waited. When he finally heard the light tread of the two women, his shoulders eased, but he forced his eyes to continue surveying the alley from the doorway.

When the door opened, he could feel his breath catch just a little as the woman from the hallway appeared, this time in full daylight and wearing a simple green day dress, her dark hair piled on her head, though the curls were impossible to contain. Her eyes were the deepest, darkest brown he'd ever seen. She was small, but she didn't have the pale, simpering look of the ladies he'd known. Her skin was several shades darker than his own, and she had an air of the wild about her. Just now, that wildness was trained directly on him.

"Well, if it isn't my burglar," she exclaimed, hands on hips, no hint of a smile. Jack winced as the maid's shocked face turned to him.

"A *burglar*?" she asked. "You come into this house and ask to speak to my lady, *oui*?"

Jack nodded.

"And yet you are this...dangerous man?"

Jack shook his head. "No, not dangerous. I swear." He turned to the smaller woman, who met his gaze and held it, challenging him to look away. He decided to be direct. "When I showed my client what I'd taken, it looked utterly worthless to me, but he willingly handed me fifty pounds for it. This raised my suspicions, so I waited around to hear him hire two assassins to come and kill the resident of this house, which I assume to be you?"

He watched as both women's expressions moved from skepticism to alarm, and then back to skepticism.

The Frenchwoman was the first to speak up. "And we trust you? Yes? A common thief?" She crossed her arms over her chest.

The mistress of the house stayed quiet at first. She looked away and chewed her lip before she looked back at him, her gaze again holding his. He felt like her eyes were two pools of water at midnight. He could see his reflection and nothing else. Finally, she asked, "What was it? What was the worthless thing?"

Jack felt himself tensing with frustration as he tried to keep one eye on the alley to be sure the assassins weren't attempting their deed right now. He took a deep breath and replied, "A locket. An old piece of tin with locks of hair inside."

The woman drew a sharp intake of breath. "My mamma's locket," she said, looking at the maid, who nodded, her lips pursed tightly together.

"Mister...?" The young woman said, looking up at Jack, one eyebrow raised.

"Covert. Jack Covert," he said, tipping a hat that would have been there had he not rushed back to the house.

"Mr. Covert," she said, drawing her back up straight, "Thank you very much for bringing me this information. I can call my man to draw you up some banknotes for your trouble."

Jack just stared at her. He started to speak, then closed his mouth shut again. He felt his color rising. "I don't think you heard me," he said, trying to enunciate each syllable. "There are men coming here to kill you. Possibly *right now.*"

The woman's forehead furrowed. "Yes, I understand. They know who I am because they found my locket." She was so matter of fact about it. It was infuriating. "The trouble for them is, I have nothing of value in this entire house, but I have a tidy nest-egg in the bank." She shrugged. "They will come. I'll offer them some money, and that'll be the end of it."

Jack almost laughed. "Offer them some—" Then he did laugh, just a short little spurt, but he felt bad about it. "My lady—"

"I'm no lady." She cut him off, crossing her arms.

"Very well. What, may I ask, is your name?"

"You may call me Millie."

Jack frowned and felt the skin between his eyebrows tighten. He took another deep breath. "These men don't want valuables, *Millie.* It was clear to me that the most valuable thing in this house to them was the owner of that locket. And not alive."

He saw almost every emotion as it passed across that small brown face. Her pert nose twitched from side to side, her eyebrows worked furiously. She bit her bottom lip, then pursed them together before they flattened out once more. He knew then that this woman would be physically incapable of keeping a secret or telling a lie. For a man who did nothing but pretend every day, it was refreshing.

She sat down at the rough table in the kitchen and the blonde woman began pouring coffee into dainty little cups. All three of them sat down and cradled their drinks in silence until finally Millie spoke.

"Here's what we know. First, they know who I am, and it's not a mistake. My mother gave me that locket on her deathbed in Italy. I've never had much use for it as it was an ugly old thing and worthless, as you say. In fact, I'd forgotten that I even put it in Anne's jewelry box in her old room, long before she moved out."

Jack nodded, sipped his coffee, then narrowed his eyes to look at Millie. "Can you think of any reason anyone would want you dead?"

Millie and the blonde Frenchwoman looked at each other and laughed. The longer Jack was here, the more convinced he was that both of them were the most naïve, flippant women he'd ever met.

"Yvette," Millie said to her maid, "Do I have any enemies?"

"Oh *oui, mademoiselle,*" the maid said, still shaking with laughter. "The men you don't ask back?" She chuckled even as she lifted the coffee cup to her lips.

"Men. Are. Coming. Here. To. Kill. You," Jack said again. "You need to take this seriously."

Millie nodded. "Of course, you're right. I'm sorry, Mr. Covert," she said, still giggling a little. "As you can see, we find the idea of my having enemies absurd. I assure you, I have lived an extremely quiet life."

"What about the new duchess?" Jack asked. "Could this be connected to her?"

Again, Millie and Yvette looked at each other and smiles twitched on their lips but stopped themselves with another glance at Jack's serious face.

"Mr. Covert, Anne Marksbury is far *less* likely to have enemies than even I. The only enemy she ever had was her own self-doubt," Millie explained.

Jack nodded and looked around the room. It was a lovely, cozy, functional place. Clean as a whistle, slightly cluttered with all the things a kitchen would usually be cluttered with. By all accounts the house was a normal Bloomsbury home, occupied by an exotically beautiful little pixie and her Viking warrior maid. He grunted.

"You say there are spurned lovers?" he asked.

"Oh, no, not really," Millie said. "You know how men are. Some get attached, but most would rather be burned at a stake.

I go for the latter, and if I somehow end up with the former, I am always sure to let them down easy."

Jack started a bit at this frank examination of the woman's exploits. He was used to women who were as debauched as the men around them, but it was shocking to hear one speak about it openly. He'd only met her three hours ago, and she had already surprised him more than any woman he'd ever met.

"All right," he said, taking a last swig of his coffee and standing up. "We need to make a plan."

Millie stood up as well and faced him, her hands on her hips. "What *we*?" she asked. "Thank you for bringing us this information, but we'll take it from here." She motioned toward the door with her outstretched arm.

Jack felt his mouth gape open. "You can't be serious," he said, keeping his voice low and even. "I am not sure you understand what is happening."

Millie's eyes flashed. "Men. Are. Coming. Here. To. Kill. Me." she repeated, mocking his voice. "Did I get that right?"

Jack felt himself sputtering to find words. He could feel his mouth moving like a fish that had been pulled from the water, gasping for oxygen.

"I understand," Millie said, "And Yvette and I will take care of it." She motioned toward the door again. "I do thank you for warning me," she said, and her eyes softened now. "You didn't have to do that."

Jack grunted again. "I am a thief, not a murderer," he said. "But I imagine I know a bit more about this underworld and how they operate than you do."

Millie nodded. "It is for that reason that I feel it's best you go," she said. "I need to get to someone I can trust."

Jack felt like someone had punched him in the middle of his chest. He stopped breathing, and every muscle locked. Her response was perfectly reasonable, so why did it hurt him like a physical blow? Why did he care so much about what happened to this woman? She was so serenely confident, and why did that bother him? It seemed there was nothing left for him to do here. He had come to warn her, and he had accomplished his task.

He nodded and turned toward the door. "Miss Millie, Miss Yvette," he said, "best of luck to you." He meant it. He snuck back out into the alley and made himself disappear.

~*~

Millie set her coffee cup down and stood with both palms on the rough-hewn kitchen table. She and Yvette shared a solemn look, and they both walked to the door to see where Jack Covert had gone. There was no sign of him in the alley, which had started to become bustling with deliveries and servants' movements. Yvette closed the door and came back to clear the table. Millie took a towel to dry the cups and put them away after Yvette washed them in the basin.

"Now, Miss Millie, you know I can do that myself," Yvette said, chiding.

"I know," Millie said. "I just need to steady myself, and I need to think this over."

Yvette stopped washing to look right at Millie, her brows drawn together with concern. Millie felt uncomfortable and shifted her gaze. She knew Yvette was worried, and she also knew that she herself was far more worried than she wanted to let on. What Jack had said had sounded outrageous at first, but his concern was very clear. For a man who probably dealt with many unsavory characters in the underworld, he had looked *concerned*, and that had sent a chill down her spine. She took a deep breath and walked to set a cup in the cupboard. Her hands were shaking as she put the cup away, and it clinked slightly against the others. She heard Yvette stroll across the room before she grabbed Millie by the shoulders from behind. She felt almost dizzy as Yvette spun her around.

"All right, Mademoiselle," she said, her gray eyes snapping. "What are we going to do? We cannot stall. What if they are coming here right now?"

Millie stopped and nodded, swallowing before agreeing with Yvette. "Of course you're right. I think I should go to Anne."

Yvette nodded. "Now you are talking sense," she said as she pushed Millie toward the stairs. "Go freshen yourself up. I will call for the carriage."

Millie almost ran upstairs. Now that she had a purpose and a plan, flimsy though it was, she was grateful to move into action. Anne was still her closest friend, though it had been some time since they'd seen each other. Anne was so busy with the new baby and social obligations; their weekly tea and chat sessions had been on hold. Anne was that rare mother of the *ton* who insisted on nursing her daughter herself. Millie loved little Maggie but had wanted to give the new family some space. She wished she weren't running there now for the reason she was, but she had a feeling Anne would know what to do. She added a few pins to her already wild curls, grabbed her pelisse from the wardrobe, and donned her sturdy leather half-boots. She took down a warm bonnet and scarf and sailed down to the entry, where Mr. Scott was already waiting with her small carriage and two horses. He nodded at her and asked, "To Sutcliffe House, Miss?"

"Yes, thank you," Millie replied, "as quickly as ever you may, Mr. Scott."

Scott tipped his hat and winked. "Certainly, Miss," he said, hopping up to the seat and clucking to the horses.

As Millie's carriage wound its way through the city morning, she leaned her head back against the cushion and exhaled slowly. It was the first moment she'd had time to think since that rogue of a thief had shown up on her back doorstep. She realized it was even colder than she had thought. The winter so far had been mild, and the Christmas holidays had passed without so much as a flake of snow. But today it felt like a deep chill had settled in over the city. Or maybe, she thought, that was the fear that had begun to encircle her heart like a vise. She wondered what Jack Covert had to gain from warning her. Or could he have been working with the assassins and playing some sort of cat-and-mouse game with her? More importantly, who on earth could want her dead, and why?

It all hinged on that locket, she thought, but the locket itself was worthless, and she had never known whose hair was in it. Her mother had simply given it to her during her last long illness. She had not told her anything about the old metal trinket or indicated that it was terribly important. She had simply said, "I suppose it's time this belonged to you." Millie had just assumed that her mother was dividing her meagre possessions and thinking of what Millie would have after she had gone. She had thought there might be a miniature portrait inside and had been surprised to discover it was just a lock of hair—light brown, faded, and brittle from age. Millie had honestly never really thought of the locket again.

Now it centered on a truly dramatic turn of events. But why?

The carriage came up sharply on a beautiful street in Mayfair. Millie heard Scott jump down, but she already had the door open. "Thank you, Mr. Scott," she said over her shoulder as she ran up the stairs. "You may bring the carriage round to the stable." The coachman tipped his hat again, and Millie rapped loudly on the door of the imposing house with a large brass knocker.

When the door opened slowly, the butler stepped aside to let her through, so well-known was she in this house. She smiled at him and began to remove her gloves, bonnet, and pelisse. "I'm so sorry, but I need to see the Duchess immediately. It's a matter of some importance."

The butler nodded, took her things, handed them to a waiting footman, and disappeared up the stairs. Millie stood there in that cavernous entry hall, chewing her lip. What would she even say to Anne? How could Anne even help? Should she ask Anne to keep it secret, or should she include Jonathan? Should she have packed her things? Was she hoping to stay here? Was Yvette safely back at the house? Her mind and heart both raced a pace, almost as if they were in tune to each other, like wheels on a train. She closed her eyes and tried to take a deep breath, but finally she heard a door open upstairs.

"Millie?" Millie sighed. It was Anne's voice. She looked up and saw Anne all but flying down the grand staircase, a dressing gown pulled loosely about her night rail, her brown hair falling in disarray around her shoulders. She took no notice of her own appearance, but ran full bore at Millie, pulling her up in a tight hug.

"What has happened?" Even held tightly in Anne's embrace, Millie could hear the shrewd note of concern in her old friend's voice.

"Can we go somewhere else?" Millie gestured around the large, dark, empty entryway.

Anne took Millie's hand and practically pulled her up the stairs. "Of course. Maggie's just been fed. Come with me to my rooms."

Millie stopped mid-landing and squeezed Anne's hand. "Is Jonathan there?"

"Yes, he's playing with Maggie in the sitting room," Anne said, then Millie could see her eyebrows furrowing. "Why? Are you in some kind of trouble?"

"You could say that," Millie said, blushing. She was suddenly aware of how outlandish her story would sound. How would she even begin to explain it? She closed her eyes and tried to take a breath again.

Millie felt Anne squeeze her hand in both of her own. "We will say hello to Jonathan and retire into my bedroom," she said. "Come."

Once they opened the door to Anne's sitting room, Jonathan's eyebrows rose in surprise at seeing Millie there at such an ungodly hour, but one quick look from Anne and he simply nodded and said, "Good morning, Millie, I hope you're well," as he bounced Maggie on his knee.

She swallowed a nervous laugh and replied, "Yes, I am,

thank you." Anne ushered her into the bedroom, closing the door behind them.

Millie's story all but poured out of her as Anne sat on the end of the bed and Millie paced back and forth on the rug at the foot.

"This...this..." Anne sputtered. "This story is outrageous!"

Millie stopped and looked at her. "I know."

"Why on earth should we trust this thief?"

"I've wondered the same thing, and all I have to answer with is the concern he showed in coming back to warn me," Millie said.

"So you have said," Anne replied with a frown.

Millie took the few steps to sit beside Anne on the end of the bed. "I know it sounds incredible. But I am so scared. If he's right..."

Anne hugged Millie about the shoulder and said, "I'm afraid, too, honestly," she paused. "Though a thief is not a particularly trustworthy messenger, there's also absolutely no reason for him to lie about it."

Millie nodded. "Yes. In fact, he could have put his reputation as a burglar on the line by betraying his client."

"That is true, too," Anne chewed her lip and ran her hand through her disheveled hair. "I think you should stay here."

"I'm not sure that's wise," Millie said quietly. "What about Maggie? I can't endanger you all."

Anne nodded. "I know, but compared to the house in Bloomsbury, this place is a fortress. We can have Jonathan call up extra men to guard the perimeter."

Millie frowned. "I suppose just for a day or two."

"You're right," Anne said, as businesslike and capable as ever, "It's not a permanent solution, but right now there's no other one. We absolutely *must* find out what is so special about that locket."

~*~

Jack lay on his bed back in his own rooms, in desperate need of sleep, but utterly unable to conjure any. He'd closed his heavy velvet drapes and his valet, Stevenson, had left a tray of food and closed the door, but he hadn't been able to do much more than move the fish around on his plate or tangle himself up in his bedclothes with his tossing and turning. He couldn't get VanHinkel's face out of his mind. The way his eyes had opened wide, sparkling with glee when he'd said *the rest when I read about it in the paper*. Jack didn't care too much about what happened to the hoity-toity snobs of the *ton*, but Millie was obviously different. First, she lived in a quiet, modest house in the artistic enclave of Bloomsbury, and second, she hadn't been particularly concerned about the loss of the locket or even about finding a thief in her hallway in the small hours of the morning.

Against his will, Jack kept reliving that encounter over and over. He could see the firelight from her room reflecting in her eyes, so dark they were almost black. He could see those curls coming loose all over her head, looking in the dimness like some sort of lovely Medusa come to turn him to stone. She'd looked at him with such a strange mix of amusement and challenge. Even in the kitchen just a few hours earlier, though she'd obviously been shaken by what he'd said, there was no breaking down in hysterics or sudden emotional outbursts. She'd listened and then she'd asked him to leave. And what else could she have done?

With a wry smile to himself, Jack thought of his own mother, the only other woman he'd ever really seen in a crisis. The difference was his mother's crises had almost always been entirely of her own making. He'd seen enough dishes hurled across the paneled dining room, enough empty bottles of claret smashed on the parlor hearth, to know to simply stay away when a scene was coming. Luckily, he'd always had his father to escape with. They'd take a swim or practice fencing, and when they came back, Mother would be asleep. But as the years went on, things got worse and worse.

Jack rolled over again and pulled the pillow over his head. He needed sleep. He had another job tonight, and he knew very well that if he wasn't at his sharpest, things would be much more difficult. He could feel his head pounding at the very idea of another sleepless night. He tried to count to a hundred, but he reached forty-seven before the image of Millie from Bloomsbury popped back into his vision. He sat up. What had her plan been? Where had she gone? He just hoped to God she wouldn't be so stupid as to go to the Duchess. VanHinkel and the assassins knew about her association with Sutcliffe and his wife. He was sure he'd told her this. Had he? He sat up and ran a hand through his hair, then down across his face, thick and scratchy with stubble. He put his head in his palms and squeezed his eyes shut. *No*, he told himself, *you have to sleep. You did your best. You tried to help. Go to sleep.*

His breath was one long ragged curse as he stood and pulled the black silk shirt across his chest and began working the buttons. He rang the little bell by his bed and heard Stevenson's businesslike gait in the hall. The door creaked open, and Stevenson came in with a look of concern on his wan face. The man was the very soul of discretion, and that was what Jack valued most about him. But he was also fiercely loyal, something that made Jack extremely uncomfortable. He was hoping to live a life without entanglements of any kind, not even servants. He tried to sound uninterested as he asked the valet to find him a fresh pair of breeches and slippers, and to prepare some coffee.

"Right away, sir," Stevenson said as he pulled the door closed behind him.

Stevenson had been one of Jack's luckiest finds when he fled home. He'd arrived in London with nothing but the coin he could scrounge from his father's study. It had been enough to rent these modest apartments, and, through his new professional connections, he'd been introduced to Stevenson, a first-rate valet who'd evidently also fallen from grace somehow, though Jack had never discovered the full story. He had always been more comfortable not knowing, just as Stevenson had no idea who he really was. He needed it to be that way. He had grown up knowing how fragile trust really was. His mother had taught him that.

Jack splashed water from the basin on his face and held his chin in the mirror. No, no time to shave. Stevenson returned with the coffee and freshly pressed breeches. Jack pulled the breeches on and downed the coffee in one gulp, enjoying the quick burn scalding his throat. He tied his silk sash around his waist, secured his dagger in its place, and grabbed his mask, holding it lightly in his palm. Stevenson was pulling the drapes open and the bright sunshine of mid-morning streamed in. Jack squinted and lifted his arm to shield his eyes.

The valet smiled. "Better to get used to it now, sir, than look like a mole emerging from the ground when you step outside."

Jack clapped the older man on the back. "Quite right, Stevenson. Thank you."

He ran down to the back entrance of the building and slipped into the alley.

He lived in a respectable, though nondescript, part of town. His neighbors were a mix of tradespeople, down-on-their-luck aristocrats, and others who didn't fit in Mayfair but weren't destitute either. It was the shadowy world of the burgeoning middle class, a place where he could usually blend into the crowd unnoticed and unrecognized. It was also respectable enough to mostly be asleep when he came and went, so being out and about now in the hustle and bustle of a London morning was quite disconcerting. He was glad he had his mask, but wearing something like that would make him stand out even more than he wished, so he slipped it in another little pocket in his sash and tried to act like any other man out at this time of day as he made his way across the few blocks to Mayfair.

As he turned up the quiet street full of stately mansions near Grosvenor Square where he knew Sutcliffe House was, his chest tightened. He would pass Danbury House. He knew no one would be there now. Since his father's death, his mother had secluded herself at the ancestral estate. As she should, considering she had killed the man. Jack felt his teeth grinding together. He turned his thoughts back to the task at hand. He walked right past Sutcliffe House, where everything appeared calm and normal, then reached the end of the block and strolled down the next street nonchalantly before slipping into the alley. Here, he flattened himself against the bricks and paused to slip his mask on, tying it tightly behind his head. With one hand on his dagger, he continued down the alleyway, his steps now purposeful and quiet, keeping close to the brick of the houses. The alleyway was far from empty, though. He could hear the clattering of pans in kitchens and the knock and rattle of coal bins. Here and there, men stood about near the carriage houses and stables, but nobody paid him any mind. Clad in all black and quiet as a church mouse, he went almost completely unnoticed. He made his way to the rear of Sutcliffe House, acting as if this were the most normal thing in the world and that he belonged there as much as the scullery maids. Finding a side gate to the spacious rear garden, he jiggled the lock just enough to cause it to give way and, looking first left, then right, slipped inside before closing it quietly behind him. He was behind a large rhododendron, carefully pruned and cultivated, but still quite green in this mild winter. From here he could survey the rear of the house and the small, but ornate, garden. There was a fountain in the center, empty now, of course, with manicured walks and paths reaching out to various smaller areas. It was a beautiful Mayfair Garden, laid out immaculately and well-groomed, but it was an empty and desolate place in the winter. His gaze moved up the golden aged brick of the back of the house itself, rising six stories in its narrow, stately grandeur, the windows across the back reflecting the bright sunlight of the morning. Jack narrowed his eyes from the glare and scanned each window as best he could, looking for anything out of the ordinary or alarming, but right now it still seemed just like any other townhouse: a waste of space and money on people who didn't know what else to do with it. He frowned and shook his head to bring his attention back to the task at hand.

Just then he heard the door from the garden room creak open and watched as a beautiful, somewhat plump woman wearing a large bonnet stepped out with a small perambulator, while another, smaller but likewise bonneted woman followed close behind, carrying a baby whom she then laid into the pram. As she did so, a few curls escaped from the bonnet and fell into the woman's face while Jack watched, fascinated. *Millie.* He surmised the other woman must be the Duchess of Sutcliffe. He cursed under his breath. *Damn that woman,* he thought, *so she was stupid enough to come here.* He shook his head. People were so predictable. He stayed behind the rhododendron while he calculated the best move to make next, but he didn't have very long to think before the hair on the back of his neck stood on end. He felt rather than heard the intruders. Jack had trained himself to be always fully aware with every fiber of his being, and now was no different. He looked up and saw two men clad all in black and wearing black silk masks similar to his own. The same men he'd seen that morning, the assassins, were creeping around the decorative finial on the corner of the house above the first floor, clinging to the outcroppings of decorative brick that adorned each level of the house. He instinctively knew that they had not yet spotted the women under the awning leading to the garden. The assassins were intent on the windows, peering in each one in the hopes of spotting their quarry. Jack knew he had to act. He crept around the perimeter of the garden against the stone wall and behind the perfectly trimmed boxwood that formed its border. He kept his focus on the women, but his eyes on the men. As he came around the corner of the garden to the rear wall of the house, he passed directly beneath them, but the stone ledge they were standing on jutted out enough that it would be almost impossible for them to see him unless they knew what they were looking for. He was far more concerned with not startling Millie and the Duchess, thus betraying their location to the assassins. Even flattened against the wall, he made his way quickly and silently toward them. He willed Millie to look up and see him. He hoped she would recognize him, and he might be able to give her an indication to keep the Duchess quiet. He stared at Millie's bonnet as if to compel her to look up and was still surprised when she did.

Her dark eyes were almost black, even in the bright sunlight. Her eyebrows shot up in surprise at seeing him, but he held a finger to his lips and pointed above him with one extended finger. He almost sighed with relief when she did not immediately look up. She nodded, then smiled into the Duchess's face and took her elbow, pointing them both back inside, lifting the baby from the pram, and disappearing back through the doorway. Jack looked up and could see the boots of the men still making their way along the ledge. He made his way to the awning the women had come out from, placed his hand on the knob behind him and slipped inside, all while watching the wall above.

"Dear God, what is the meaning of this?" hissed a voice nearby. He pulled the mask off, put a finger to his lips again, and stood just inside the door, his entire body on alert.

"Anne, this is Mr. Covert," Millie said quietly, and Jack was annoyed to hear the faintest hint of amusement in her voice. He wheeled around and faced both of them, the Duchess holding the baby against her shoulder and wearing an expression he could only describe as utter disbelief. He motioned to an inner passage outside the garden room, away from the windows.

He leaned his head toward both of them, and they brought their own faces closer, as if on cue. "They're here," he said.

Anne scoffed. "Impossible," she said. He was relieved that she didn't seem prone to hysterics.

"They knew of your connection, and I assume when they

found you had gone from the Bloomsbury house, they came straight here."

Millie nodded. "I was worried about that," she said.

"But so quickly?" Anne asked, the fear starting to appear in her eyes. "We've barely had time to explain everything to Jonathan. He's out now, rustling up extra security."

"I'm afraid it's too late for that," Jack whispered, genuine regret in his voice. "We must get Millie away from here."

"*Miss diRossi* has nowhere else to go," Anne said, a steely edge in her voice, and Jack knew what they said about the new Duchess was true. She may not have been born to the role, but she filled it quite well.

"Leave *Miss diRossi* to me," Jack replied with a hint of sarcasm. "We need to get her as far away from you and the babe as possible."

Anne stiffened, and they both turned to Millie, who was standing with her hands on her hips, looking back and forth between them like she was watching a cat playing with a ball of yarn.

"Are we through discussing me as if I were not here?" she asked.

Jack and Anne looked at each other, raised their eyebrows, then nodded back to Millie in unison.

"Yes."

"Yes, I believe we are."

Millie frowned, and her eyes narrowed. Jack could tell that she was irritated with both of them. He also saw the corner of Anne's mouth twitch just the tiniest bit, and he wanted to respond, but there was no time to argue.

"Millie, we must leave at once," he said, training his face to become serious again. "We'll go to my lodgings."

Millie looked at Anne, and some unspoken communication passed between them before Anne nodded.

"Your Grace," he inclined his head toward Anne. "Take the baby upstairs immediately and situate yourself in any normal pose like you had been there for hours. Be sure to go upstairs; they're going to go floor by floor looking. Make yourself easily seen from a window."

Anne nodded, hugged Millie, pulled back, and said, "Take care of yourself, do you understand me?" Millie nodded and dropped a kiss on the baby's forehead. Anne rushed off and disappeared up the stairwell. Millie looked after them for a moment before turning back to Jack. Her eyes were moist, but she shocked him when she grabbed his hand and held it in her own.

"Lead the way," she said.

Chapter 3

The touch of Millie's small fingers twining lightly with his own sent a shock up Jack's arm and seemed to warm his whole body. He pulled her along the same passage and headed straight for the front door. The butler and two footmen stood there, apparently awaiting instructions. Jack nodded to them, then adjusted his own clothing. He looked down at Millie and gently tucked her stray curls back under the bonnet. He pulled the tie under her chin tighter.

"A jacket? A Spencer or pelisse, please? Not Miss diRossi's," he said to the servants.

"Right away, my Lord," one of the footman said as he rushed off.

Jack shook his head. "Just Mister—" but the man was already out of earshot. "Covert," he muttered.

The footman returned quickly with a smart Spencer jacket. He held it open, and Millie shrugged into it. It was a little large on her, but close enough. She pulled it down in front and adjusted her cuffs. Jack sent her a questioning look. "Ready?" he asked.

"As I'll ever be," she said and slowly let out a deep breath. "Let's go."

Jack walked to the door. "No, we can't be seen leaving together," he said, turning to the footmen. "I'll sneak out the back. Wait for five minutes and send Miss diRossi out the front." Jack took Millie by the shoulders and looked into her eyes. "Meet me on the path by the Serpentine in the park. Just walk like you're strolling. I'll find you." She returned his gaze, unflinching, and nodded. Instinctively and without thought, Jack bent his head slightly and dropped a kiss on the top of her ridiculous bonnet. "Don't look back," he said.

Millie watched as the mysterious Jack Covert disappeared down the hall, back toward the garden. She was still absolutely stunned, but she felt a strange calm and sense of purpose. She wondered again, for the hundredth time, what had compelled this burglar to help her, but she was nonetheless grateful. The reality that there were men climbing on the outside of this house right now who were hoping to find and kill her still felt distant, despite the fact that Jack seemed to be telling the truth. She wished wholeheartedly that she had had more time with Anne. She wondered what had happened to Yvette. Had they harmed her, or had they simply discovered that Millie wasn't there and left her alone? She didn't really believe in God, but she found herself praying fervently for the latter. The five minutes she spent standing there, waiting, felt like an eternity. She fidgeted with the buttons on the Spencer and the ribbons on the bonnet. She found herself touching the top where Jack had kissed it. It was a chaste and friendly gesture, but her mind dwelt on it. Could it have been only last night that she'd enjoyed her dalliance with Peter? Millie felt dazed. She'd received an amazing orgasm not twelve hours ago, and now she was bemused by a kiss that had never even touched her skin. She frowned. It was amazing what a near death experience could do for one's perspective.

Just at that moment, one of the footmen moved forward, grabbed her elbow, and guided her to the door. He touched his forelock out of respect and farewell, and Millie nodded. She took a deep breath and walked into the street.

Don't look back. Don't look back. Those were the last words

Jack had said to her, and she repeated them over and over as she made her way to Hyde Park. Though it was winter, the day was bright, and there were several other young ladies and gentlemen doing the same. A morning constitutional along the Serpentine was a common enough occurrence, and if the men were busy looking for her in the back of the house, they wouldn't notice her leaving out the front door. She just prayed that they'd make their search thorough enough to buy Jack time to find her.

Millie found the path by the river and followed it, slowing herself to move at a normal, leisurely pace for a woman at this time of day, even though all her muscles were tensed to run. Her senses were on high alert for Jack, a flash of black here, a sound in the trees there. She didn't know if he'd be hiding or if he, like her, would have tried to make himself look normal so they'd blend in.

Despite this constant heightened awareness of her surroundings, she was still startled when he appeared beside her. She cursed under her breath. "How do you do that?" she hissed.

"Practice," he said, and he took her hand and placed it on his arm. She looked up at him from under the brim of the bonnet and was astonished to see that he was now wearing a waistcoat, cravat, greatcoat, perfectly polished Hessians, a hat, and a round pair of spectacles. He did not look anything like himself.

"How did you—?" she began, but he cut her off.

"I told you," He said, smiling, "Practice." He patted her arm, and she frowned. "Now," he continued, looking around them, "We need to enjoy this walk before we make a run for it."

"A run for what?" she asked, starting to become annoyed at the way he made plans and carried them out without letting anyone else know what they were.

"We'll go to my rooms," he said, "Not even my own servants know who I really am. We'll be safe there until we can figure out the next steps."

She nodded. That sounded very reasonable.

Jack went on. "The problem is," he said, stroking the stubble on his chin with two fingers, "how to get there."

"Hire a hack?" Millie asked, wondering if she was missing something. People hailed and rode in hackney cabs all over the city, including from Hyde Park.

"It's one possibility," Jack acknowledged, "but I'm a little worried they'll be checking hacks leaving Mayfair once they realize you weren't with the Duchess."

"Checking hacks?" Millie asked, shocked. "Can they do that?"

Jack looked over at her and she could feel the muscles in his arm tightening beneath her fingers as they walked, though he betrayed no tension on his face or in his gait. She'd have to ask him how he managed that.

"They can't and they shouldn't," Jack said wryly, "but believe me, they will."

Millie swallowed hard. "I still don't understand what they could want with me," she said quietly.

"I cannot either," Jack replied. "All we know is it has something to do with that locket."

"My mother gave me the locket," Millie said, trying to keep her voice even and calm. "I knew it was worthless, even then. She said nothing when she gave it to me except 'this is yours now,' and it seemed to have little importance to her either. I believed she was just trying to settle her affairs because she knew the end was near."

"How did she die?" Jack asked, and Millie wasn't offended by the question. It was so rare that anyone asked about her mother. People always assumed the story was too tragic or too hard to relive. Millie had never been particularly interested in reliving it, that was true, but she also wasn't ashamed of her past.

"She died of syphilis," Millie said softly. "She was an opera singer and a whore."

"Like the new Duchess's mother?" Jack asked. All of London

had heard Anne and Jonathan's amazing love story.

"No, not like Anne's mother," Millie replied. "My mother drank. She lost all her money gambling. She left me home in our rooms for days at a time by myself." She paused and looked up at Jack to see that he was looking at her, his intense gaze a brighter shade of blue in the sunlight. "Annelise Heatherington was a *courtesan*. That much is true. She sold her body for a price, and it kept her in that house in Bloomsbury, singing and doing what she loved. But she was a *mother*, too. Not just to Anne, but also to me."

Jack raised his free hand and placed it on her own fingers that were still lightly twined around his bicep. "I'm sorry," he said. "I didn't mean to pry."

"No need to apologize," Millie said, and she meant it. "It feels good to talk about both of them, honestly. I've never shied away from it."

Jack only nodded. "What about your parents?" Millie asked, and she regretted it right away, for as soon as the words left her mouth, his lips became a thin line.

"They're both dead," he said, biting the words off like a tough piece of meat. "We'll leave it at that."

Millie pursed her lips and went no further. She could respect his questions, but she could also respect his secrets. They were nearing the end of the path at the park, and Jack surprised her by laughing heartily. He reached up and squeezed her fingers and she, too, began to laugh, probably a bit too loudly. But then she'd never really playacted before.

"Keep laughing and don't turn around," Jack said quietly, smiling between guffaws. Millie did as he said, but it went against her nature not to look back, and this was the second time today she'd had to control the impulse.

"I'm not cut out for this," she said, in a singsong, still laughing. Her laughter sounded like two ha'pennys on a cheese grater. It rang so false to her own ears, but she dared not stop. They'd reached a cross path away from the Serpentine and Jack turned them down it as nonchalantly as if they really had been two lovers having a quiet tête-à-tête. Here there were several large trees whose beautiful branches created a leafy green canopy in summer, but whose stately trunks still provided a lovely vista even in winter. Jack walked her off the path to one of them, then turned and pushed her back against its trunk. His brow furrowed, and she had just enough time to see a slight frown before he bent his head slightly and slanted his mouth over hers.

Millie felt a shockwave from her lips to the depth of her belly, to the backs of her knees, which weakened slightly as he kissed her. She felt the rough bark of the tree on her back as she slipped a little from the shock, but then Jack's arms came up behind her and pulled her in closer to him. She could feel the muscles in his chest tightening against her, and she instinctively moved her arms around to his back, where broad sinew was barely contained beneath the fine fabric of the coat he'd scavenged. In spite of herself, she moaned a little, but she dared not deepen the kiss. She knew this was all part of the show, but damn, his lips felt so...*good*. Her body fit into his perfectly, and she longed for even more contact. Just as she felt she could no longer contain herself, he pulled back and looked around the tree.

"They're gone," he said, his voice ragged. He dropped his hands and pulled away from her. "I do apologize, Miss diRossi," but she could almost hear the pounding of his heart from his flushed face.

"None needed," she said, "And I suppose if I'll be staying in your apartments, you may call me simply Millie."

Jack's face was inscrutable. "Very well." He straightened his cravat and reached toward her to straighten the bodice of the Spencer and pull on the strings of the bonnet. It was a strangely gentle gesture, and Millie's eyes narrowed again. Who *was* this man?

"They went toward Kensington," he said. "I don't know if

they were our men or not, but we can't be too careful." He doubled back across the grass to another path headed back east to Mayfair.

"We'll catch a hack at the corner gate," he said, pulling her at a faster pace now. "It should be bustling at this time of day. With any luck, we'll be lost in the crowd."

Millie felt the need to look behind her, but she willed herself to remain calm and to look straight ahead. Her heart was pounding so hard and so loud that she was surprised she could hear anything else at all. Not only was her entire body tense due to the danger they were in, but she was also in a heightened state of awareness of the enigmatic man beside her. She'd felt drawn to him even last night in her hallway, but now she was physically *aware* of him in a whole other way. She could feel where her skirts brushed his leg beside her, her fingertips tingled where they rested lightly on his arm. It felt like there was a heat radiating from him that warmed her whole body. They continued walking, trying to act as normally as possible, until they finally reached the great gate at the southeast corner of the park, where any number of carriages, carts, hacks, and single riders could be seen riding back and forth along Knightsbridge, Park Lane, and around Hyde Park Corner. Millie felt nauseous, fighting the desire to turn around and see if they had been followed. But Jack just stepped out into the street, holding his hand up like any gentleman wishing to hail a hackney. Soon enough, one pulled up next to them, Jack shouted an address to the driver, and they stepped in and pulled the door closed.

Millie sat, her back straight, on the edge of her seat and leaned forward to peer through the dingy window. She was not unused to hackney cabs, but she nonetheless found them distasteful.

"Too low-class for your liking?" Jack asked, watching her.

She frowned and turned to look at him. "On the contrary, Mr. Covert, I'm quite used to low-class. I'm just not a fan of dirty. I prefer to walk whenever I can."

"And take private carriages from your highborn friends?"

Millie bristled at the note of mockery in his voice as he turned to look out his own window. Who *was* this man, she wondered for the hundredth time.

"I will take any carriage offered to me," she said, biting the words out. "But, as I said, I prefer to walk." She decided to change the subject. "Do you think anyone has followed us?"

"It doesn't look like it," he said. "We've made quite a lucky escape."

"You certainly know how to do it," she said, finally allowing herself to relax a bit and leaning back against the cushion. "I suppose you've had a lot of practice."

"For the hundredth time," Jack said, turning back toward her, his eyes flashing in the dim light, "I'm not used to dealing with any people at all. In fact, that's the reason I'm in this business."

"Fair enough." She put out her hand. "At any rate, I owe you my life."

He looked down at her offering, and she had trouble reading his emotions as he took her hand for a moment and then dropped it. He seemed at first to recoil from her touch, then he softened, and she realized his guard had lifted just a bit before he snapped it firmly back in place. She shook her head. This poor man needed a good roll in the sack.

She inched her bottom over the cushion toward him until their bodies were touching again from foot to shoulder, just as they had been during the harrowing walk through the park. She put one hand on his knee, and his face swiveled toward hers in surprise.

"What the devil..." he began, but she cut him off by taking his face in her hands and pulling him toward her.

The kiss in the park had been chaste, full of alarm and action, and a ruse to appear like simple lovers taking a lovers' walk. This one was different, because Millie wanted it to be different. She ran her tongue across first his top lip and then the bottom, tasting him before moving her mouth fully over his. She felt his response as he softened and took hold of her shoulders. She darted her tongue in his mouth and felt his own respond. She moved her hands from the sides of his face to the back of his neck, and she grabbed the hair that grew longer at his nape, pulling on it slightly. She was starting to realize this could be fun. Maybe more fun than Peter.

So, she was surprised when Jack pulled back from her, grabbing her wrists and pulling them gently back down to her lap. "What are you about, Miss diRossi?" he murmured, his breathing ragged and uneven.

"We both need to relax," she said, shrugging her shoulders. "When you kissed me in the park, I liked it. I thought I might like a real one even more. And I did. Didn't you?"

"Did I...like it?" he asked, seeming taken aback. "Miss diRossi..."

"Please, dear God, stop with the *Miss*. I'm Millie. Just Millie."

"Millie," he said in a ragged whisper, then paused. "I'm unused to women—"

"Pursuing their own pleasure?" she finished his sentence. He laughed.

"I suppose one might put it that way," he said, running a hand through his black hair. "At least not respectable ones."

"Who said anything about respectable?" she laughed. "I think we can both agree that's one word that doesn't describe either of us."

To her relief, Jack chuckled. "That's true," he said. "I believe we've both eschewed that label by choice." The cab slowed and Jack leaned forward to look out the window again. "Here we are," he said, and stood just as they came to a stop. He opened the door and turned to help Millie out. She took his offered hand and ran her fingers across his palm suggestively as she stepped out. He made a face that was exactly between a smile and a frown. That pleased her.

They stood at the curb briefly while Jack paid the driver, and Millie looked around. She was surprised to note that they were in Covent Garden.

"You live in Covent Garden?" she asked, her eyebrows raised.

"Not quite," he said, and once again placed her hand on his arm and pulled her forward. She rolled her eyes and followed.

Chapter 4

Jack felt rather than saw Millie roll her eyes at him, and he tried to hide his smile as he propelled them forward through the crowd at Covent Garden. It was a smorgasbord for the senses: vendors hawked their colorful wares, various carts offered up steaming meat pies and other street foods, and the entire area teemed with life from all the varied strata of society. Jack had always loved Covent Garden, even as a child. But they were not here for a pleasure stroll. He took them right through the heart of the market, dodging other pedestrians and heading for the other side. He was confident that, even if they had been followed in the hack, there was no way anyone would know where they were now. He allowed himself to let his guard down, just a bit, but he still wanted to make absolutely certain. Getting back to his rooms safely would be worthless if someone had followed them.

Finally, after weaving in and out of the market for what seemed like an hour, they turned down a side street. There were still plenty of people around, horses and carts and walkers alike, heading to and from Covent Garden, but now it was much quieter, and they could try to work some things out.

"About that kiss," he began, clearing his throat. He felt her fingers tighten on his bicep, and he involuntarily tightened the muscles in his arm. He almost cursed aloud at himself. She had certainly aroused something in him that he hadn't felt in a long time, something he'd told himself was unnecessary for life. He frowned. "It shouldn't happen again," he said.

Millie turned her face up to him, her dark eyes narrowing beneath the brim of the ridiculous bonnet she still wore. "I was under the impression you liked it," she said, searching his face. "I'm so sorry if you didn't." He could tell she meant it, and that should have given him some relief. But that was the problem. It didn't.

"I did like it," he said, "But that sort of thing is not for me."

"Kissing is not for you?" she asked, laughing a little. "Kissing is for everyone." She made a grand gesture with her free hand. "It's part of the human experience."

"I just prefer to live without...entanglements," he said, trying to choose his words.

She moved her free hand and clapped it on top of the one already holding his arm, and she shocked him by laying her head against his shoulder briefly. "Good news," she said. "I also prefer my dalliances to be, shall we say, uncomplicated?"

He smiled and shook his head. She wasn't making this any easier. "My experience is that all dalliances are complicated, as any relations between two or more humans must be."

She nodded and acknowledged his words. "Generally, I believe that to be true, but I also believe that in many cases, it's worth it. Close friends, lovers, all can add meaning to life. I do not buy into the idea that one must be attached and tied down to one's lovers." She shrugged.

"I know quite a few men who take that view," he said, "But you may be the first woman I've met to say so."

She laughed out loud, and he couldn't help but smile in response. Hers was an infectious laugh, a clear, high-pitched sound, full of genuine mirth. "You just haven't met the right women."

He wanted to tell her he'd barely met any women at all, but he wasn't about to start sharing his soul with this little minx.

"But if you say no more kissing," she went on, her face more serious, "Of course I will acquiesce."

He squeezed her fingers, and she squeezed his arm back as if to acknowledge their agreement. "But that doesn't mean I won't still be thinking about it," she said, and she looked back up into his eyes, her own turned up at the corners with good humor, but with something else, as well. She really did desire him, he realized, and the thought was not unpleasant. Though it was certainly complicated.

Finally, after making their way through several blocks and streets, they arrived at his nondescript building, a three-story townhouse with a residence on each floor. "Here we are," he said, gesturing for her to ascend the front stair first. He took one last long look up and down the street to be sure they were still unnoticed, then followed her up the stairs through the entrance. Her hips swayed slowly as she made her way up the narrow flight of steps, and he imagined grabbing hold of those hips from behind. He shook his head and closed his eyes. He must stop this. He would help her to safety, and then he would be rid of her and back to his normal life.

"It's the third floor," he said, motioning her forward at the landing.

When they came through the door to his parlor, he realized he'd have to explain her presence to Stevenson. Before he could even finish the thought, the valet appeared from his own room. He betrayed no surprise upon seeing Millie standing there, and Jack congratulated himself again for having found the man.

"Stevenson, this is my friend, Elizabeth," he said. "She'll need to stay with us a few nights, so if you could prepare a bed for me in the sitting room, and get us some lunch? Tea?" He realized he wasn't even sure what time it was anymore.

Stevenson nodded at both of them and withdrew into the

kitchen.

Jack turned to remove his jacket and loosened his cravat. He went to the bar under the window and poured two glasses of water from the carafe. He turned to offer one to Millie, who was still standing in her Spencer and her bonnet, looking around at the room. He cleared his throat.

She looked back at him, and his stomach dropped upon seeing how pale her face had become. She was just so fetchingly *open.* He wasn't sure he'd ever met a woman like her. One always knew what she was thinking—she wore it all over her face.

"Here, have a glass of water to steady yourself," he said.

The furrow between her thick black brows deepened. "You don't happen to have anything stronger, do you?" she asked.

"No," he said, and she laughed a little. "I'm not joking," he said, frowning. He knew it was uncommon for a man of his age, and especially of his reputation, but it was the truth. He'd never enjoyed alcohol, not after what he'd seen it do to his family.

"Very well," she said, shrugging. She took the offered glass of water and sipped, turning around and surveying the room. "This is a lovely bachelor set," she said. "Quite comfortable."

"It suits me," he said, sitting on the settee. He motioned to a chair across from him. "Please, make yourself at home. Stevenson will take your jacket and bonnet when he returns. I'll set you up in my bedroom and sleep in my sitting room. We don't have a lot of spare space here," he said, chuckling.

"Of course," she said, "That will be more than agreeable. I could take the sitting room, though," she said. "I'm quite used to simple arrangements."

"My work has led me to some terribly uncomfortable lodgings," he said. "It will be quite all right for me. And hopefully, with any luck, you will not be here long."

She turned her head to look at him, and for once, he wasn't quite sure what she was thinking.

"So, what's the next move?" she asked.

"We must find out why that locket was so important," he said. "That's the key to everything."

"I agree. Fortunately, Anne and Jonathan are already looking into that." She paused and looked to the window, deep in thought. "Will we be able to get messages to them from here?"

He nodded. "Yes," he said, "As you experienced on the way here, I have a few ways of getting around the city in secret." He added a wink, thinking he needed to put her at ease. When she smiled in response, he felt warmth rise from his belly and spread upwards.

"So, tell me again what you know about the locket," he said, leaning back against the cushion of the settee. "Your mother gave it to you before she died. Where was that again?"

"Venice," Millie said. "We traveled for mother's singing roles but had a permanent lodging in Venice."

"Where was your father?"

Millie stared at him, blinking. "I never knew him."

"Do you know his name?"

"No," she said. "Mother was always adamant that I do not know. She called him a no-good scoundrel, accused him of walking out on us, and said I'd be better off imagining that I had no father."

"You had no reason to doubt her?"

Millie gave a very undignified snort. "I had every reason to doubt her. She drank, she gave herself away to men who cared nothing for her, she made herself ridiculous for them, never protected me from them, and eventually the whore's disease killed her. I had no reason to trust her, which is another reason why the necklace is so baffling." Millie took a deep breath and flattened her lips. "She never did anything sentimental for me in her life. She never viewed me as much more than a burden, or, occasionally, a confidante or fellow traveler. The most loving thing she ever did was ask Annelise to care for me."

"Perhaps she had a change of heart on her deathbed," Jack

said, turning the water glass back and forth between his thumb and forefinger. "People do, you know. So often that it's a cliche." And some never do, he thought, clenching his teeth together so tightly that his jaw hurt as he stood to and gave a little bow to her "If you'll excuse me." Without a second glance, he walked out of the room.

Alone in his sitting room, running a fresh cloth over his face and neck and enjoying the bracing shock of the cold water, Jack thought about their conversation. Given Jack's own experiences, he could understand why her mother might want to spare Millie from her other parent. Jack had often prayed for just such an enlightened view from his own father. Instead, his father had left for London for weeks at a time, believing incorrectly that the nanny and tutor would be capable of caring for Jack in the way a child needed. Jack couldn't remember a time when his mother wasn't deep in drink. She had been occasionally affectionate when he was a young child but was still distant and often absent from the nursery. However, when in her cups, she was prone to fits that ran the emotional gamut from overly affectionate, to raging and blaming, to weepily attempting atonement. Jack had learned to hide from her early, and his nannies and tutors had often tried to help him, but his mother was their employer. If they didn't give him up to her, she'd sack them. In this way, Jack had learned you couldn't trust anyone but yourself.

When Jack hit his teen years, his rage at his mother started to transfer to his father. *Why do you leave me here?* He'd demanded on holidays home from Eton, where he'd finally found an escape and the ability to be his own man. He had loved his studies, and part of him wished he could become a scholar and live at Oxford or Cambridge, fading into the happy oblivion of books. But it was not to be. His father was not only insistent on his returning to the estate, but often drilled Jack's responsibilities in to him during long lectures about filial piety, duty, honor, and other such nonsense. Jack was an only child, heir to the title, and responsible for caring for everyone once his father was gone. Jack had always supposed as a young man that his mother's ruinous behavior would mean she would die long before his father, but it was not to be.

He surveyed his face in the mirror. If he squinted a little, he could see his father in his own dark countenance. He had his father's height and features, but his father had been softer. He'd tried to care for Jack in the only way he knew how, but Jack knew that, in truth, it was his father's love for his mother that had ruined him. Now when Jack saw himself in the mirror, his eyes flinty and slightly narrowed, his mouth set in a hard, straight line, he knew that was the difference between them. Plenty of marriages in the *ton* were brought about due to convenience, and very little affection on either party's part. This was normal and could be dealt with by both men and women, with friends, lovers, the interests of the children, the business of the estate, and involvement in parliament. There were loveless but amicable arrangements all over the kingdom. Not so for Jack's parents. The Viscount Danbury and his bride were undoubtedly a love match. Jack had heard it whispered his whole life. *Such a shame. Such a beautiful couple.* It was bad enough for his mother to ruin her own life, but to take advantage of genuine love given was unpardonable. He'd never forgive her for what she'd done to their family, and he'd never forgive his father for putting up with it. He knew that he would never make the same mistake. He'd been tempted by many women, but he knew the temporary pleasure wasn't worth the risk. He'd always been able to move past any unwanted feelings he might have had, and it would be the same with Millie. He just had to help her see her way to safety, and he'd soon forget about her.

Millie tossed and turned in Jack's big bed. She tried to imagine the most mundane and comforting things: holding Maggie, dusting the mantel in the house, the words to an aria she'd been learning. Nothing worked. Her mind's eye just kept being filled with the irascible, silent, incredibly attractive man in the next room. She could picture the way his muscles moved beneath that silky black shirt, the broadness of his chest in the elegant waistcoat and breeches, the way his unruly black hair fell down into his face when he was concentrating deeply on something, the sparkle in his blue eyes when he'd bantered with her, and the way that sparkle disappeared and his mouth set in a grim line when she got too close.

Most of all, she kept thinking about those two kisses. She'd truly enjoyed her night with Peter—could that have only been the previous night? He was a sweet man and a satisfying lover, but in her mind, it was as if he never existed. All her thoughts just kept returning to Jack Covert's lips on hers. Even though he had made his feelings about their kisses clear, she knew he couldn't deny the electricity that had passed between them. He must have his own reasons to keep out of entanglements, and she vowed to respect them, but that didn't stop the craving to feel the soft press of his mouth again. She closed her eyes and tried to relive last night with Peter. She imagined him trailing kisses down her stomach, and his skill with his tongue. She had just gotten to the good part when he'd looked up at her from between her thighs, but the face in her mind was that damned Jack Covert's.

Frustrated, Millie got out of bed and pushed her curly hair out of her face. She padded over to the washstand and splashed some cool water on her face before patting dry with the towel that hung there. As she held it to her face, her whole being reeled as the scent of Jack met her nose. His shaving soap, she assumed, but she held the cloth still and breathed deeply. She really was going mad, she thought. It was not the first time she'd smelled shaving soap, but none of the others smelled like *him*. She finished wiping her face and started to pace about the room. The sooner they could find out what was going on and what these murderers wanted from her, the faster she could put Jack Covert—his sparkling eyes, his hard chest, and his soft lips—behind her.

When she woke, she was pleased to find that she had a restful sleep. Even a mind as anxious as hers had to eventually be quelled from exhaustion. She looked for sunlight to signal the morning and was slightly confused. She had no idea what time it was. It was still dark as midnight in the room, and she was completely disoriented. Had she slept the whole day away? She'd slept in just a chemise, and after a brief search of the room yielded no women's clothing, she found a silk robe near the bed and pulled it tight about her. Though Jack was not a particularly tall man, his robe still brushed the floor when she put it on. She cinched the cord at the waist and pulled the door open. She had to squint as the bright sliver of light entered the room. She held her hand up to shield her eyes and was still disoriented for a few moments before she realized it was morning.

"Jack?" she asked. She didn't want to wake him. She pulled the door open further and stepped into the little sitting room. Everything was straightened and set to rights as if no one had slept there the night before. This made her slightly concerned. *Had* Jack slept? Seeing that the room was empty, she walked over to the little bar and poured herself a glass of water. She'd barely moved toward the settee when the double door swung wide, and Stevenson, the valet, asked her to join Mr. Covert for breakfast in the drawing room.

She stood. "I'll just change," she said, and made for the bedroom, but Stevenson's lips twitched as he replied, "No need, Miss. Mr. Covert keeps a relaxed home."

She nodded and followed the man to the next room, where a beautiful table had been laid with a steaming pot of coffee, a smaller pot of chocolate, several scones, several coddled eggs, and more fruit than she had seen in quite some time. Fruit was rather scarce in winter, especially after Christmas. She took a seat, and the door opened again. Jack walked in, properly washed and dressed, in a fresh pair of his usual black breeches. She wondered how many pairs he owned. There was no trace of the dandyish, elegant outfit he'd stolen yesterday in Mayfair. He wore his black silk shirt, but it hung open at the neck with no cravat, and she felt herself blush as she spied the hint of black hair peeking out from the deep V on his chest. She looked away. She was hungry for more than just eggs, she admitted, but the breakfast would have to do.

"I trust you slept well?" he asked, grabbing a piece of toast and slathering butter on it.

"Not at first," she admitted, "But when I finally fell asleep, I must have been like the dead. I was so disoriented when I woke in the darkness that I wondered if I'd slept all day."

He chuckled. "Yes, the nocturnal life does take some getting used to," he said. "But I find now I prefer it."

Millie broke the top of a coddled egg and pulled it open. "I lead a somewhat nocturnal life myself," she said, reaching in to get a spoonful. "But I could never wake without at least some sunshine."

"I think some of us just have more need of shadow," Jack said.

"What made you seek the darkness?" she asked.

He was quiet. He took a sip of coffee and leaned back against the chair. His eyes met hers, but she couldn't read his expression. "My family," he said, but he said it in a way that warned her not to ask any follow-up questions. She could respect that.

"I guess neither of us had great fortune with our parents," she said.

Jack nodded. "Yes, and at least I don't have murderers after me because of mine."

"Speaking of which, have you thought of a next step for me?"

"The first plan is to get a message to your ducal friend and find out what he's been able to discover. We'll make much more progress if we work together."

Millie nodded in agreement. "Can we also make sure Yvette is safe?" she asked.

"Yes, that's going to be part of the message," Jack said. "Though my instincts tell me that if they found you out of the house, they would not have bothered with her or anyone else there."

"I agree," Millie said. "Is there a way to make sure Yvette knows I am safe? She's more than a servant."

Jack nodded. "Yes, but I cannot give her any details. Anything she knows could put her in danger."

"I understand," Millie said.

"Now, for something more fun," Jack said, leaning back and sipping his coffee. "We need to get you out of those clothes."

Millie choked on the piece of egg she'd just eaten and took a sip of water. She blinked her eyes and looked up to see Jack smiling that wry little grin.

"I'll send Stevenson out to get you some serviceable dresses. We're not sure how long you'll be here. Might as well wear clean clothes. And I'll need my robe back eventually," he said, tilting his head and glancing at where said garment had slipped down her shoulder a few inches. She followed his gaze and pulled it up.

"Of course," she said, "I would be grateful."

He swallowed the last bit of coffee and stood. "I'll see about getting those messages back and forth." His eyes narrowed as he asked. "Can you keep yourself busy here?"

She stood. "Yes. I saw some fine books in your room I'm interested in reading."

His eyebrows went up briefly before his face became expressionless once more. He stood and touched his forehead to her in a little salute and said, "Then I'll be off. Back by luncheon." She heard him finish preparing to go out and then heard the door close behind him.

She finished her breakfast and returned to the room. Millie sank into the settee and let out the longest sigh she believed she'd ever released. Her arms hung limp at her sides, and she stared up at the ceiling. How did this man manage to madden her like this? When he'd suggested removing her clothes, her mind had jumped right to the tangled heat of coupling rather than the more obvious meaning, especially given the context. She'd always had a healthy appetite in that area, but she'd never been particularly obsessed. She also realized Jonathan might be the only man she'd ever spent time with just as a friend. But it wasn't really that she avoided men, rather that she preferred to avoid *complications*. She was lucky enough to be the rare London woman with a truly independent life. She had plenty of friends, acquaintances, and men she could take to bed when the need arose, but the idea of keeping one in the house was as preposterous as the idea of adopting a peacock—it was a pretty idea, but the logistics would never work.

She took a deep breath, rose, and went to one of the shelves lining the walls of the sitting room. She realized there were shelves lining the walls of the entire suite of rooms. Jack didn't appear to be the type of man to keep books just to show them off. In fact, she knew in his line of work he probably did not have callers or visitors. He was more and more a curiosity to her as she ran a finger along the spines. There were several of the usual volumes she'd expect in a genteel, educated man's collection, the usual histories, some of the classics in original and translation, but she was surprised when she arrived at a whole section of novels. Not only did she see *The Mysteries of Udolpho*, but several other popular novels. She smiled approvingly. Her fingertips found one in three volumes, titled *Sense and Sensibility,* and took down the first volume. She knew this was the first of the novels released by the anonymous lady who'd written *Pride and Prejudice* and Millie had been dying to get her hands on it. She cracked it open and smiled at the pages, which had been marked in pencil. Perhaps she would learn something about the enigmatic Mr. Covert after all, she thought as she settled into the cushions of the settee, curling her legs beneath her.

~*~

Jack made his way through the city slowly, making sure he wasn't followed or recognized. The best disguise was usually confidence, he knew, and he was adept at pretending he had nothing to hide. He stopped at several shops, just as if he were a gentleman out on an excursion. He purchased two new books and a set of fresh cedar pencils. Armed with a satchel of purchases, he looked even more nondescript and innocuous. First, he wound his way to Bloomsbury to check on Yvette. Even with his confidence and his purchases, he dared not go to the house himself, but he knew many of the large network of street urchins who could be prevailed upon to deliver a message for a few coins. He had a reputation among those who knew him for paying much higher "wages' than most of the n'er-do-wells around London, so he also could command the most discreet and talented of these young lurkers.

A few blocks from Millie's house, he found one such young helper, a girl who'd done this sort of work for him before. He told her the house number, described Yvette, and sent the girl off. He stayed in the shadows near the carriage houses in the alley and cracked his new book. This one was called *Emma*, and it was by the "lady author" who'd written some of his favorite books in the past several years. He found the descriptions of the gentry to be biting, hilarious, and familiar, but he also found comfort in the plots and characters who managed to find the best in each other and themselves. He knew real life wasn't like that, and that's why he loved to read about it in books. He began reading while keeping one eye on the direction from which the girl would be returning, and his senses on high alert for anything out of the ordinary.

He'd only just started to get acquainted with Miss Woodhouse and her hypochondriac father when the little girl returned, breathless, but with information.

"The blonde French'oman is there, milor' but she's not alone. There's two other women there. Right proper gentlewomen, I'd say, sir."

Jack felt his brows furrow and his eyes narrow with suspicion. "Describe them," he said curtly.

"Both short, both slim little things they were, milor', an' they were both very serious sorts, very dour faces."

"How did Miss Yvette seem?" he asked. "Was she being threatened, do you think?"

"She was right serious, too, sir, but she didn't seem scared or uncomfortable."

Jack pressed his lips together and took a deep breath. "All right, thank you Bette. You'll get an extra coin if you can deliver a message for me."

The little girl's eyes brightened. "Of course, sir!"

Jack ripped the back blank page from his book and hastily wrote a note to Yvette with one of the new pencils. He folded it twice and handed it to the girl, then strolled into the street to wait for Yvette in the square where he'd directed her.

The square was beginning to fill. Nannies with prams walked, and artists carefully setting up their easels. There was something about Bloomsbury that always set him at ease. He never had much cause to come here professionally, since most of his clients were intent on the valuable contents of more fashionable neighborhoods. Another reason he should have been more suspicious about the locket job, he thought, shaking his head. Still, it was a beautiful morning, and he felt sure he was about to finally have a small break in the mystery of Millie's pursuers. The sooner he could solve it and get her safe, the sooner he could get back to his normal life.

He opened the book again, but only pretended to read as he kept his senses alert for Yvette. It wasn't long before he saw her tall, blonde form making its way across the square. As she neared, he lowered the book and called her over, trying to make it look like he was a stranger asking her the time. She stopped, pulled a little pin watch from a pocket on her jacket, and he nodded his thanks. Unlike her employer, Yvette was quite good at acting.

"Lovely weather we're having, isn't it?" she asked in her light French accent.

"Yes," he answered, nodding, "maybe we'll finally see some snow."

"I always say winter in London just isn't right until it snows," she said, and then lowered her voice, "I've got company."

"Yes, I heard," he said. "Who is it?"

"Two ladies," Yvette replied. "Gentlewomen. Looking for Miss Millie."

Jack's eyebrows came together in confusion. "Did they seem threatening?"

"Not at all," Yvette said, leaning forward to speak even lower. "In fact, they seemed excited to see her and disappointed she wasn't there."

Jack shook his head. What the devil was going on?

"They said they'd been looking for her for so long," Yvette said, "But they wouldn't give me any more information. They are quite eager, though, I can say that."

"Are they still there?"

"No, sir," Yvette shook her head and looked down. "I tried to keep them, but they said maybe they needed to go to Venice."

Jack's head shot up at that. He looked Yvette in the eyes. "Are you sure? They said Venice?"

Yvette pursed her lips before replying. "Yes, sir, that's what gave me a fright, knowing about Millie's past. They've got the right Mildred diRossi, I'm sure."

Jack brought his fingers to his chin, deep in thought.

"Yvette," he said, "I can count on you not to breathe a word of this to anyone?"

She nodded and took one of his hands. "You'll protect her?" she asked, less a question and more a demand.

He squeezed her hand in his own. "Yes, I will."

She pulled back and then waved. "Good luck with your search, sir. I hope you find the right milliner."

"Thank you, Miss," he responded with a light tone to match Yvette's. "I cannot thank you enough. Good day."

Jack walked away from the little square in the opposite direction from which he'd come. He made his gait measured and even, strolling for all the world like a man just out for an errand or a morning constitutional. Under this calculated calm exterior, however, he was all turmoil. Not only did this latest information confound him, but it also meant he was likely stuck with Millie for a while longer. What did it mean that there were both common murderers *and* well-to-do people trying to find her? Could these two wildly different factions somehow be working together? Were they competing interests or just differing ways of trying to track her down? Did they all mean harm to her? Yvette had proposed that the visitors she'd had appeared eager. Was this because they were excited about finding Millie or excited about eliminating her? Not knowing the answer to any of these questions left them in an even more precarious spot than the one they'd originally found themselves in. Complications were always messy and always meant delays. Not only was he further from the goal of securing Millie's safety, but now he'd have to spend even more time with the damned woman, something he'd promised himself he'd try to avoid at all costs.

After a winding and circuitous adventure through London, Jack was sure no one had followed him when he finally arrived at his own lodgings. He made his way up the stairs two at a time but slowed down as he approached his rooms. What would he say to Millie? He took a deep breath, took hold of the doorknob, and pushed the door open.

What he saw when he entered made his heart seize, despite its being the most normal thing in the world. Millie lay on the settee, still wrapped in his dressing gown, her bare feet propped up on one arm and her head resting on a pillow against the other. One arm was thrown behind her head, a copy of one of the latest novels open on her chest, rising and falling with the steady, even rhythm of her sleeping breath.

She was so beautiful he felt almost lightheaded looking at her. Those unruly curls stood out against the skin of her forehead, her long black lashes lay curling against her cheeks, and her sharp little chin came to a perfect point beneath the bow of her lips, dark pink and slightly open as she slept. He remembered the feel of those lips against his and he could feel himself flushing with heat. He shook his head and looked up at the ceiling, counting breaths to calm himself before he looked back at her and then cleared his throat.

When she didn't respond, he did it again, trying to be louder this time. She smiled a little in her sleep and rolled over, pillowing her hand underneath one soft cheek. Jack watched, waiting, as the book slid from her chest and down to the floor with a loud thump.

Millie jumped up, clutching the dressing gown at her throat, her curls standing out all over her head like some kind of gorgeous Medusa. Jack couldn't help laughing, but he regained composure and nodded to her.

"Sorry if I woke you," he said, trying to keep the mirth out of his voice.

He realized he needn't have bothered, as Millie filled the room with her own laughter. "Well, you certainly gave me a fright," she said and made her way over to where he stood. She surprised him again by taking both his hands in her own and kissing each of his cheeks before she pulled back and eyed him with a furrowed brow.

"You don't look as if you have good news," she said in a flat tone. She walked back to the settee and sat, patting the cushion next to her. Jack followed and leaned back, rubbing his fingers on his temples.

"Actually," he started, "I do have several pieces of good

news. Yvette and the Duchess are both very safe and happy to hear you are safe."

Millie sighed with relief.

"As we suspected," he continued, "They are of no use to these assassins if you're not with them. I assume they'll be watched, but also that they'll be left alone."

Millie pursed her lips together. "But that's not all," she said, and it wasn't a question.

"No." Jack paused, unsure of how to tell her what he'd found out from Yvette. He decided that frank honesty was the best route. "Someone else is looking for you."

Millie's eyebrows shot up in surprise. "Who?"

"We don't know. But these were two gentlewomen. They visited Yvette today and were distraught not to find you."

"Could it be a trick?"

"Yes," he said, echoing his thoughts from earlier. "It could be, but it doesn't seem likely."

Millie leaned back into the pillow and puffed out her cheeks before blowing the breath out slowly. "Well, we've got complications, then, haven't we?"

Jack nodded slowly. "We do." He turned to her and took her hands in his. "I have an idea, but I don't think you'll like it."

Millie raised one perfectly shaped black eyebrow, and the smooth motion made him warm all over.

"I think we should go to Venice," he said, and she laughed at that, dropping his hands and standing up.

"Preposterous," she exclaimed as she went to the window and crossed her arms. "Impossible."

He stood up and strode to her, keeping his touch light as he grabbed her shoulders and turned her to face him. "I know," he said. "I have jobs lined up. I have plans."

"I have *friends*," she almost shouted. "I have a *life*. I have *more* than just plans." He felt the heat rise to his throat and cheeks as her words struck him almost like a blow.

He turned around. "Yes, I suppose you're right; I don't have a *life*," he bit off.

She came up from behind him and wrapped her arms around his waist. And he could not have been more surprised had the Prince Regent himself walked into his rooms. Nonetheless, he could feel himself melting into her. She lay her head against his back and whispered, "I'm sorry, Jack. That was uncalled for. Of course you have a life. And you've given so much of it up for mine already."

He closed his eyes and almost by instinct raised his hands to cover hers where they lay clasped on his stomach. He felt a tingle where she touched him, a tightness across his abdomen, and a warmth in his chest as he allowed himself one deep intake of breath before he squeezed her hands and pulled them gently away.

He turned around and pulled her in a hug, but it was a chaste one. "Thank you," he said, his voice gruff, "Thank you."

He pulled himself away and returned to the couch, but his entire body felt cold where hers had been. How would he manage being in such proximity to her for any length of time? He sat and ran a hand through his hair, scratching the back of his head. She went back to the window and stood, staring out, silent. She hugged herself with her arms folded across her chest as if to ward off a chill.

It seemed like an age before she finally said, her voice soft, "You're right. We should go."

He sighed, and it felt like part of his soul was leaving his body. "It won't be easy," he said, warning.

She snorted and turned around, a smile spreading across her face. "Of course it won't," she said. "You forget I've made this trip once before."

His smile was grim as he thought about that. "I can't promise this trip will be any happier than that one."

She came back to sit beside him and put her hand on his leg. "That one was very happy," she said. "I was coming to a place where I was safe and cared for." She leaned back on the cushion again and stared up at the ceiling. "This time I don't know what I will find at the end. I'm being chased by murderers. I'll have to entrust my life to a devilishly handsome thief. And I'll have to make the whole journey without so much as kissing him." She laughed, and he was starting to realize that she used flirtation as a way to prevent deeper conversation. As soon as their talk moved toward her past or the danger she was in, she brought up the attraction between them. He obviously could not deny it was there, but the thought that she was only using him to escape her sadness made him frown. She noticed and her tone was still light when she continued, "Don't look so sad. I won't bother you about it."

He shook his head and covered her hand with his own, squeezing it a little. "It's not that, Millie. You can't think I don't feel what's between us."

She swallowed and looked up at him, those dark eyes wide.

"I am not interested in being a plaything, or a way of escaping reality."

Millie's eyes narrowed, and she pulled her hand away. "What's so wrong with trying to escape reality?"

Jack paused and tilted his head. "Because reality is never far away," he said. He thought of his mother. "Some try to push it away with drink, some with sex, some with work..." He trailed off.

"Some with a life spent in the darkness?" Millie said, but her tone wasn't accusing.

He nodded. "Yes, some with that."

"Who are you really, Jack Covert?" Millie asked.

He looked at her and wanted to tell her the whole truth, but he wasn't ready. He could tell her *a* truth though. "I'm Jack Covert, Millie," he said. "At least that's who I am now. It's who I want to be. I made that choice."

She nodded and her lips flattened, turned down a bit at the corners but not in a frown, more in a gesture that said *fair enough*. She shrugged. "Why can't Jack Covert let himself have a little fun?" she asked, and her tone was not flirtatious anymore. She was asking like she was really curious.

He had to admit her question took him aback. Why *couldn't* he let himself have a little fun? He relished his life and the fact that he'd escaped his responsibilities and his mother. He loved being alone, he loved having time to read, he loved the challenge and thrill of his work. He loved that what he did needled the aristocracy without causing anyone any real pain. But he couldn't say he was happy. Not really. And he certainly hadn't had any fun in a very long time. In fact, he couldn't remember the last time. That is, until he met Millie.

"The chase in the park was fun," he said, realizing the truth of it even as he said it.

She smiled. "It was terrifying," she said, laughing.

They looked each other in the eyes. He squinted just a little and tried to glean what she was thinking. "We're going to Venice," he said, and it was not a question.

"We're going to Venice," she repeated back to him, in the same flat tone. Then the corner of her little pink mouth upturned just the slightest bit and the edges of her eyes crinkled. "And it might be *fun*," she added with a wink.

Chapter 5

Millie stood with Jack at the door of the tiny cabin. Jack had been lucky to secure passage on a packet ship going around the continent and into the Mediterranean at the last minute. They had the good fortune, funded by Jack's actual fortune, to secure private accommodation. It had only taken them a day and a half to pack, get the necessary messages to Anne and Yvette, and arrive at the docks at Margate. Millie just hoped it had been quick enough, and that no one else knew where they were. She realized with a sinking stomach that one of the *not fun* parts of this adventure was the constant worry and suspicion of every stranger. It was not her way to distrust people. She generally liked to keep an open mind and an open heart, and it wasn't unusual for her to make friends with unlikely people. She frowned to herself and looked at the man beside her. *Including a common thief*, she thought. She took a deep breath and looked back at the interior of the little cabin they'd be sharing on this journey, and her eyes were just becoming accustomed to the dim light when she gulped.

"Why, there's only one bed," she exclaimed, and she could hear Jack groan before she even looked over to see the reaction on his face. He pushed past her into the tiny little room and looked around him, running a hand through his hair. He turned around once, then turned around the other way, as if he were expecting to see something different from the new angle. Millie laughed in spite of herself.

"My contact told me one wardroom, two bunks," he said, his tone icy.

Millie shrugged. "I guess they were wrong." She came into the little room, where there was just enough space for them both to stand next to the single bunk. There was a simple closet for their belongings, a chamber pot on the floor, and little else. The cabin opened directly into the shared passenger dining room, and it was meant only for sleeping. Millie had fond memories of her first voyage on a packet boat with Annelise. She'd been little more than a child, then, and she'd spent most of her time scampering about on deck, learning sailor lingo, and entertaining all the old, conscripted men in the sailors' quarters belowdecks. It had been a pleasant time, and she remembered with special fondness the nights spent curled up in Annelise's arms. It was the first time in her young life that she had been wanted.

Now, though, the idea of sharing this tiny bunk with Jack did not carry the same warm feelings. Not only would it be deuced cramped and uncomfortable, she thought, but it would be *uncomfortable* in more ways than one. She could sense that the tension in Jack's body was due to this second problem. She shook her head again as she peered up at him in the dim light.

"I'm sure we'll manage," she said, trying to keep her voice light. She knew she was treading on thin ice with Jack's mood. "It's only ten days at the most. And hopefully we'll get a lucky spell of weather and make it even sooner."

Jack grunted but nodded again. "I can see if there's any space for me belowdecks with the sailors," he said.

"Please don't make yourself uncomfortable on my account," she said, starting to put her carpetbag and hatbox in the little closet. "We can just take shifts, that's all. We're both used to sleeping at all hours. We'll manage."

Jack took a deep breath, and she felt his exhale from several feet away, so forceful and ragged it was. "Very well," he said in a resigned tone, and he moved beside her to begin making the bed. There was so much Millie didn't know about traveling, but Jack seemed to know what to do in every situation. For example, one must bring their own bedding on the packet ship and it counted toward their luggage allowance.

Jack grunted again. "At least we'll be warm with the extra bedding," he said, almost as if he'd been following the train of her thoughts.

"True. A silver lining," she said, "See, fun already."

They both laughed.

"Come," Jack said, taking her hand. "We should be on deck when the ship sails. It's always a sight."

Millie smiled and squeezed his hand, holding it tight in hers. "If I didn't know better, I'd think you were looking forward to this," she said.

"I love sailing," Jack said. "Accompanying my father on his travels was the highlight of my childhood."

Millie narrowed her eyes but knew enough not to prod him to provide more information. He was opening up to her slowly, but she didn't want to force it. She sensed that in some ways, they needed each other. She had never thought she needed more friends. Her life was full of people who cared for her and would listen to her troubles when needed. Anne would drop everything to help her, as she'd demonstrated quite clearly in the last few days. But Jack put her at ease in a way that none of her other friends did. She couldn't explain it, but she felt *comfortable* around him. She wasn't conscious of the class difference between them, like she was with Anne or even Yvette. Though she felt a strong attraction to him, she wasn't thinking about bedding him all the time the way she was with men she dallied with. She supposed those men weren't really *friends*, though. She shook her head. She had used them, just as Jack had said. Maybe that was another thing that made her so comfortable with him. He seemed to know her better than she knew herself. And that was something because Millie prided herself on self-awareness. She had known deep hardship and sorrow and had learned at an early age that acceptance was one of the keys to happiness. She let go of that which was not in her control and sought to have control over as much as possible. That's why her Bloomsbury life suited her. In fact, that's why life as a maid also suited her. She knew what her tasks were each day, she knew where her next meal was coming from, and she knew she would not be mistreated. That had been enough. Now that she had her freedom, and no longer needed to work, she had sought to control other aspects of her life. When she was lonely, she sought company. It shouldn't be shocking that, having lived in a courtesan's house all her life, she sought male company of the sexual kind. She had never felt shame about it. Unlike Anne, Millie had never disapproved of that lifestyle. She had known her own mother's vices and failings, but none of them had to do with her choice of profession. Her mother had been one of the least good people she'd known, and Annelise Heatherington was one of the best. The fact that they had both been essentially whores had no bearing on that.

They reached the deck, and Jack kept hold of her hand. They were traveling as a young married couple, and it was important to keep that ruse. Still, her hand was growing warm in his, tingling as she thought of what his palm would feel like grazing her bare skin from her waist to her— "You are deep in thought," Jack said as they arrived at the deck railing next to the dock. Sailors, dockworkers, and merchants all stood, waving handkerchiefs.

"Do they have family sailing with us?" she asked.

"Some," he answered, "Mostly they're just here to mark our going. It's part of their routine."

She smiled. "That's nice," she said, and she meant it. It *was* nice. Millie realized she knew very little about the world outside London. She'd been so young when she'd left Italy, and even when she lived there, her life had been circumscribed by the small lodging she shared with her mother. Her best companions had been the landlord's cat, employed as rodent control, and the books she managed to scrounge from the streets.

"Where did you travel with your father?" she asked, thinking enough time had passed that she might broach the topic again without his clamping up like an oyster being poked with a stick.

"Not very far," he said, his tone flat but not strained. "I took the packet to Calais with him several times when he had business in Paris." He smiled at the memory and turned to her. "It wasn't the journey or what we did that mattered," he said. "It was being away from my mother."

Millie raised her eyebrows in question, but Jack looked away, and his eyes seemed to see even further than the horizon. He wasn't clamping up so much as disappearing into himself. Less like an oyster and more like a turtle, she thought with a little exhale at her own cleverness.

The anchor had been raised and the gangplank pulled in when the ship began to move as the dockmen pushed her away into deeper water. The deck swarmed with commotion, with the few other passengers staying out of the way with Jack and Millie while the sailors buzzed back and forth on the deck and up and down the masts, readying the sails and rigging for when they were far enough out in the channel to unfurl and catch the wind. Millie found it endlessly fascinating, and she watched the commotion with wide eyes.

Jack laughed, and Millie looked up at him. The corners of his eyes crinkled with joy. "What?" she asked.

"You," he said. "You look like a child."

She frowned, and he rushed to explain. "No, no, in a good way," he said. "You look so innocent, and your excitement is infectious. It's quite fetching, in fact."

Millie looked up at him and then nudged him in the arm. "I thought we weren't supposed to flirt," she said.

He smiled. "It's not flirting, if I mean it," he said. "I can't make an entire sea voyage without being honest with you."

She smiled and nodded. "I'll accept it, then," she said, and just then the big main sail unfurled above them, catching the wind and snapping into place with a loud clap. She laughed with glee and then ran to the other side of the deck to see the horizon in front of them as they picked up speed. When she reached the railing, her foot slipped on a wet spot, but no sooner had she felt herself lose balance than she felt the bulk of Jack's strong chest against her back and his arms wrap around her protectively. She couldn't help herself when she sank back against him. It was a relief, yes, but it was also because it felt so good. His muscles tensed with holding her steady and she brought her hands up to his strong forearms, twined around her waist. She allowed herself a quick squeeze, and she sighed. He really was an incredible specimen of a man, she thought. *Serves me right that he's the only one I can't have.* She let go of his arms and squirmed a little to break free of him.

"Thank you," she said, pulling her coat around her.

"You just need to get your sea legs," Jack said as if nothing had happened, but his eyes told a different story. There was a coldness there. They were such a clear blue they looked like little chips of ice. "Why don't you go down to the cabin, and I'll leave you alone to rest awhile." His tone was solicitous, but not at all warm. She just nodded. He helped her find her way back below, and she lay down on the bunk, realizing that she was quite sleepy after all the excitement they'd been through. She closed her eyes and was soon lost in sleep.

Jack leaned back against the rowboat on the deck of the ship, turning the page in his book back to the previous one for the fourth or fifth time, realizing that he had read two full pages without understanding or remembering what had happened. He slammed the book closed and laid it on the deck next to him. He put both hands behind his head and leaned back, surveying the clear blue sky. Though it was still quite cold, the seas were calm, and the sun was bright and warm. Above decks, one could stretch out and soak up what sunshine was to be had before being stuck back below in the darkness, cold, or bad weather that might come. Jack tried to spend as much time as possible on deck, and he had tried to get Millie to do so as well, but it was taking a while for her to become accustomed to the roiling and rocking of a ship at sea. He knew she was embarrassed to retch in front of him, so he tried to leave her alone as much as possible, though he wished he could help her in some way.

He still marveled at that. He always wanted to help her. From that night when she bumped into him in the hallway of her own house, to their first day on the ship when he'd caught her in his arms, he had an overwhelming desire to protect this woman. It was very unlike him, he thought, but then again, he'd deliberately chosen work that didn't involve people, so how was he to know what was like or unlike himself? He had never wondered about this before, and this was one of the uncomfortable things about being around her. She made him think these thoughts about himself. He smiled and shook his head.

He looked back down at the book he was holding. This anonymous female novelist seemed preoccupied with the idea that love conquers all. He wondered, not for the first time, why this idea compelled him in literature but repulsed him in real life. His parents were proof that love was a weakness. It worked in novels, and it probably felt great at first, but it wouldn't take long before it destroyed you. Jack had noticed all these novels ended with the proposal or the wedding. He frowned. What about the lifetime afterwards? He realized, much to his chagrin, that he would get no more reading done today. He decided it might be well to go and check on Millie.

He made his way down the tiny staircase that led to the cabin level. He heard—and smelled before he saw—what was happening around the dining table. Raucous singing and the strong smell of Caribbean rum wafted up to him before he rounded the corner and saw them. Several off-duty officers sat around the table, their shirts open at the throat and their jackets slung across the chair backs. The lyrics of a bawdy ballad were being sung badly by the four men around the table, and quite well by the small but mighty curly-headed diva who sat at the head of the table. The rousing chorus ended, and Millie's strong, sweet soprano rang out:

I caught her all aback,

and she shifted her main tack,

but Maggie, she had busted her main stay

Jack thought of rushing forward to stop her antics, but he knew he held no power or control here. Watching her sing the naughty song, her cheeks flushed with laughter, her eyes dancing with her joy, all he could really think about was how happy he was that she was no longer ill. He also took a moment to note exactly how beautiful her voice was, and how much it fitted with her open and lovely face. He stayed in the shadows for a moment while she finished, worried that his presence might give her pause. He loved looking at her when she wasn't aware of him. He realized that, even though they were honest and forthright with each other, she was still guarded around him. He supposed he was guarded himself now that he thought about it. But as he stood there, watching her pound the table and finish off the song with the chorus, he realized that he hadn't felt this close to anyone since his father had died. The song ended with all the men taking draughts of rum and pounding their tankards on the table and Millie stood, bowing and blowing kisses in an exaggerated mimic of a real performer, and as her eyes roamed around the room, thanking the men for their applause, they finally lit on Jack, who had stepped forward from the stairs just a bit. Her smile widened, and she rushed over to him.

"I see you're feeling better," he said, cocking his head to the side as she approached.

"So much better," she said, breathing fast. "When I woke up, I was so hungry and exhausted, I had no idea where I was or what time it was for a moment."

She gestured to the men. "I heard these fellows out here taking a meal, and I crept out to see if I could get a bite to eat. As you can see," she nodded to them, "they welcomed me to join them."

Jack tried to look stern, but he couldn't help a little quiver of amusement at the corner of his lips as he said, "I don't think rum is what you should be having on such an empty stomach."

Millie frowned up at him and narrowed her eyes. "I didn't have any, if you must know," she said, the petulance making her voice rise just a bit, "Just some salt tack and weak ale with lemon in it." She put one hand on her hip. "Not that it's any of your business."

"Given that I must sleep in the same bed," Jack said, nodding toward their cabin door, "I do think it's my business not to have to clean vomit from the sheets."

Millie's chin rose. "I've been very good about the chamber pot," she said with some pride, and Jack had to laugh.

"Aye, that you have," he said. "Now, have you had enough to eat? I think you might need some rest. Seas are calm for now, and hopefully you've gotten your stomach used to the journey, but you must be exhausted."

As if on cue, the ship lurched just a little bit, and Millie fell into him, her face landing square on his shoulder. He couldn't stop himself from wrapping his arms around her to catch and hold her, but he blushed and pulled back, mindful of the other men in the room staring.

He nodded toward them. "Thank you, sirs, for taking such good care of my wife," he said in an even tone. "Now I think I must get her back in bed."

One of the men gave a merry little laugh and said, "Aye, I'm sure you must." The rest of the men laughed heartily until Jack's scowl silenced them. He took Millie's arm and led her through their door, closing it with force behind him.

Millie slumped down onto the bunk, laughter shaking her shoulders. She pulled herself down to the pillow and pulled the blankets up around her neck, but then scooted to the edge of the bunk against the wall and pulled the cover back at the corner, gesturing with her hand for him to join her.

He tried to keep his face empty, but he must have scowled because she rolled her eyes and said, "Don't worry, Covert, I won't try any funny stuff."

Jack frowned at her. "I can go back up on deck," he said. "I was trying to read. You need some rest."

She yawned in response. "Yes, I do. But I'm cold," she paused and then looked right into his eyes, "and a little lonely."

He had read in novels about one's heart melting, but he had never been able to conjure what that might feel like until this moment. She looked so pathetic, so open, and so adorable that he had absolutely no power to resist her. He sat on the bunk, then stretched his frame out next to her, his bulk pressing against her from their shoulders all the way down to their ankles. He secured the blankets around her, tucking them in and staying on top of the covers himself.

She grinned and closed her eyes, nuzzling her face into his shoulder. She made a small noise and sounded for all the world like a purring cat. He could feel his breeches tightening around his arousal, but he ignored it. He brought his free hand up and rubbed her head, her curls soft as silk beneath his rough fingers. "That's it," he said, whispering softly. "Get some rest." Soon he could hear her breath becoming even, just the tiniest little snore escaping occasionally, and he knew she was well and truly asleep. He started to sidle off the bunk to leave her, but her arm came across his chest and held him there, so he sighed and closed his eyes. He might as well try to rest, he thought. It wasn't like he'd get any more reading done now, anyway.

~*~

It was full dark when Jack opened his eyes. He blinked a little, realizing that he couldn't even see his hand in front of his face. Since they'd embarked on this trip, he'd spent most of his nights out in the dining room or up on the deck, preferring the dim starlight to the close, suffocating air of the cabin. He was used to sleeping during the day anyway, so it startled him to be utterly sightless. He could feel, rather than see, Millie next to him, as she shifted her position.

"We seem to have slept the day away," she said, stretching her toes.

"You must have really needed it," he said, concern in his voice.

"I think you did, too." He felt the tips of her fingers drawing a line from his temple to his chin. He tingled everywhere she touched him, from the light touch of her fingers on his face to where the edges of their hips met, all the way down to where her toes lay, falling sideways on top of his ankle. He felt like he was burning despite the chill in the air.

He drew in a ragged breath and brought his hand up to wrap around her fingers. He didn't know what madness held sway over him, but he pulled her hand across his lips and placed the lightest of kisses on her palm. She let out a soft gasp, and he stopped breathing.

"I'm sorry," he said, pulling her palm away from his mouth. "I shouldn't have—"

"Jack," she said, and her voice was scratchy with sleep and need. "I want you." Her tone was not flirtatious in the slightest. Instead, it was open, even, honest. "I admit I want you because I am comfortable with you," she said, squeezing his fingers where they still held hers, "but that's different from *using you for comfort.*"

Jack swallowed. He knew she was telling the truth, and he

knew he felt the same. He'd never felt so tempted in his life. In fact, though he had the normal physical urges of most men, he'd promised himself not to do this. He had to explain.

"Millie," he said, "I have to tell you—"

"Don't," she said, pulling away as if he'd slapped her. "Don't bother. I understand. I'll stop trying."

He turned on his side and pulled her in toward him, holding her head against his chest and running his fingers through her hair. "No," he said, "It's not that. I want you, too."

Their mouths found each other in the dark, and he felt an explosion of exquisite pain in his chest as they kissed. They just lay there, their lips together, his hand caressing her head for long moments before he pulled back. "I've just," he stammered. "That is to say, I've never—"

"Jack Covert," she said, and her voice was almost teasing. "Are you telling me you're a virgin?"

"It's Redstone, actually," he said, "Jack Redstone. And yes."

Millie's body tensed. "The lost Viscount Danbury?" she asked, her voice incredulous.

He laughed. "I suppose that was the only thing I could have told you more shocking than the virgin thing."

She leaned forward and whispered against his lips, "I don't find it shocking at all. Just surprising. But I know better than anyone that everyone's got their own story." She brought her lips down on his with more force this time, then pulled back again. "I'm just surprised I'm sharing a bed with a nobleman. It must be something in the water at that house in Bloomsbury."

He laughed out loud at that, but then became serious. He wanted her so badly, he wasn't sure how to tell her what he had to say next. He cleared his throat.

"Millie," he said, "I swore to myself I'd never give my body to any woman...that way."

She dropped several small kisses on his cheek. "We can bring each other pleasure in any number of ways," she said, and her voice was husky. "I won't take anything from you that you don't want to give."

He groaned. She was so open and gentle with him, so accepting of something that should be embarrassing for a man of his years.

"I want to," he said, his voice catching a little, "But I don't want to disappoint you."

"That," she said, bringing her mouth down to his again, and whispering against his lips, "Would be impossible, Jack *Redstone.*"

Chapter 6

Millie felt herself growing wet and swollen between her legs as she kissed him. She'd never bedded a virgin, and she'd never had an interest in it. But Jack wasn't just any man. He was *Jack*. Something about the total darkness made it feel even safer, and even more intoxicating. She lay on her side, her body pressed tightly against his in the space of the small, narrow bunk. As she kissed him, she ran a hand across his chest, the fabric beneath her fingers sliding over his skin, and she thrilled at the groan he released in reaction. Her hand moved slowly down, and she pulled his shirt from his breeches before sliding her hand up his bare stomach. She darted her tongue in his mouth, and their kiss became even more voracious.

His stomach and chest were downy with fine hair, and she ran her fingers through it, luxuriating in the feel of its softness next to the hardness of muscle beneath. She hadn't realized just how much she'd been dreaming about this until she was touching him. She pulled her mouth from his and leaned down to whisper in his ear.

"I wish it weren't so dark," she said. "I want to see you."

Jack groaned again, and she felt him physically lift her,

sliding his hand underneath her side, and pulling her on top of him. His hands roved up and down her back, pulling her closer to him.

"I've imagined you for so many days," he said, his voice gruff and low, echoing her own thoughts. "Since that night in the hallway at your house, I've pictured what you would look like with your hair down, what you would feel like," he whispered against her neck as he dropped small kisses there. She sighed in response, and he cupped her buttocks, pulling her tighter against his arousal. She moved against him through their clothes and felt close to exploding already.

"Jack," she said, "May I touch you?"

"Please, God, please," he said, in response, clearly losing control.

She reached her hand down between them, sliding her fingers between the laces of his breeches to loosen them, then pulling him up and into her hands. His cock felt hard with need already, and she used her thumb to get wet drops from the tip and rub up and down his shaft. He writhed beneath her, and she felt his head tilt back. She buried her face in his neck and licked him there, his whiskers rough against her tongue. She just drank in the sheer *maleness* of him. Her hand tightened and loosened while she stroked him, stopping occasionally to run her thumb across the tip and around the head. He gasped at each new touch, and the sound of his arousal was like lighting a fire in her belly. She rubbed herself against the muscled expanse of his leg where she knelt.

Jack's hands explored her body while she moved. He pulled the cap sleeves of her dress down over her shoulders and kissed her neck and the top of her bare chest. His hands came around and cupped each of her breasts, and she felt her nipples tighten into sharp little buds, straining at the fabric of her chemise and stays. When his thumbs came up to flick across them, she gasped and stopped what she was doing.

"You can't do that much more," she said, panting, "Or I'll

come."

Jack licked the top of her shoulder and up her neck before whispering in her ear. "Please do," he said, his own voice a barely controlled whisper. "Please. I want you to. I want to give it to you."

His hands stayed on her breasts, teasing her nipples through her shirt, and she writhed against his thigh in an increasing rhythm until she finally could take it no longer. "*Jack*," she cried out, shuddering, a bright light exploding behind her eyes in the darkness of the room. He pulled her face down and kissed her deeply. She lay there, very still, for what seemed like forever, but was surely just moments before she started to come back to herself. She kissed him again, and he bucked his hips upward.

"No," she said against his lips. "Don't rush."

She kept her hand wrapped around his cock, and she was pleased to feel how hard it was. It felt like steel covered in velvet in her palm, and she reveled in knowing she had done this to him. She squeezed but did not move her hand, and he wrapped his arms around her and held her upper body close to his chest while her hand between them teased him. She took him close to the edge, then pulled back, kissing him, nuzzling his neck, nibbling at his earlobe, until she could tell he could take it no more. She pulled her hand up and down quickly, running her thumb against that sensitive spot near the head, and she sighed with contentment when his seed finally released over her hand. She kept stroking him until she was sure he was finished, then she lay back down next to him with her head on his shoulder, running her index finger up and down his stomach.

Jack put his finger under her chin and tilted her face back up to his. He kissed her again, this time chastely, just the feather of his lips against hers. "Thank you," he said in a whisper.

"Thank *you*," she said, and she laughed, a husky, satisfied, languorous sound. "And just look," she said, "we never even removed our clothing."

"Next time," he whispered, rubbing her back absently. "Next time."

She smiled to herself and closed her eyes. A next time would be just fine by her.

They finally fully woke in the morning when the dim sunlight from the stairwell shone through the dining room and under the crack at their door. It was still very dark, so Millie got up and lit the little lantern that hung in the cabin. She surveyed the room, trying to avoid looking at Jack as long as possible. The lingering satisfaction from last night made her blush, and she was worried he would have regrets. She didn't. Unless he did, then she would feel like the worst sort of flirt and harlot. She took her pleasure wherever she could, and never felt shame about it, but taking advantage of Jack would break her. She couldn't explain it. How had a person who'd been robbing her when they met become such an important part of her life? He'd had no motive in coming back to warn her about the assassins. He'd only done it because he was a good person. She'd been around good people living on the margins of society all her life, so it didn't surprise her that a thief could be good. But she was surprised by how protective she felt about him. Learning he was a virgin was surely part of it, she knew, but she'd felt this way about him from the beginning. He was so knowledgeable, so competent, so skilled at what he did, but there was a part of him that was vulnerable, and that was the part she wanted to protect. She felt it so fiercely it caused a physical pain in her heart.

He yawned, and she finally turned to look at him. She was so afraid of what he might say or how he might react, but she also couldn't avoid him forever. He stretched, his eyes still closed, and she just enjoyed looking at him for a moment. He really was a fine specimen of a man. Though he wasn't the tall, imposing figure one usually read about in novels or the scandal sheets, he had his own kind of quiet power in that compact frame. His breeches pulled tight across muscular legs, and she felt heat flush all the way from her neck to her temples as she remembered riding that thigh the night before. His shirt still fell open to reveal the dark hair that grew there, and she felt herself becoming wet again, thinking of him holding her face against his shoulder and the feel of that hair beneath her fingertips. Her gaze traveled up, slowly, to the muscles in his neck and jaw, which opened again for an even larger yawn, then, just as she looked up to his face, his eyes fluttered open, those dark lashes in stark contrast to the icy blue beneath. She couldn't quite read his thoughts in those eyes, but she was sure he could read hers.

"Good morning." Her voice came out in more of a squeak than a greeting.

He chuckled and her whole body relaxed. His voice was hoarse with sleep. "Good morning," he said. He patted the bed next to him, asking her to sit down. She complied, but she held herself still so as not to touch him, wary of how he might react.

She needn't have worried, because Jack pulled her down against him, hugging her close, dropping a chaste kiss on her forehead, before letting her sit back up. He pulled himself up, arranging the pillow behind him and leaning against the wall.

"Last night was—" he began, but she cut him off.

"A mistake," she blurted out.

Jack pulled his eyebrows together in confusion. "That wasn't what I was going to say," and his voice trailed up at the end like a question.

Millie grabbed some of the sheets in her hand, toying with them and staring down to avoid his gaze. "I don't want you to think I took advantage of you," she said.

He laughed out loud at that. "Millie, I'm a virgin, but I'm not quite an innocent," he replied. "I'm a grown man. I don't do anything I don't want to do. I thought you knew me better than that by now."

She smiled but didn't look up yet. When had she ever been this nervous the morning after a tryst? Then she remembered— she usually never let them stay until the morning. She sighed.

This was all uncharted territory for her, too. A fine mess she'd gotten herself into.

"I've been thinking," Jack said, then he put two fingers under her chin to pull her gaze up to meet his own. She had to close her eyes again in response. His touch had so much power over her. But he let his fingers drop, and she opened them again. She realized just the piercing blue of his eyes had almost the same effect as the warmth of his fingertips. She felt flushed, and she licked her lips almost against her will.

"About what?" she asked, and she cursed her voice for being squeaky again.

"When we get to Venice, it's going to be all business. We'll be hiding, we'll be tracking down clues. We'll be on edge and distracted. It will be dangerous and frightening, and even if we succeed, we'll just be gaining the freedom to return to our own lives. The next few days on this ship, we are free in a way we might not ever be again, either of us."

Millie swallowed and nodded, trying to keep her face from betraying her thoughts. If he was going to say what she thought he was going to say—she flushed again, cursing herself for it.

"I have a proposition," he said, and his tone was flat, even while his eyes flashed with something she couldn't quite name.

She nodded again, still unwilling to speak for fear of breaking the spell or making him change his mind.

"I have been lonely," he said, keeping his gaze trained on her face. "I like my life and have no regrets, but being with you has helped me see I shouldn't deny myself pleasure."

Millie literally squeaked at that.

"I have no intention of marrying, or changing my life when I get back," he began, "But it doesn't mean we can't be friends. Friends who—"

She couldn't take it any longer. "Yes," she said, the words tripping off her tongue. "Yes. Don't say any more. I agree."

"Let me just finish—"

She took his hand. "No. I agree. I mean yes, I agree. No, you don't need to finish."

He laughed and placed a palm on each of her cheeks, pulling her in for another kiss, just a quick brush of their lips.

"I'm glad you agree," he said, touching his nose to hers. "But we must lay some ground rules."

She swallowed again but nodded. Her voice was a whisper against his lips when she said, "As long as you don't change your mind."

He shook his head, rubbing his nose across hers in a gesture that was somehow more intimate than anything they had done the night before. "I won't," he said, "I promise."

She nodded. He pulled back and held up his hand, counting on his fingers. "First, no complications. We agree this will end when we get to Venice." She nodded again. "Second, we do whatever feels good, but only after gaining the enthusiastic consent of the other." She giggled at that. She couldn't imagine *not* consenting enthusiastically to whatever this man wanted to do to her. "Third, no more shifts in this bed. When you're in it, I'm in it," he said, and she was surprised by the flinty edge in his voice.

"Agreed," she said.

He held his hand out. "Very well," he said. "Let's shake on it."

She took his hand in hers, but instead of a gentlemanly shake, she gave it a tug and pulled him down on top of her, wrapping her arms around him and kissing him like she'd wanted to kiss him all morning.

Jack grunted in visceral response to her embrace, but he pulled himself back with reluctance. "I think we'd better have some breakfast first, don't you?" Her eyes narrowed at him, and her lips pursed into a little frown.

He shook his head. "Oh, no you don't. Enthusiastic consent, remember?"

She picked up the pillow and hit him with it. Hard. He threw his head back and laughed, and he realized he rarely laughed like this. It made his stomach hurt. "Listen," he said, leaning forward and trapping her wrists in his hands. "You have been very sick. As far as I know, you've only eaten hard tack, some watered-down lemon ale, and my mouth."

She giggled but went limp in his arms, looking up at him with those big brown eyes, her long dark lashes batting. She frowned but reached her face up to his for one more kiss on the cheek. "Fine," she said, "Let's go eat."

They got ready quickly, having slept in their clothes. Jack needed a fresh pair of breeches, and they both needed to straighten themselves out, but it took only moments. Jack stood, leaning on the door frame, watching her worry about her hair in the tiny little glass that hung above the washstand. She jabbed pins in, winced, then tried other angles. He found himself smiling at her. He walked up behind her and took her hands down. He found the few pins that had made their way in and started removing them, dropping them in the empty basin on the washstand, satisfied by the little clinking sound each one made. When he was sure he'd got them all, he met her eyes in the mirror and lifted his hands to the mass of her hair.

"I couldn't stop thinking about this last night," he said, running his fingertips through the thick curls and rubbing them on her scalp. She closed her eyes and almost purred. "I have wanted to see this hair wild since that first night in your hallway."

She turned her head to let him massage different parts of her scalp as she laughed. "This hair has been the bane of my existence since childhood," she said. "It never stays where it should."

"I think that's what I like about it," he said, bending down to whisper in her ear. "It's just like you."

She laughed again, picking up the brush. "Well, be that as it may, I can't very well go out and have breakfast looking like this," she said, her voice practical.

He grabbed the brush and gently combed through the tangles down the lengths. Once he'd worked out the worst of the knots, he pulled the whole mass of it up to the back of her head, and he was amazed by the sheer weight of it. He began twisting and smoothing, then held out his hand for the pins. She dropped them in his palm. Her eyes were wide in the mirror. He put the pins in his mouth to hold them, and started placing them one by one, working quickly, and trying not to hurt her. Though she winced a few times when he got it wrong, he was very pleased when he turned her around to face him. The simple topknot was held in place, but he reached up and pulled a few curls out around her face. "There," he said, "those are for me."

His groin tightened again when she turned her face up to his. Her cheeks were flushed, and he knew what they were both thinking. That made him feel even hotter. He pulled her to him and growled, a low, feral sound. "We've got to get out of here now, or I'm never letting you out again," he said, placing one more kiss on her forehead before pulling back.

When they emerged from their cabin, they blinked a little in the bright light pouring down from the deck into the dining room. It must be late, he thought. The sun was quite high and there was no one else in the room. He went over to the galley and found a couple of hard-boiled eggs. He was so pleased to be on a short packet voyage and not to have a want for fresher food. He rummaged around in the galley storage cabinets and found a jar of water, a huge chunk of cheese, and half a loaf of good, if not slightly stale, bread. "Eureka!" he shouted, balancing the items on his arms as he brought them over to the table where Millie sat, eyeing him.

Her eyes grew wide as saucers. "I really am famished," she said. "I hadn't realized how much until just now."

He lay the food on the table and placed one of the eggs in front of her before unwrapping the paper from the crusty loaf of bread. There was a knife already stuck in the cheese, and he set these out between them, the pungent odor of it making his mouth water.

They ate with such gusto that it was silent in the galley except for the sound of the bread ripping, the paper crumpling, and the banging of the eggshell against the scored wood of the tabletop. He smiled. He couldn't remember the last time he'd enjoyed a meal so much. He guessed hunger really was the best seasoning. Or maybe it was the company. He pushed that thought aside. He was going to enjoy this time with Millie and not over analyze it. He wasn't sure what he'd been thinking when he told her his real identity. That could cause huge problems for him, but he'd have to cross that bridge if and when they came to it. If he had any regrets from last night or this morning at all, that was the only one. He knew deep inside that, though he really didn't want a commitment or to enter into a marriage or even a long-term agreement with anyone, he did want companionship and friendship. And, more than that, he had to admit to himself that part of the reason he'd denied himself these things for so long was as a punishment. He knew he'd abandoned his responsibilities when he'd left Danbury Grange, abandoned his father's legacy just as sure as he'd abandoned his mother, maybe when she needed him the most. He didn't deserve friendship. He knew he'd done the right thing for himself, but that didn't mean it was the *right thing*. He sighed.

Millie looked up from the egg she was still picking apart and paused before popping a piece of yolk into her mouth. "Is something wrong?" she asked. "Don't tell me it's the cheese. I really want that cheese."

He smiled back at her, but he knew the smile didn't reach his eyes. "No, just lost in memories, I suppose."

She frowned. "They seem like bad ones." She paused, then set the rest of the egg down in front of her, leaning forward, one little errant curl falling into her face. "I hope they're not from last night."

He laughed. "How can you think that?" he said.

She sighed with relief. "It all seems too good to be true," she said. "Usually when that's the feeling, it's also the fact."

"Well, not this," he said, ripping off another hunk of bread and stuffing it in his mouth. He chewed a little, then said, his mouth still a little full, "I was thinking about my family."

Her bow of a mouth flattened into a line and two tiny wrinkles appeared between her eyes as she stared at him. "Do you want to talk about it?"

"Not particularly."

She nodded and picked her egg back up. She drew one knee up to her chest and sat, looking for all the world like the statue of a seraphim one might see hanging off the side of a church. He chuckled at the comparison and took another bite of cheese. "Thank you for not prying. I'm not sure it would help to talk about it. I'd rather not."

"Of course," she said, chewing. "I know exactly how you feel."

"But you're so open," he said, surprised at her answer. "You told me your whole life story the first day I met you."

She shrugged, and the curl on her forehead bounced with the movement. "That's true." She leaned forward and ripped a hunk of bread from the loaf. "But it doesn't heal. I'm just an open person. I don't keep secrets well, and I'm not ashamed of that." She stopped to chew for a moment, then swallowed. "But it's really time that heals. What you do in the meantime makes very little difference."

He frowned. Time hadn't done much at all to heal him. He wondered if there was something wrong with him. Maybe he did deserve to be punished. Maybe he had made the wrong decisions and done the wrong things. Did time heal for everyone else but him? He shoved these thoughts aside and tried to focus on Millie's face. Maybe it was Millie who was remarkable. Maybe time only healed for her, and why wouldn't it? She was just a tiny ball of energy and hope, he realized. And that's what drew him to her. Of course, she was beautiful, but in that dark hallway in Bloomsbury he hadn't fully been able to see that. No, it was her energy that had drawn him, her openness, her refusal to be afraid of him, her sarcasm, and her strength. Her ability to laugh at everything, including herself. As he watched her, she took the knife and leaned forward to cut another piece of cheese. She brushed one of those wayward curls back behind her ear, then sat back in the chair. He felt himself getting hard just looking at her. Nothing she was doing was arousing. In fact, she was eating with gusto, crumbs falling to her lap, which she would then just brush off her skirt without even thinking. She took a quick drink of the ale and wiped her lips with the back of her hand. He almost groaned, remembering how those lips had felt against his. He couldn't wait to get her back in that cabin. He knew he didn't deserve her. He didn't deserve to be truly happy. He'd given up on his mother and given up on himself. He knew he was making the right choice to keep himself away from other people. He and Millie could enjoy each other's bodies and company on this trip, he thought, but it would be absolutely essential to let her go when it was over.

Chapter 7

Millie lay in the sun on the deck, wrapped up in a blanket from below, trying to enjoy some fresh air, light, and warmth. She had slept so well in Jack's arms and had felt so much better after their improvised yet hearty breakfast. She almost felt like a new woman. In a way, she supposed she was. Though she had never been a shy and retiring wallflower, she had also never sought adventure. She'd lived through enough uncertainty and mayhem with her mother, she thought with a frown. But this was an adventure of a very different sort, and of course, Jack was a companion she trusted and could rely on. She clutched the book she held, one of Jack's novels they'd brought to help pass the time on the ship. She'd read the first few chapters, and she was eager to find out what happened to these poor Dashwood sisters, so ill-treated by their brother. But what had kept her attention the most was Jack's precise, cramped handwriting on each page. The notes he had taken while reading gave her an insight into him that she felt all the conversations in the world never could have. It felt sneaky and intimate to read them, but he had told her to feel free. He marked figures of speech the author used, tracked his opinions of characters and how the author was developing them, and underlined little similes or turns of phrase that he found particularly striking. They were mundane, really, Millie thought. But it was the fact of their existence at all that was so revealing. Jack was a student. Not just of writing or literature, but of human nature. He was a sensitive reader of character, she realized, and that was part of what made him so good at his job. His instinctive knowledge of how a pursuer might act allowed him to elude them easily. His ability to anticipate people's responses and actions was what made him a good thief and what had kept him alive. She cocked her head and looked out at the sun glinting off the waves. That ability to anticipate moods and learn to avoid them was something she was very familiar with. If you had a parent who drank, it was how you learned to survive your childhood. Millie leaned back and closed her eyes, images of her mother filling her mind. The blank stare that meant a bender was coming. The rheumy eyes that meant she was entering a spiral of shame about her drinking. The red cheeks that meant she'd soon turn to anger, an anger that sent a young Millie hiding under the table. Yes, Millie knew and understood all of this. She could see it very clearly in Jack's behavior, the way he tensed up when a new person entered a room, his constant state of alertness, waiting to decide whether to stay or leave any situation.

But there was something else in this man, too. The annotations in the romantic novel were only the beginning of the depths he was hiding. He cared about learning. He cared about thinking. It was important to him not to always accept things as they were, but to question and to ponder. It had been a long time since Millie had considered any man her intellectual equal. She liked to surround herself with creative friends who engaged her in philosophical and artistic conversation, but the men she took to bed were rarely from this set.

And now she was taking Jack to bed. *Their* bed. This ship had flung them together against their will, but even these two headstrong, stubborn people were bending under the weight of their desire for each other. And why shouldn't they, she thought, with a little toss of her head. She narrowed her eyes and stared at the shapes the clouds were making in the sky, basking in the bright, warm sunshine.

"Where are you?" Jack's voice interrupted her reverie just as his shadow fell over her. She shaded her eyes and looked up at his face.

"Hmm?" she said, so surprised by his arrival that she hadn't the faintest idea what he meant.

He pointed at the book. "In *Sense and Sensibility*," he said, "Which part are you in?"

She laughed and then sighed. "I'm not making much progress, I'm afraid," she said, pulling the book back up from where it had fallen against her stomach. She scanned the page that was open, then flipped back a page, running her finger down the fine, creamy paper. "Ah, yes," she said, remembering, "They'd just gotten to Barton Cottage. Chapter six."

Jack lowered himself down next to her, and his body exuded a warmth almost as strong as the sun's. He took the book from her. "Oh, then you're just about to meet Mrs. Jennings." He scanned the page and chuckled, then handed the book back. "You're in for a treat."

"Would you like to join me?" Millie asked, not wanting him to leave, but knowing she wouldn't be able to focus on her reading with him sitting so close to her.

"Do you want me to read aloud?" he asked, and he sounded unsure.

She turned to him, delighted by the idea. "Yes! How wonderful! We can take turns."

He smiled, and his blue eyes seemed to reflect the blue of the sky and the glinting sunlight from the water. He took the book back from her, and when their fingers touched, she felt a *frisson* of energy between them. She'd wondered if their little escapade in the bunk last night would have taken some of the edge off her desire, but instead it seemed to have only increased it. She sighed, and Jack looked up at her, his brow furrowed just the tiniest bit.

"What is it? Are you cold?"

Millie smiled. "No," she said, "No. Please. Start reading." She cocked her head to indicate the book. "Please."

"Very well. 'Mrs. Dashwood and her daughters were met at the door of the house by Sir John, who welcomed them to Barton Park with unaffected sincerity,'" he began. Millie closed her eyes, and she could see Barton Park almost as clearly as if it existed right in front of her. The silly Lady Middleton, the jolly Sir John, and the inveterate gossip and busybody Mrs. Jennings were all figures who were as alive to her as if she knew them in Bloomsbury. Jack's voice was soothing, but also lively. He modulated his voice with each new character, and Millie found herself laughing time and again. She lay her head on his shoulder and listened in bliss, and Jack moved to prop the book on his knee and held it with one hand. The other found its way between them, where his fingers twined in hers. Millie felt her eyes becoming wet with tears that she couldn't explain, but Jack never stopped reading.

Though it was warm and sunny and calm, it was still January, and soon enough the sun was setting. As the captain and first lieutenant walked the deck for inspection, they stopped to greet the couple, and Millie knew that they looked like the perfect picture of newlyweds enjoying their first trip to the continent. She was glad their ruse allowed them this public intimacy. The captain and lieutenant exchanged pleasantries with them, and they all remarked that they looked forward to a communal dinner tonight, now that Millie had recovered from her seasickness.

Millie and Jack smiled and thanked the men, and they moved on, continuing their rounds. Jack turned to Millie and whispered behind the book. "And to think, you thought we should travel as brother and sister."

Millie laughed so loudly it turned into a snort. "As usual, you were right," she said, finally, her shoulders still shaking. "Can you imagine how our arrangement would look if you had listened to me?"

He leaned in and nuzzled the top of her head. "It would have been impossible," he whispered against her hair. "I find I quite like it this way."

She almost purred in response. Her fingers tightened around his. "Keep reading," she said, and he did, the sound of his voice and the adventures of the Dashwoods making her utterly unaware of time passing until Jack slammed the book shut. She sat up with a start.

"Why did you stop?"

He held the book in his hand and gestured to the sky. "Not enough light."

She sat up and stretched. "How long have we been sitting here?"

"We're on chapter nine now," he said in response, chuckling. He groaned a little as he stretched his legs out and then came to his feet. "It must be close to dinnertime."

Almost in response, Millie's stomach made a rather unladylike noise. "You don't say," she said, as she carefully stood, trying to be graceful with all the skirts caught in her legs.

In the cabin, they barely had enough room to maneuver around each other as they made their ablutions. Millie found it much easier to wear the same dress as long as possible, but she did wish she could put on something smarter. She wanted Jack to find her attractive, she realized, and the thought was disturbing. She had never before in her life dressed for a man. She liked nice clothes, and she liked to experiment with her hair. In fact, choosing outfits and creating hairstyles had been her favorite part of being a maid for Anne and her mother. But she hated the idea that women only loved fashion to attract men. And it wasn't helped by the fact that Anne had never thought about fashion a day in her life. She would have worn the same yellow morning dress every day until it fell apart. In fact, Millie thought with a wry smile, she was probably wearing it right now.

But Millie loved to choose a dress, bonnets, jewelry, and jackets, and then to plan how she could tame her curls into something more becoming to fit a certain occasion. She chose according to the function, though, not according to the tastes or interests of those attending. Now, though…she turned around from where she had been fussing in her carpetbag and caught her breath when she saw the muscled expanse of Jack's back as he was pulling on a fresh shirt. Her heart skipped a beat as she watched the shirt ripple down over his skin. He turned around and smiled, and she blushed, knowing that he had seen her watching. She quickly averted her eyes, but it was only a moment before he closed the small distance between them and swept her up in his arms.

"I want to see you, too," he said, his lips brushing her ear. "Tonight."

She grew so weak in the knees that she was afraid she might fall. He held her tight in his strong embrace, though, and traced tiny kisses from her ear down to her collarbone before he pulled himself away. She felt cold where his face had been. "Tonight," she whispered in response. Her voice was as weak as her knees.

She turned back to her bag and chose a light Spencer to fight off the chill that would settle in the dining room now that darkness had fallen. She went back to the little mirror over the washstand and sighed at the state of her curls.

Jack sat on the bunk and patted the blanket next to him. "Come," he said, and his voice was a command, though gentle. She obeyed and sat next to him. He turned and grabbed her shoulders to face her away from him, and he methodically pulled out every pin he'd placed earlier that morning. She sighed as she felt her heavy hair falling around her shoulders. He sighed, too, as his fingers made their way up her neck and moved along her scalp, rubbing the soreness from the tight pins out. "Your hair is glorious," he said, his voice full of awe.

Millie turned and laughed. "It's a giant pain in the neck," she said, then turned back, "Literally."

Jack's fingers moved back down her scalp and back to her neck, rubbing and massaging the muscles there. It felt so good she thought she might melt.

He kneaded and used his knuckles on the tops of her shoulders, then squeezed her shoulders again before pulling her hair back up. He started to pull the hair near her right temple with a gentle tug, and she realized he was braiding. "Where on earth did you learn to braid?" she asked.

"I used to braid my mother's hair," he said, but did not continue.

He finished that braid and made an identical one at her other temple, then pulled them together at the top of her head and pinned them in place. He started pulling pieces of hair from around the rest of her head and pinning them to reach the braids on top, and it seemed like only moments had passed before she had a perfectly coiffed updo. She stood up and went to the mirror and admired herself. The most becoming braids pulled up from her temples and accentuated her large eyes, and the bun on top seemed to hold all her curls in place, a neat, prim, and becoming little knot.

"Amazing," she said, turning first to the right and then to the left. "How on earth?"

"I told you," He said, and his voice was gruff now, "I used to help my mother. She loved it when my father or I 'played with her hair,' as she called it."

Millie came back to sit beside Jack again and she made sure her voice was gentle. She did not want him to close himself off again. "You hadn't mentioned any good memories of your mother."

"There aren't many," he said, and his eyes were sad. The hollows beneath them were accentuated by the dim lantern light, and he looked away from her, not focusing on anything in the room, but obviously seeing right into the past. "But there are some."

She took his hand and squeezed. "I have some wonderful memories of my mother," she said. "They almost all involved singing." She smiled. "My mother really was amazing at what she did. Sitting in the wings, behind the rigging at the opera, those are my favorite memories. She sang soprano, so she was always the star. And the entire theater would hush in response."

Jack smiled. "That sounds wonderful," he said. "I've never been to the theater."

Millie drew her face back in shock. "But you're a Viscount."

"That happened after I ran away," he said. "I was only a viscount's son before that."

"Still. It seems shocking you wouldn't have gone. Were you in society much?"

Jack paused and stared past her, lost in thought. "No," he said, and though it was a simple word, his tone made it seem like the final one on the subject. Millie squeezed his hand again. "Come, let's eat. I believe the other passengers are waiting for us."

~*~

The other passengers and the ship's complement of officers were indeed waiting for them when they stepped out into the shared dining room. The officers and cabin passengers generally shared a more formal meal at dinner, but Jack and Millie hadn't attended one yet due to Millie's illness. Now, though, Jack thought, they seemed most welcome.

They all made their pleasantries and sat down at the big table, laden with several delicious-looking dishes arranged down the middle, family-style. Officers and passengers passed bowls and platters around, serving themselves. There was fresh fish, freshly baked bread from the galley ovens, stewed vegetables, and potatoes. Jack's stomach growled audibly, and he stole a glance at Millie, who covered her laugh with her napkin.

She really did look radiant, he thought. Now that they had relaxed into the routine of the ship, and she was no longer ill, he was coming to truly appreciate her beauty, even more than he originally had. He loved the flush that came to her cheeks, and he loved most of all when he was the cause. She was laughing *at* him and not *with* him now, but even that brought him some sense of accomplishment. He wanted to keep her laughing, he realized. He'd do anything to keep her laughing.

As the dinner progressed, with jokes, stories, and thoughts about the weather and their destinations, he realized something else. He enjoyed the company. Even when he'd lived at home, he'd never eaten at a table full of people. When he was young, he'd eaten in the nursery. He'd sometimes eaten with his father as he grew older, but his father was often absent, especially toward the end of his life. At Eton, he'd never been entirely comfortable with large groups of his classmates, and he'd never fit in. Now, though, he could see why some people had large families. There was something very soothing about sharing a meal with others, even when he had nothing to contribute to the conversation. Just that sound of laughter felt like a balm to him. He had been content to live alone and in darkness, but it had never occurred to him to wonder what he'd been missing.

Almost as if she could read his thoughts, Millie turned to him. "This is nice, isn't it?" she said, sipping a glass of claret.

"It is," he assented, with one nod. "It really is."

Millie leaned back in her chair and took another long draught of wine. "It really makes me miss Bloomsbury," she said, sighing. "Tonight, I would have been to Lady M's *salon.*"

"*Salon?*" he asked, curious.

"That's just the pretentious name we give it," Millie laughed, setting the wine glass back in front of her and moving pieces of fish around on her plate. "We get together every Thursday, eat a fine meal, and then hear lectures and performances. Lady M is always finding some new scientist, mathematician, or poet to introduce to us. We enjoy the performances and contribute to the patronage of those we find to have talent or need—preferably both." She pulled a bite to her mouth.

"That sounds lovely," Jack said, trying to show his sincerity with his tone. "I'd like to attend one of these *salons*."

"You should," Millie said. "You wouldn't be the only aristocrat there. Lady M herself is landed gentry, though that's just a pseudonym."

Jack grunted. "I'm not an aristocrat anymore," he said. "I gave that all up, remember? The *lost* Viscount?"

Her smile in response was so wide, he felt warm just seeing it. "Oh, no, I remember. You'd be surprised how many disgraced aristocrats are lurking in Bloomsbury."

He started as if she'd physically smacked him. "*I'm* not disgraced," he said, offended.

She narrowed her eyes. "I caught you stealing from me in the middle of the night. I think you're disgraced now, My Lord."

He looked around. "Keep your voice down," he hissed.

She smiled again, but this time it was the smile of a mother scolding a child. "You are far too nervous," she said, and she picked her napkin up again to dab at the corners of her mouth before carefully arranging it back on her lap. "The trick to not being heard is to sound like you don't care if anyone hears."

He frowned. He was the expert in subterfuge, was he not? Who was she to give him lessons in keeping his identity secret? He leaned back and crossed her arms, grunting a little.

Millie laughed, a light little trill that made him shiver, just a little. He narrowed his eyes.

She pointed her fork at him before putting it in her mouth. "You, sir, look like a person trying to hide who he is."

He rolled his eyes and relaxed his arms, leaning forward to take a sip of water. He decided to change the subject. "Tell me more about these *salons*," he said. "What have been some of your favorites?"

"We had Mary Shelley, but before she wrote *Frankenstein*,"

she said, with a satisfied smirk. Clearly, she had seen the work on his shelves.

"That's my favorite novel," he said, his eyes wide.

"It's one of mine as well," Millie replied, taking another bite. "Mary is an absolute pill, though."

Jack laughed. "Who else?"

"Oh, a few French mathematicians, some very interesting surgeons, several philosophers, and not a few inveterate bluestockings."

"I read quite a bit," Jack said, leaning his head on his fist, thinking, "But the idea of all those people in a room, real people, *talking* about these things—" He trailed off, unable to even fathom a good word to describe it.

"It's wonderful," Millie said, agreeing. One of the other passengers from down the table heard them and asked Millie about one of the mathematicians he'd heard of, and Jack had a moment to think while Millie was otherwise engaged. He tried to focus on his meal, but he couldn't take his eyes off her. He realized that it was not just his body that was longing for hers, it was all of her that he wanted. He closed his eyes and thought back to that afternoon when she'd lain, her head on his shoulder, and they'd read the novel together, the warm sun on their faces, and it had seemed as if the entire world around them no longer existed or existed only for their sole enjoyment.

And, in a way, didn't it? Wasn't he, of all people, the kind of person who should be able to reinvent the world around him? Hadn't he spent his life doing that? Suddenly, he felt like the air in the dining cabin was stifling. He folded his napkin and made a quick apology to excuse himself, then went up the stairs to the deck.

He braced his legs to stand firmly in the gentle rocking of the boat and took a deep breath of the cold, frosty air. It was a still night, and the cold was so complete and so clean it felt like standing in space itself. The stars seemed so close he felt he could reach out and touch them. He took another deep breath, so deep it almost hurt, then he walked to the rail and grabbed it, looking out across the starlit sea to the horizon, only visible in the line between stars and no stars.

He knew he was in dangerous waters. Not the sea that spread out before him, but the vast ocean of feeling he had been treading to stay above for his whole life. When his father had been alive, he had been able to feel, been able to love. He knew his father loved him, and he had even known, somewhere deep down, that his mother loved him. As the years had gone on, though, it had become increasingly clear that neither loved him *enough*. He knew if he could just be more loveable, his mother would realize she needed to stop drinking. If she only loved him just a *little* more, that would be what it took to make her realize what she was doing. He had always believed that, and he still did.

With his father, it was different. The viscount had loved Jack. He knew that for sure. But he also knew, as sure as he was of his father's love, that he must have loved the Viscountess more. He must have known all along that it would be better for Jack to take him out of that house, but he couldn't bring himself to do it. Jack had watched his father struggle against that his whole life. He had watched the pain cross the older man's face every time he had come back to Danbury Grange. And every time the Viscount had gone again, Jack had retreated more and more inside himself, wondering what it was about himself that kept his father from taking him back to London. Why had he left him there with his mother, in that house of pain and sorrow? He'd asked this question over and over, and each time, his father's answer was the same.

"I can't do that to your mother, Jack," he'd said, tears in his eyes.

"How can you do it to *me*?" the little boy had cried.

Jack winced, remembering. How could love be a force for good when it had been the cause of all his pain and suffering?

No, it couldn't.

He thought of Millie, sitting downstairs, enjoying the company of all those people, able to open up and go out in society. She shared herself willingly with others, but she, too, kept her friendships and her romantic life separate. In fact, she claimed to have no romantic life, only a sexual one, and that seemed to be working well for her. But was Jack just built differently? Was he just not able to keep himself from falling in love? And what would he do if he did fall in love with this woman, this bewitching, lovely, open woman, and she didn't love him back? What then?

Chapter 8

Jack's reverie on deck was interrupted by the distant flash of lightning on the horizon. It was so far away, he heard no thunder, though he strained his ears to listen for it. So far, they'd had such lucky weather on this voyage, he wasn't surprised that they'd eventually run into a storm, but it still worried him, especially for Millie's poor stomach, only just now recovered from the movement of a calm sea. He turned to go below and check on her, but as he made his way toward the cabin stairs, he saw her coming up toward him. The lamplight from below outlined her small frame, and the way she took the stairs two at a time revealed her energy and excitement. As she came fully out into the chilly night breeze, she pulled her jacket closer around her and shivered.

"It gets cold so quickly at night," she said, her teeth chattering as she came toward him. She looked up at the stars. "But the beauty is just breathtaking, is it not?"

He smiled, but then jerked his head toward the horizon. "It is, for now," he began, "but it looks as if a storm may be heading our way. I was just coming to check on you." He pulled her close and held her against him. She was shivering. He couldn't be sure if it was the thought of the storm, the cold air, or the closeness of his body. He hoped it was the latter. He rubbed her back briskly to warm her up, and she circled her arms around him in response.

"This feels nice," she said, turning her face up to look at him. "How do you stay so warm?"

"Nervous energy, I suppose," he laughed.

She turned her face toward the horizon. "I just saw lightning," she said.

"We'd better go belowdecks and make ourselves comfortable," he said, grabbing her hand in his. "Still no thunder, so we might miss it, but better to be safe than sorry."

She leaned her head against his shoulder. "Yes," she said, squeezing his hand. "Safe."

When they got belowdecks, the crewmen were scrambling to be ready for a possible storm, and Jack and Millie busied themselves helping to put away the dishes and food from dinner. It didn't take long before everything was clear, and the dining room deserted. He and Millie followed the rest of the passengers and made their way to their own cabin, where Jack lit the small hanging lantern and began to busy himself with straightening the bedclothes. His entire body was tense, not knowing how Millie felt, not knowing how to tell her that he wanted her. It was only that morning that they'd made their agreement, but he wasn't sure if she was feeling well enough, or too worried about the storm. It felt crass to ask, and he'd never been the type to flirt or seduce. He didn't even know where to begin. So, he kept his eyes carefully averted and pretended to keep himself busy while he waited, his breath almost locked inside his body.

He reached down to grab his soiled clothing from earlier and try to arrange it neatly, but as he stood to fold his breeches, he felt Millie's arms come around his waist from behind. She clasped her hands together over his belly, and he could feel her gentle breathing as she rested her head on his back. He closed his eyes and dropped the breeches, covering her arms with his own and twining his fingers with hers at his waist. He just stood there, the silence broken only by the sound of their breath and the gentle constant lap of the waves on the side of the ship. When the distant rumble of thunder wound itself around the room, he shivered. He had always loved thunderstorms, and even more so at sea. He supposed it was no surprise he'd picked a profession that kept him riding that knife edge of danger. He'd always been attracted to it.

Millie's hands untangled from his, and he felt her pulling his shirt from his breeches. He still wore the waistcoat he'd donned for dinner, but she didn't touch it. Instead, she freed the bottom of his shirt and then slid her hands up under, her fingertips grazing the skin of his belly. He groaned but dared not move. He wanted nothing more than to turn and take her into his arms, but what she was doing felt so good, he didn't want it to stop. Her hands slid up the bare skin of his stomach, moving in circles, feeling every inch of him. He felt her breath next to his ear as she said, "I want to see you, Jack."

She ran her hands back down his stomach, and his skin felt cold when she pulled away. He watched her, frozen, as her fingers began working at the buttons of the waistcoat. Once she finished, he shrugged out of it as she pulled it from his shoulders. Finally, he turned to look at her, and her eyes were dark with desire. She smiled at him and took his face in her hands. He turned to place a kiss on her palm, and he felt the pad of her other thumb caressing his cheekbone. He closed his eyes again. It was all too much. He wasn't sure he could bear it.

Millie's hands moved down to his neck, where she began to unknot the cravat he wore. She was clearly taking her time as she unknotted it, then slowly pulled the length of the fabric away. His shirt hung open now, and he felt exposed in a way that was both delicious and frightening. He brought his hands up to her waist, but she took them in her own and placed them back down by his side.

Her voice was low and breathy with need when she said, "Let me lead you." She pulled his shirt open and dropped her face to his throat. His head fell back as she began placing little kisses on the side of his neck. Surely, she could feel his heart pounding, he thought, and her tongue darted out to lick the place where it pulsed beneath his jawline. He wrapped his arms around her and pulled her closer to him, but again she brought his hands back to his sides. She bunched his shirt up in her hands and brought it upward, then allowed him to lift his arms to get it off, and he felt seared by every inch of cloth that made its way up his torso as she pulled slowly just to torture him. When she finally got it free and flung it across the little cabin, she took a step back, her head cocked. Jack was panting, feeling like a tiger crouched and ready to pounce. He licked his lips.

Millie let out a low little noise from the back of her throat that sounded almost like a purr. Her breathing was ragged, and he watched her chest heave with each intake. She smiled. "You're a finely made man, Jack Covert, you know that?"

He could only grunt in response. He had never been naked in front of a woman, never received a compliment from one, save the leering jests thrown his way in the East End or down by the docks. He felt himself blushing, unable to speak. He looked away in his discomfort, but she moved toward him and took his jaw between the thumb and forefinger of one hand. She was gentle but firm as she turned his face back toward her own. Her eyes narrowed slightly, but were still kind as she whispered, "Say thank you."

Jack brought his eyebrows together, posing a question without asking it.

"That's what you do when someone compliments you," she said, as if instructing a child. "You say thank you."

He could only rasp out, "Thank you, then," in response, but her smile broadened, and her eyes crinkled with her pleasure as she brought her face up to his and finally kissed him on the mouth. She brushed her lips against his, just the barest whisper of touch between them, then she dropped smaller kisses around his mouth, stopping at one corner to dart her tongue out and run it across his top lip. He shuddered and could take it no longer. He wrapped his arms around her and brought her close against him, his need straining against his breeches and pressing into her belly. He cupped her backside and pulled her up against him until his erection nestled between her legs. She gasped, but responded with her kiss, plunging her tongue into his mouth. He responded with all of himself, meeting her heat and intensity, but never feeling like it was enough. He wanted her, all of her, and he wanted her *now*.

He realized she was still wearing the Spencer jacket she'd had on at dinner, and he pushed her torso away just enough to get his fingers to the buttons. It seemed like there were two million of them, but he unclasped each one, starting at the bottom, his hands brushing against her breasts as he moved. Finally, freeing the last top button, he yanked the material down her arms and threw it onto the floor. She snaked her arms up around his neck and pulled him down to kiss her again, but he was single-minded in his desire to get her out of her clothes.

"I want to see you," he growled, grabbing her face with one hand, and holding it inches from his own. "I want to see all of you."

She nodded and turned so he could undo the buttons on the back of her dress. As soon as it was unbuttoned enough to remove, she pulled it off over her head and turned back to face him. She was the perfect woman, he thought. She wore no stays, and her chemise clung to her breasts and hips, the thin fabric only enhancing her shape. Her nipples were hard and dusky, straining against the muslin. Jack took her breasts into his hands and rubbed his thumbs across them, and he thought he might burst when she let out a deep moan.

He pulled her back against him and buried his face in her neck, pulling the chemise down roughly across her nipples and making her gasp again. He ran his tongue along her earlobe and down into the hollow of her throat. She clutched his shoulders, and he felt a sweet pain as her fingernails bit into his skin.

"I want to make you come again," he said, his lips against the tender skin at her jawline. "This time, I want to watch your face when I do it."

She gulped and nodded, her fingers still trying to find purchase on his back and shoulders, as if she could pull herself closer to him somehow. Jack bunched up the chemise where it was still pooled at her waist, and he tugged it down inch by inch, kneeling to follow it with kisses. He ran his tongue around her belly button and pulled the chemise down to the floor. He pulled her stockings down to follow, then stood and took a step back to stare at her. Instead of covering herself up, or trying to be modest, she just looked right into his eyes and let her hands stay at her sides.

"You are so beautiful," he said, his voice soft with wonder. "Even more beautiful than I'd been imagining."

"You've been thinking of me naked, Jack Covert?" she said, her lips twitching up at one side in that insolent smile he loved.

"Every minute," he said, "And dreaming about it at night."

They still stood a foot apart, staring into each other's eyes, and Jack felt like there was an invisible fire burning between them. Her skin was flushed with it, and he felt out of control at the sight of her. She reached up and pulled the pins from her hair, and the dark, lush curls fell past her shoulders, the ends lightly brushing her nipples. She brought her hands up and cupped both her breasts, pinching her nipples between her forefingers and thumbs. He never broke eye contact with her as he unlaced his breeches and dropped them to the floor. He took his cock in his hand and stroked it, relishing the hunger in her eyes as she watched him.

He knew they were playing a game, and he couldn't shake the sensation of wanting it to last forever, even as he knew he could barely contain himself for even a few more seconds. She smiled at him again, this time full of desire, intensity, and passion. She reached one hand out and beckoned him toward her.

He pulled her up into his arms and laid her on the bunk. She grunted a little as her head landed on the hard wall, and he started. "I'm so sorry, are you—"

"I'm wonderful, Jack," she said, reaching up to stroke his chin. "I just need you. *Now.*"

Jack straddled her and kissed her again, hard and full of need. She took his cock in her hands and fingered it lightly. He took her earlobe in his mouth and bit it, pulling it between his teeth and playing with her. Her hands clasped around his erection in response, and he moved down to her breasts, taking first one nipple and then the other between his teeth, nipping at her gently, then pulling back and blowing on them softly. She writhed beneath him, her hips bucking up toward him.

"Not yet," he whispered, against the curve of her breast.

He brought his hand down between her legs and brushed his fingertips along the hair that grew there, drawing back when her hips moved to press herself against him. He held his hand just above her, daring her to move again. He pulled his head back up to look at her and her eyes were wide and intense, meeting his gaze without flinching or blinking. He didn't move for long seconds, then placed his hand on her mound and rubbed gently. Her eyes closed and her head fell back on the pillow, her hands gripping the sheets on either side of her. He slid his finger into her slit and rubbed up and down again, not entering her yet. He had never been with a woman, but he'd certainly consumed a lot of naughty pamphlets. He knew to use his fingers, but he was unclear where. He bent his head in embarrassment, his breath coming faster.

"You're going to have to show me, Millie," he said, his voice barely above a whisper.

Her fingertips left the sheets and came up to his face, tracing the line of his jaw, his nose, his brow. "Of course I will," she whispered. Her fingers were like feathers brushing him, down his shoulders, across his chest and belly, and finally she took the hand that rested on her womanhood, and moved it down between her legs, one of her fingers pushing his into her. He felt her then, slick, wet, and hot. She bucked her hips again, but this time he did not stop her.

"Does that feel good?" he asked, and she could only murmur her assent. She brought both her hands to cup his buttocks, and she kneaded him as he stroked her.

She put her hand back between them and moved his thumb to a place just above her slit. She showed him how to brush it gently while he moved his finger in and out and she writhed beneath him. He felt both weak and powerful as he looked down into her eyes. He was making her feel this way. He was mastering her like he'd mastered hiding, like he'd mastered blending into a crowd. He could learn and practice, and he could make her feel like this. It was like a drug to him. He felt like he was floating above himself, like he might have an orgasm without even touching his cock. It was maddening, and it was delicious, and it was the most dangerous thing he'd ever done.

Their eyes locked again while he stroked her. He bent to kiss her one more time, but he had been telling the truth earlier: he wanted to watch her come. He lifted his head again, his other hand toying with her nipple, and he watched her turn and twist. Her passion was uncontained as her curls splayed out across the pillow and her soft lips panted with need.

"Jack," she moaned, her breath coming faster and faster, "Oh my God, Jack."

He teased her, pulling his finger out and rubbing her thigh, her mound, her belly, then playing with her nub with his thumb again.

"Please, Jack," she said, "Please."

He slid his finger back inside her, and her body tensed beneath him. He pulled it out and slid two in, rubbing her with his thumb again in slow lazy circles, watching her face the whole time. Finally, she shuddered and cried out, her eyes closed, her entire body going still while he kept rubbing until she relaxed and smiled. He smiled, too. He had never felt such a sense of mastery.

Millie looked thoroughly satisfied, but her eyes were shining in the lamplight. She squirmed up and took his face in her hands. "My turn," she said, getting off the bed and laying him down. He stared up at her as she climbed atop him and watched those curls cover her face and fall across his stomach as she kissed her way down his torso. She cupped his balls in her hands and squeezed them very gently, then pressed her fingers into the sensitive skin beneath them. He almost exploded right then. He'd never seen that in any of his pamphlets. And when he took care of himself, it was more routine than anything. Think of breasts bouncing, stroke, come into the chamber pot, take a bath. This was nothing at all like that. He moaned and leaned his head back when she wrapped her fingers around the base of his cock, but his eyes flew open when he felt her mouth on it. He *had* seen this in his pamphlets, but he'd never imagined having it done to him. Soon he could no longer form a rational thought. He watched her take him into her mouth, lick him, and stroke him, and he knew he had never seen anything so beautiful in his life. He had never felt anything like it, and he couldn't take his eyes off her. She took him all the way into her throat and moaned, and he felt it all the way down to his toes. When she looked up at him and their eyes locked again, he knew he was going to explode. He knew he should warn her, but she drew up and smiled knowingly. She pulled her hand up to follow her mouth and stroked him a few last times, and finally his seed spilled over her hand and onto his belly. She cupped his balls again and felt them pulsing, then she stretched herself out beside him, her fingers playing with the hair on his chest.

"In two days, we'll be in Venice," Jack said, his voice hoarse.

"Then we'll have to make the most of these two days," Millie said, her cheek against his shoulder.

Jack brought his hand up to her hair and pulled a strand

straight, then watched it spring back to a curl when he let it go. It pleased him in an absurd sort of way, and he let out a soft laugh. "I love your hair," he said. "I can't get enough of it."

Millie laughed. "I love that you love it." She propped herself up on her elbow and looked down at him, her eyes deep and dark. She traced his lips with her fingertips. "I love your lips," she said. "I really love them when they're laughing. They don't do that enough."

He smiled. "They have done so much more in the past week than they ever have. And I have you to thank for it."

She kissed him, and he felt his groin tightening again with desire. She felt it too, because she lifted her head, mischief in her smile, and said, "Why, Jack Covert, I believe we *will* make the most of these two days." He kissed her fiercely again, pulling the sheet over them both.

~*~

The rest of those two days were a blur for Millie, she thought, as she stood on the deck of the ship and watched Gibraltar looming into view. They had taken their pleasure from each other in the cabin, where Jack was an apt pupil in the art of pleasing a woman. She had never really had to teach a man how to make love to her, but she found she was enjoying it immensely. But it was all the time they spent together out of the cabin that was worrying her. She enjoyed it quite as much, maybe even more— than she did the bed sport. In fact, when she closed her eyes, she didn't dream of Jack naked anymore. Instead, she dreamed of him on the deck of the ship, lazing against a pile of rope, one arm flung behind his head as he lounged, eating an apple, and telling her stories about his life as a thief. They were equal parts thrilling and hilarious, and she listened in rapture as he regaled her. She had always enjoyed being around interesting people, and nobody in the world could say Jack Covert wasn't interesting. Jack Redstone, she corrected herself. A *Viscount*— who'd have ever thought. She shook her head. She was in dangerous territory, indeed. And, though she'd entered into the deal with Jack willingly, and had completely agreed with him that they could enjoy each other's company as friends on this voyage, while also enjoying each other's bodies, without danger to their hearts, she now knew that was no longer true, at least not for her. She was, slowly, a little bit every day, losing her heart to this man—this infuriating, wonderful, handsome man.

She didn't want it to happen. She was fighting against it every second, but it was happening, nonetheless. Perhaps the best thing that could happen was for them to reach the port in Venice and get back to the task at hand. But she felt an emptiness when she thought of it. The idea of being with Jack and not touching him, not sharing her bed with him at night, was unbearable. She closed her eyes and gripped the railing in front of her, taking a deep breath of the bracing salt air. It was much warmer now that they were readying to enter the Mediterranean, and they had been lucky to experience calm seas. Even the night that they had seen the storm turned out to be only some gentle rocking and rain. And they had been so engrossed with each other they had not even noticed it.

Now, here they were, the rock of Gibraltar looming larger and larger as they sailed toward it. She knew they'd be stopping to deliver mail and packages at the port on Gibraltar, and she was thrilled to see it again. The last time she'd only been a child, but the memory of the monkeys, of Annelise holding her hand and walking her along the street, had stayed with her all these years. She found herself full of excitement at the idea of seeing it with Jack. She shook her head again, willing herself to banish such thoughts. She had spent the entire morning waffling between the thrill of relishing one more day—and night—with him, and the sense of impending doom she felt with the knowledge that soon their deal would end. She knew no good would come of her perseverating on the situation, yet she couldn't seem to stop herself. Her dreams were full of Jack when she slept, her thoughts were full of Jack when she woke up, and even when he was with her, her whole self was still full of Jack. There was nothing for it: she was falling in love with the man. Damn it all. She had always been able to separate her body and her heart. Why was she having so much trouble controlling herself now?

She shook her head and turned around, leaning her back against the rail and shading her eyes as she looked up at the mast, the large sail full of wind, pulling them toward port. Perhaps part of the appeal was losing control, she had to admit to herself. She had vowed never to do that after watching what had happened to her mother but wasn't there something wonderful about letting one's guard down and not being sure what would happen? It wasn't always dangerous or sad or frightening. It could be thrilling. This sense of movement on the ship, having taken her out of her routine and her normal comfortable life, was thrilling. It was taking her toward answers, ones she had never sought, about her childhood and her mother. It was taking her toward a foreign land, where she no longer knew the language, taking her to spend more time with Jack. She closed her eyes, blew air into her cheeks, then puffed it out quickly.

"Are you feeling all right?" Jack's voice, though gentle and soft, startled her in her reverie. He was striding toward her across the deck, concern clear on his face.

She smiled. "No, no, fine," she said, turning around to look back out at the rock.

"I was worried you might have a touch of seasickness again," he said, coming to stand next to her and covering her hand on the railing with his own. "It sometimes happens when one is coming into port."

She pulled away from him and started walking toward the bow, and she didn't know if she hoped he would follow or hoped he'd let her go. She reached the front of the ship, and it was amazing how much stronger the wind was there. Millie had to brace herself against it, and it was so loud that she felt rather than heard Jack come up behind her.

He laid his hand on his shoulder and said, "Tell me what's wrong." She smiled to herself and shook her head but did not turn around. She tried to sound nonchalant as she threw a "nothing" over her shoulder back at him. His laughter in response was loud and clear, and she frowned.

He came to stand beside her and bent down to shout against the wind. "I may not have bedded any women, but I've studied my share," he said. "I know what *nothing* means."

She laughed as well, but it was a rueful laugh, mirthless. She decided to tell the truth, though maybe not the full truth. "I'm getting nervous about Venice," she said. "I don't know what we will find."

When he replied, "I thought as much," she was half relieved he didn't guess the rest of her meaning, and half disappointed. He pulled her against him to shelter her from the cold of the wind, and wrapped his arms around her, his elbows leaning on the rail. She felt like every inch of her that touched him was glowing, from where her calves pressed against his strong legs to where the back of her head rested on his shoulder, to where his arms crossed in front of her belly. They stood there like that for long minutes, silent, listening to the wind whip by and the shouts of the sailors as they adjusted the rigging and prepared to dock at Gibraltar. Soon enough the sea birds were dipping and screeching above them, and the ship glided through the Strait, the hills rising above them on both sides, until finally they maneuvered toward the huge sharp point of stone and into the port.

Millie turned to look up at Jack, and he loosened his hold on her. "It's so much smaller than I remember," she exclaimed.

"No, you're just much bigger," he said, pulling her back in against him. "Funny how life happens that way."

She thought about what he said and knew it was true. What would Venice look like now from her adult eyes, eyes that had seen so much, that had become so essentially British? She certainly looked Italian, but she had no accent, barely remembered any of the language, and had only vague impressions of the city and her mother. She wasn't even sure she'd be able to find the *pensione* where they'd lived. But she'd have to cross all those bridges, literally and figuratively, once they arrived. Still, it was unnerving to imagine how her perspective had changed. In fact, she thought as she relaxed into Jack's strong arms around her, her perspective had changed on everything, and for some things, it hadn't taken almost two decades. It had taken only five days on this ship for her strongly held opinions and ideals about sex and love to flip upside down. She had always been open to new experiences, always been willing to reexamine her beliefs in the face of new evidence, but this was different. Wasn't this the exception that proved the rule? She'd only proven to herself how weak she was, and how easy it would be to go down that path, to lose her solitude, her serenity, even her sanity.

Once they docked, the deck was full of men skittering this way and that, offloading cargo and letters, and bringing on supplies and more packages. She and Jack went below to stay out of the way and get their things for a short walk around the port.

She shrugged on her Spencer and set to work on the endless tiny buttons on the front while Jack found his greatcoat and wrapped himself with it. He put on a fashionable hat, and he looked absolutely dashing. Every bit the scoundrel, and every bit her friend. She reached for her own bonnet and Jack shook his head in sorrow. "What a shame to cover up those curls," he said, sighing. She smiled and tied the ribbon below her chin but met his eyes as she pulled one lock out to hang next to her cheek. He reached forward and brushed it back, then pinched her earlobe playfully. "Let's go."

They made their way up to the big gangplank that had been lowered, and she rested her arm in his. She knew they looked every bit the young couple in love, and she felt a sense of satisfaction watching the reactions of passersby. She could hear at least four different languages on the docks as they made their way toward the long street of shops and restaurants that faced the port. Other couples passed them, the gentlemen touching their hats and Jack responding in turn. It was a gorgeous sunny day, and the sky was filled with fluffy white clouds. She looked up at the huge promontory of the Rock and said, "I wish we could climb it."

"Maybe on the way back," Jack said. "This packet is only in port for an hour or two."

They strolled along the avenue and stopped to look in at the shops. Mostly they just enjoyed the feeling of the solid ground beneath their feet, and that exhilaration that comes with being in a foreign land. The air smelled just a little different, the sky looked just a little different, the people looked and sounded just a little different. Millie had forgotten how much fun it was to travel.

When they reached a cross street, they heard a shriek, and soon two of the famous Gibraltar monkeys came running out of the alley, having surprised a pedestrian and made off with her meat pie. Millie shouted with delight, and she and Jack sprang apart to let the monkey pass. They fell back toward each other in peals of laughter.

Once they'd gotten hold of themselves again and had continued walking, Jack spoke. "You know," he said, his voice hesitant. "I'm going to miss this."

"Me, too," Millie said, unsure what he meant, but holding her breath and waiting for him to elaborate.

"You will?" he asked in surprise.

"Of course," she said, searching for her next words. "It's been an adventure."

She stole a side glance up at him and saw his jaw set in a hard line, the muscle twitching where it met his throat.

"That's not what I meant," he said, through clenched teeth, and it was clear it was taking him some effort.

She looked down at their feet on the cobblestones. "I know," she whispered, then went on, "Earlier," she said, "on deck, you asked me what was wrong. I told you I was nervous about what would happen in Venice."

He nodded, keeping his gaze straight ahead.

"I was only half telling the truth," she said. "I *am* nervous about Venice. I am terrified of what we might find, worried the killers will have followed us there, sad at the thought of my childhood and seeing those places that brought such misery to my mother." She paused as they drew up to a scenic view across the port. They stopped walking, and she turned to look up at him, leaning back so she could see his face clearly under the brim of her bonnet.

"But I'm also in mourning already," she said, holding his hands in her own. "I'm going to miss the way it's been with you." She looked to the side, embarrassed at the emotion in her voice.

"That wasn't our agreement," he said, and she couldn't read his voice. It was calm and steady, but there was something else as well. She dared not look back up at him, for fear of what she'd see in his face.

"I know," she breathed.

He put his forefinger under her chin and tipped her face back up. When her eyes met his, she was shocked to see his brow had a deep furrow and his mouth was pressed into a tight line. "I don't want it to end, either, Millie," he said, and her name sounded like music when he said it. He pulled her into a tight hug, and she rested her cheek against the lapels of his greatcoat.

"Jack," she said, her voice a sigh, a lament, and a prayer all at the same time, "What are we going to do?"

Chapter 9

It was dark when they pulled into port at Venice, but the city was so bright with lantern light that they could see it for almost an hour before they finally docked. That was one thing Millie remembered about Venice, this amazing city of glass and water—it came alive after dark. Perhaps it was just her mother's lifestyle, but Millie's most vivid memories of the city were of the Rialto Bridge lit at night, the cafes full of people on the sidewalks, the gondolas gliding at one's side as they walked the ancient cobblestones. They were sensory impressions more than memories, but they were beautiful and vibrant, nonetheless. She found herself with a mix of emotions that felt almost unbearable in their contradictions. She was excited, anxious, sad, overwhelmed—the positive and negative energy seemed at war within her.

Again, she stood on deck watching the destination grow closer, but this was different than it had been just the day before when they'd stopped at Gibraltar. Now, she was truly alone. Jack was readying their things and helping out belowdecks. She knew he was just making a pretense of being busy to allow her some time to herself, and she was grateful for it. She needed to collect her feelings, to gather herself back inward, and put on a brave face to the world, and that world included Jack, though sometimes it felt like there was little separation between them, especially here on the ship. But Millie knew there was a part of herself she could never let Jack into, no matter how close he got or how much she wanted it. Their words on that pier in Gibraltar had proven it: their hearts were no longer safe with each other. If they both wanted to stay unentangled and unencumbered, they were going to have to end it now. She knew her heart was unwilling, not to mention her body, but that was precisely why she had to keep her head in control. There could be no more whispered confessions, no more tear-filled emotional outbursts. There could be no more embraces. She could simply not allow it to go on like this. They'd made an agreement, and they were both going to stick to that agreement, whatever it cost them. Because the alternative was worse, Millie thought. The alternative would cost her her *self*, her very identity. And what about Jack? Hadn't he had very good reasons for choosing the life he had? Who was she to come and compromise that for him? No, for both their sakes, their little dalliance was over now. She'd have it as a memory, and that would have to be enough. She thought of Anne Elliot in *Persuasion*. She'd lived with her memory of her romance with Captain Wentworth for seven years, and it had sustained her in its own way, hadn't it? Never mind that love conquered all at the end of that novel, Millie thought wryly. Everyone knew happily-ever-afters didn't exist in real life. Happily-for-nows, maybe, and wasn't that just what she'd enjoyed on the journey here? A happily-for-now that had lasted for five full days. She'd relish the memory of it forever. Her only regret was that she hadn't taken Jack's virginity, in the technical sense, but she respected his decision on that just as much as she respected his feelings about romance and love. She'd just have to leave that part for her dreams, which she was sure would be full of this man for years to come.

She sighed and gripped the railing in front of her, trying to ground herself in the cold, solid wood of the ship. She set her lips in a grim line and walked around, watching the sailors work. Everything they did was in such harmony. Each man had his task, and each man knew he could depend on the next. They worked like a chorus. Each had his part, and only when their parts were put together would the ship sail properly. It was inspiring, and a little draining, for her to think about. She hadn't really seen the work of a real team since Annelise's time on the stage. She supposed the time she'd spent with Anne and Jonathan helping to quell a smallpox outbreak in his village counted, too. They'd worked together and overcome something dangerous. Her life, and Jack's life, was the opposite of that. They achieved what they did individually. Millie, for her part, enjoying a quiet life in Bloomsbury, and Jack living out his own escape plan.

But since she'd met him, they had been a team. First, he gave her orders to help protect her, and she followed them with little question because he was so capable. But now they were ready to start a new adventure in Venice, one where the outcome was uncertain, but where their success absolutely depended on the trust they had in one another. She took a moment to be grateful she'd met him that night. Imagine if it had been any other thief who'd been hired to take her locket. She shuddered at the thought. She'd be dead now, most likely. Whatever luck had brought Jack to her had also kept them both safe and one step ahead of the assassins. She just hoped their luck would hold when they arrived.

Almost as if on cue, Jack stepped up beside her. She turned to look at him as he set down their bags at his feet.

"We're here," he said, and his voice was flat.

"Yes," she replied. "The city is beautiful from the water, isn't it?"

He nodded. "I've never been this far from home," he said. "Even with my father, we usually sailed just across the channel and traveled over land. Paris, usually."

"Just wait," Millie said, smiling. "You're in for a treat. Venice is a delightful city, though it's fallen on quite hard times lately."

"I've heard stories about the Venice of forty years ago," Jack said, shaking his head. "It was once a very proud Republic."

"A lot has changed," Millie nodded. "But hopefully now that Napoleon has fallen, it might build back some of its vibrancy. At any rate," she continued, winking, "I'm quite sure certain parts of the city remain unchanged."

"You mean the whores," Jack laughed. "Yes, I suppose any city needs those, regardless of politics and war."

"Maybe *especially* because of politics and war," Millie said with a touch of sarcasm. But she smiled again, thinking of her childhood. "But the whores are some of the best people you'd meet. And they know everything."

"Then we'll start with the whores," Jack said.

"We'll need to head to the Rialto bridge," Millie nodded ahead to the city looming now in front of them. "Find a *pensione* near there for lodging and make our rounds among the ladies of the night."

"Have the lions been returned to St. Mark's square?" Jack asked, gazing out at the city. "I've always wanted to see them."

"The last I read, yes," Millie said. "It was a condition of Napoleon's second surrender." She looked up at him and saw the dreaminess in his eyes. "I'm sure we'll have time to see them," she said.

He smiled, and he had never looked more boyish. "Good."

They both turned back to watch the bustle on the docks below as the ship was brought into its berth in the port. "We'll have to take a ride in a gondola of course," Millie said, starting to count on her fingers, "the bridge of sighs, the basilica, and naturally we'll eat every single thing we can get our hands on."

"You make it sound like we're two young swains going on a Grand Tour," Jack laughed.

"Well, I'm certainly no swain," Millie said, "But we can tour all we like. We came all this way. And," she continued, her voice softening, "though my very life depends on it, there's not much for you on this whole adventure."

His eyes burned as he looked down at her. She couldn't tell if he was a little angry with her, if he desired her, or both. "There's been plenty in it for me," he said, between clenched teeth.

Millie smiled, but she knew it must look tight and fake. She didn't want to think about what had happened between them right now. To be reminded of what they were set to lose was not helpful. She wanted to break the tension but didn't know how, so she said nothing.

Soon enough, the ship was fully docked, and they were lowering the big gangplank. The other passengers had also come to the deck in anticipation, and the sailors stood aside to let them all pass first before the cargo. There were Venetians waiting down on the docks, shouting in Italian, some selling food and wares, others offering passage to the city proper. Millie and Jack both paused at the bottom of the gangplank, looked at each other, then entered the din and crowd.

It was like nothing Jack had ever seen. The crowd was loud and boisterous, as docks at night often are, with people waiting for arrivals of ships, packages, and supplies, and even more people waiting for foreigners to whom they could ply their trade. There was no shortage of carriages available, looking for passengers, but Millie walked right past them, motioning her head for him to follow. They walked a short way until they reached the other side of the road, and he realized they weren't on a street at all, but more of a pier. There was a river on the other side, and he looked down into the water, inky black in the night, with the lantern lights reflecting on it like stars. He realized that Venice had a smell, too. It was an ocean, salt, fish smell like a port, but something more as well. There was the warm smell of bread baking, the sharp smell of meat roasting, and the unmistakable smell, though light, of human waste. The combination was not unpleasant, he thought. It was certainly singular. He couldn't think of anywhere else in the world that smelled quite like this.

As he stood there, just trying to be present in the moment, he realized Millie was staring at him. "Am I that obvious?" he said.

She laughed. "It really is a wonderful city," she said, then she motioned to the canal. "Ah, here we are," she said, holding out a hand as a gondola pulled up, its gondolier dressed in the sort of livery of his profession. Jack smiled. Of course, they didn't need a carriage. They would be floating to the city center.

"*Al Ponte di Rialto, per favore*," she said, and once again he stood in amazement at her. Somehow, she was even more beautiful when she spoke Italian, halting though it was. He shook his head. He had to stop having thoughts like that.

"*Si, Signorina,*" the gondolier said, bowing. Jack realized there were steps leading down into the canal, made just for entering and exiting the gondolas that frequented the port. He set down their baggage and held out his hand to help Millie down into the boat. She took it and lifted her skirts, lowering herself carefully. She looked back up at him and smiled—a knowing smile—where the tips of her eyes crinkled together with mischief. She held her hand up so he could pass down the bags, then she sat on one of the benches in the narrow little boat.

Jack followed her down, and they sat together. The gondolier nodded, Millie nodded back, and the man braced himself in the stern of the boat and pushed them off with his tall pole. A lantern hung at the bow, and the gentle swaying of the vessel threw a moving shadow on the water around them. Jack was charmed by the entire scene.

The canal near the port was the equivalent of a side street, but when they reached the end, Jack was amazed by what he saw. A wide avenue, made of water, but as busy as any street in London. Packed with gondolas and other small boats traveling both ways, and more of the small vessels tied up all along the edge where grand palazzos grew from the murky water like they had sprouted there. Lanterns were lit all along the canal, at the doors of the homes, and at little cafes where the sounds of music tinkled out in the air.

The gondolier moved them expertly out into this bustling scene, and Millie took Jack's hand. "It's so beautiful," she said. "I'd forgotten exactly how beautiful it is."

Jack could only swallow and nod. He was charmed by this city, which seemed to pulse with excitement and activity.

"*Sei qui per Carnevale?*" the gondolier asked, motioning.

"What did he say?" Jack whispered, embarrassed that he knew no Italian.

"He asked if we're here for *Carnevale*," Millie said. "I'd completely forgotten it's that time of year. But..." she counted on her fingers, "yes, Ash Wednesday is in two weeks."

Jack cocked his head, thinking. He'd heard about *Carnevale*, of course, but London had had no such celebration in over 200 years, since it had ceased to be a Catholic country. He'd, of course, observed Lent in the Anglican way since birth, like any noble family would, but *Carnevale* was something utterly foreign to him, and thus completely interesting.

He leaned forward in his excitement, taking in the sights and sounds around him. It was still early in the season, so there were no harlequins or masks to be seen, but there was a sense of revelry. It was everywhere in the streets and the canal. People singing, hefting large bottles of wine, and lovers in embraces one would be scandalized to see in daylight. The whole scene was intoxicating, he thought, and without a drop of hard drink.

Soon enough, he could make out what appeared to be a series of white arches over the water. It wasn't until they were closer that he realized it was a bridge and not his imagination. It looked unlike any bridge he'd ever seen. Gleaming white even in the dim lantern light, it rose from each shore to a point in the middle, where a huge arch was framed with a pediment resting on two columns. Like stair steps rising to this central arch were several smaller arches on each side, and Jack could see lanterns moving along the bridge as people walked across in both directions. There were vendors along the bridge, as well, selling all the usual things: food, souvenirs, and other items, but there were also *Carnevale* vendors, as well, with elaborate masks, torches, and more lanterns.

Their gondola slid into place alongside a dock, and between huge poles for tying the boats up. The gondolier stepped out, and Millie paid him with a coin from her purse before he held his hand out to help her. As they stepped onto the bustling street next to the canal, Jack felt more alive than he had in months, maybe even years. He held his arm out to her, and she took it, giving it a small squeeze as they made their way toward the bridge.

They stopped halfway across and went to look out across the canal.

"It seems we do a lot of standing side by side, staring at water," Jack quipped.

"A very pensive lot we are," Millie said with a laugh.

"So much weighing on our minds every day," he said, trying to match her tone.

She looked up at him and started counting on her fingers. "Let's see. Assassins out to get me, fleeing our homes in fear, mystery of the locket," she trailed off, but Jack knew what they were both leaving unsaid. Everything they'd been through was frightening, full of stress and uncertainty, but the thing weighing on both their minds the most was the end of the arrangement they'd made on board the ship.

After their emotional confession in Gibraltar, Jack had realized what a mistake the whole experiment had been. He wasn't sure what he'd been thinking about starting it in the first place. In fact, he was certain he hadn't been thinking at all, at least not with his head. He'd thought it was with his body, his unruly betrayer of a body, but now he knew it was part of his heart, too. This minx had stolen a piece of it, and it was essential that he not allow her to take the rest. He had done many things in his life that required emotional strength. In fact, he'd been raised with the necessity for it from childhood. He knew how to lock out his emotions, how to push people away. He was an expert at it, in fact. It would take all of his willpower and not a little magical thinking, he thought, but surely he could do it.

"Shall we get a room?" Millie asked, picking the satchel at her feet back up. "With *two* beds," she added, almost as if reading his thoughts.

He nodded his assent and followed her to the other side of the bridge, which bustled with activity and where there were several hotels and *pensiones* for travelers. Jack paused for a moment to look up at the architecture. Everything here was breathtaking. Even the most run-down inn was charming in the way the stucco peeled off the walls. Each building featured arched windows, many rising several stories in the air due to the lack of precious dry land on which to build. The fronts of the buildings were painted in bright colors, and together they were dazzling. Porticoes stuck out into the street, often columned, with those signature arches, and the city, though still reeling from all the political upheaval, was clearly starting to revive its tourist trade at *Carnevale* time. He hoped they'd have the luck to find a room with two beds, he thought with a frown.

But his worries were for naught, for they found a comfortable room for a fair price at only the second hotel they tried, and it wasn't long before they were each safely tucked into their own beds. Though he was exhausted from the journey, and from the lateness of the hour, Jack just lay staring up at the ceiling, where little cracks had appeared in the stucco, flickering in the lantern light that peeked through the curtains from the street. Though they were in separate beds, the room wasn't large, and Jack felt an almost magnetic pull to Millie in the few feet between them. He listened to her breathing and knew she wasn't asleep, either. He had never felt such torture in his life. He turned on his side to face the window and away from her, but when he closed his eyes, all he could picture was her naked body writhing beneath him, the way her eyes had looked when he pleasured her, the sounds that escaped from the back of her throat, and, more than anything, the way that pleasuring her had made him *feel*. He pulled the pillow over his head and squeezed it against his ears, thinking if he could just stop listening to her breathing, he might be able to banish the images. But being alone with his own thoughts was even more torturous. He had to force himself to admit how much he cared about her. He cursed himself and stood.

"Where are you going?" Millie's voice sounded small and distant from the other bed. He shrugged on his shirt and stuffed it into his breeches before grabbing his waistcoat from the chair where he'd lain it.

"Out," he said, and his voice sounded harder than he'd meant it to.

Millie gasped audibly, and he closed his eyes. He didn't want to fall all the way in love with her, but he didn't want to hurt her, either. He turned around and met her gaze in the dim light.

"I'm sorry," he said. "You know it's not you."

She nodded. "I know," she said. "If you hadn't gotten up to leave, I would have." Her smile was rueful, almost a frown really, when she continued. "It's torture being with you like this."

"I can't sleep," he said, not feeling it necessary to agree with her, since they both knew the truth. "I'm used to doing my work at night, anyway." He pulled the waistcoat on and busied himself with the buttons so he could sound more businesslike. "I'll just take a look around and get the lay of the land."

She closed her eyes and nodded, pulling the blankets up to her chin. "I'll try to get some sleep so you can have the room when you get back," she said.

"I wish you good rest, then," he said as he tied his cravat.

She rolled over and plumped the pillow beneath her before settling in a more comfortable position. She was a vision, with those curls splayed out against the white linen, the pink curve of her cheek resting on the pillow like the petal of a flower. He turned and grabbed his hat.

"Jack," she called before he walked out the door. "Tomorrow we'll explore."

He smiled. "Indeed, we shall," he said, and pulled the door closed behind him.

The night was chilly and starting to turn more silent. Revelers stumbled down the streets and a low fog had settled along the canal. Lanterns were being put out, and the darkness hung all around him, matching his mood. He turned and walked back toward the Rialto, climbing the stairs up the bridge slowly, not even bothering to look around him. Occasionally, another pedestrian walked past, sometimes weaving in their drunkenness, sometimes with fast steps, obviously someone heading home from less enjoyable activities. Jack leaned against the cold marble at the top of the bridge and stared down into the dark water of the canal. There were no jams of boats bustling here now, only the occasional splash of a gondola pole taking the last of the partiers home.

It was at moments like these that Jack truly wished he could drink. He had vowed never to do so, after what he'd seen it do to his mother, of course, but there was a certain attraction to it for him. When he was alone, in the dead of night, knowing the woman he was falling in love with was just yards away in a soft, warm bed, when he could picture her face and the way her lips tasted...that was a time that called for a strong drink.

He turned and walked back down the other side of the bridge, only to come upon a group of women gathered around a small fire burning in a pit. They were wearing the clothing of upper-class ladies, but their heavy makeup, low bodices, and worn faces belied their profession. Clearly, they were working, and when one of them spied Jack, she called him over. "*Mi Amor*," she cried, beckoning with her hand. "*Vieni al scardarti.*"

Jack splayed his hands out and shrugged his shoulders. "I speak only English," he said, slowly, hoping they would understand.

"*Ah, Inglesi!*" one of the older women said, clapping her hands. "I speak it a little," she said in a halting accent. "From England?" she asked, gesturing to the sea.

"Yes," he nodded, holding his hands out over the fire. "Just arrived tonight."

"Not many *Inglesi* here anymore," she said, her voice tinged with sadness.

"No," Jack replied, cautious, feeling his way around this woman's thoughts. "But hopefully there will be again."

The woman spat at the ground behind her. "Now that *bastardo* Napoleon is gone," she said, and Jack relaxed a little. The woman sidled closer to Jack and ran a finger up his arm. "I miss my young Englishmen," she said, looking up at him with a coquettish batting of her lashes. Her eyes were rimmed with kohl, and she was flirting with him expertly, but he felt no stirring in his body.

He patted her hand, then lifted it off his arm. "Not tonight, I'm afraid, dear," he said, and his voice was gentle.

"Bah, I'm too tired to work anymore tonight," she said, and she lifted her skirts to sit astride a stool around the fire. "Come warm yourself, anyway, *tesoro*," she said.

"I thank you," he said, nodding.

"*Grazie*," she said, showing him what to say.

"Yes," Jack replied, smiling. "*Grazie*."

He looked around at the other women who'd been gathered by the fire. One by one, they'd been approached by men and led off, and now some were in conversation in darkened corners, some sat in tete-a-tetes on the steps of the bridge, and some were walking away to other, more comfortable locales.

Jack gestured toward them. "I'm not keeping your business away, am I?" he asked the woman.

"No," she said. "I'm the grandmother here now. I don't need

more than one in a night." She laughed. "Keep me company while I keep an eye on these little *pulcini*."

"How long have you been out here?" Jack asked, eyeing her closely.

"Only a few hours," she said. "*Carnevale* is an easy time for business. No need for long nights"

"No," Jack said, trying to explain, "How long have you been working the Rialto? Are you from Venice?"

"*Sì*," she said, smiling, "born here and, God willing, I'll die here. I've worked the Rialto since I was a child. First pickpocketing while my mother worked the men, then learning the trade from her."

Jack watched the woman and was surprised to hear not a hint of sadness in her voice. One might think it was a rough life, living as a prostitute on the streets of Venice, but this woman had no shame about her occupation, and she even seemed to enjoy it.

"You're thinking, how sad is this woman, this old woman, still selling her body," she shook her head and the cheap wig she wore turned just half a second slower than her scalp, causing her to look strange indeed. She laughed and it completed the look. Her big bosom heaved, and her smile widened. "It's not such a bad life," she said, and she reached down into the satchel she carried and pulled out a flask. She offered it to Jack, but he shook his head, and she took a big swig.

"The old ones looked after me," she said, "Now I look after the young ones. We're all together, you see?" she gestured around her. "We protect each other, nurse each other, and help each other have our babies. And we don't need to depend on any man to do it."

Jack crossed his arms against the chill but nodded his respect. Their motivations were quite similar to his—independence, a lack of entanglements, a desire to make one's own life and be in control of one's own destiny. "It sounds familiar to me," he said.

The woman lifted her flask in a toast. *"All'independenza!"* she said and downed another swig.

Jack lifted his own hand as if he had a drink in it, and repeated her phrase, poorly accented though it was. It was clear what it meant in any language.

Jack moved to go, but at the last minute decided to take a chance. "What is your name?" he asked, not knowing if her answer would be true or not, but curious nonetheless.

"Francesca," she said, "My Englishmen used to call me Fanny." Her eyes sparkled as she held out her hand in greeting.

"Well, Fanny," he said, as he made a gallant little bow over her hand. "A pleasure."

"Come back and see me tomorrow," she said, "I'll be here."

"I just might take you up on that," Jack said over his shoulder as he walked back toward the bridge.

He continued his stroll, enjoying the quiet of the very late night, or, he thought as he looked up, the very early morning. He could still hear the occasional splash of a gondola on the canal, and the sound of a stray cat knocking over a pail. But in general, a soft silence had fallen over the city, and Jack relished it. He realized he hadn't experienced a true silence since he'd met Millie. Every minute since then had been full of activity, and of course the constant hum of the wind and waves on the ship, not to mention the near-constant activity of the sailors.

Now, though, he could try to impart some of the peace and serenity of the night into his exhausted brain. It was lucky he'd struck a tenuous friendship with Fanny. She could prove a valuable source, especially if she'd been a prostitute in Venice all her life. He loved that feeling, of discovering information, working sources. It was one thing he didn't get to do much in his life as a thief. He was very good at pretending to be someone else, occasionally gaining people's trust. But it was all in the service of a singular goal: the job. Now, though, he supposed he did still have a job, but it felt different. He wanted to help Millie discover the truth about the assassins. It seemed nothing from her childhood was a secret. It was puzzling, indeed. He wondered if Millie's mother could have gotten involved in criminal activity of some kind, or if someone was trying to find revenge on the late singer by hunting down her daughter. It didn't seem likely.

He knew plenty about Millie's past, but now he allowed himself to wonder about Millie's life in the future. Once they were able to secure her safety and find out what was going on, what would she do then? He assumed she would return to Bloomsbury and continue living her life as she did before. Friends, parties, salons. Lovers. The last thought made his blood run cold. Part of what he loved about Millie was her openness and her lack of shame about her pleasure. But when he thought of her beneath another man—when he thought of her face when another man brought her to her climax—he stopped in the middle of the street and realized he'd been walking in circles around the block where their hotel was. His fists were clenched so tightly that he was digging his fingernails into his palms. He loosened them and stretched his fingers out, shaking his shoulders and willing himself to think of something else.

What would *he* do when they got back to London? Go back to being one of England's finest cat burglars, he supposed. Though there would likely be damage to his reputation on that front if VanHinkel had discovered his betrayal and his helping Millie. He shook his head. He supposed he could go back to his mother's house, become the Viscount Danbury. He laughed at himself, then, out loud. A cold sound that shook him with its malice. He knew in the back of his mind it was always possible to come back and reassume his identity, and he supposed that's what made it so consistently repugnant to him. Even if he did go back, even if he did assume the title and managed to avoid any scenes with his mother, if he moved to the stately mansion in Mayfair, what then? He supposed he'd have to take his seat in the Lords, look to the accounts, manage the household and the estates. These were all tasks he would be good at and was not averse to doing, but it was the expectations, he thought. There was the rub. An unmarried young Viscount in the prime of life arriving in the middle of a London season would be the talk of the *ton*. Every mama of every darling debutante would be beating down his door. He could hide away in Danbury House and attend to his duties, but it would nonetheless be torturous. He wasn't sure he could do it.

And then there was his mother. What would he do about his mother? He'd known all along he couldn't escape forever. It had been four years since his father's death and his own disappearance. Every year he'd promised himself he'd go back, that he would just live this life a little longer. That once he got hold of himself and came to terms with his past and his feelings about his mother, he would be able to return.

And he'd gone on living his life, cultivating his clients and sources, getting better and better at what he did. But the answers never came. He never did 'get hold of himself,' whatever that would look like, and he certainly never came to terms with his past. He had developed personal ideals based on his experiences. First, never steal from anyone not obscenely wealthy; second, never drink; and finally, never get emotionally entangled with anyone. They had all been easy ideals to uphold, until he'd met Millie. The first two were still easy. He could uphold them the rest of his life. He'd never had any true inclination to drink, and he still didn't. But he knew it was too late for the emotional entanglement. He knew it as well as he knew his own body. He was falling in love with Millie, and there was nothing he could do to stop it, not to mention he was utterly powerless over his feelings. But the feelings and the entanglement were two different things. As long as he could keep away from her here in Venice, his ideals could still win out.

Chapter 10

Millie stretched and yawned, feeling as rested and contented as a cat waking up in a beam of sunshine. Once Jack had gone, she had finally been able to sleep, and she was so physically and emotionally exhausted, she'd slept for what felt like hours and hours. Though it wasn't entirely dreamless, it had been restful, and some of the memories of the good dreams lingered with her, warm thoughts of Jack's body against hers, his lips on her skin. She stretched again and felt that strange twinge of sadness, longing, and pleasure at the memories of him, the real life him, that she had experienced on the ship. She knew it could never happen again, of course, but it didn't mean it wasn't a sweet memory. She turned to her stomach and stretched out, smiling, luxuriating a bit in waking up and not having to jump out of the bed. She wondered where Jack had gone. There was a small sliver of sunshine coming through the curtains, so she knew it was well and truly morning. She had no idea what time she'd finally fallen asleep, but she knew she must get up, if for no other reason than that Jack needed to rest whenever he got back. She rubbed her eyes and sat up, holding the blanket to her chest, her curls falling in front of her face.

"Good morning," she heard from the corner of the room, and she started, huffing her lips out to blow her hair away from her eyes. She clutched the blanket more tightly around her, though of course she was fully dressed beneath it.

Jack chuckled from the chair in the dim corner. She wasn't sure she'd even noticed a chair there last night. She sighed and fell back against the pillow. "How long have you been here?" she asked with another yawn.

"Not long," he said. "I didn't want to wake you, so I sat and tried to read a while. I dozed off myself."

"Well," Millie said, sitting back up and turning her legs to the edge of the bed, "You can have the room now." She pulled her boots on and quickly did the laces before standing and straightening her dress. "I am so sorry to have kept you waiting. You should have awakened me."

"Nonsense," Jack said, standing, and she was once again overcome by his presence. He was so magnetic, so male, so compelling. She felt drawn to him, and powerless over how drawn to him she was. She needed to get out of the room, and fast.

She moved toward the door and put her hand on the knob. "Have pleasant dreams," she said, turning it and moving out into the little hall. She pulled the door closed but paused just for a second as his eyes met hers. They were full of something she couldn't quite decipher, but she didn't stay to find out.

Once Millie stepped out onto the street, she could take a deep breath of the fresh salt air. There was a murkiness in the scent of Venice from the still water of the canals, but the breeze always carried a freshness from the sea. Millie's strides were purposeful as she made her way away from the Rialto, trying to get to a cup of coffee as quickly as possible. Luckily, Venice was still the coffee capital of the world, and all along the Grand Canal were little cafes with sidewalk tables, filling up even at this early hour in the chill February air. Millie stopped at one, gave her order to the waiter, and leaned back to stare out onto the canal, watching the boats float by—gondolas with their individual passengers, larger boats with cargo being pushed by their captains, and the even larger ferries, transporting people and cargo longer distances through the city.

It was cold, but Millie found it bracing and invigorating. She felt like she was ready to start anew, to put her feelings about Jack behind her, and to get to the bottom of the mystery of the locket. She also felt like she might be ready to face some of the things about her past she'd avoided thinking about for all these years. It had always been easy to view her mother as a pathetic sort of character, the mildest of villains, one so sad she was not even worth hating. Millie had no strong or hard feelings about her mother either way. Millie's childhood had been terrible and even traumatic in some ways, but she had also been cared for by a community of women who were similarly ground down by the choices life had forced them to make. And one of those women had taken her home, to England, to be cared for and allowed the space and freedom to grow as she pleased. Millie had been blessed in many ways, and, at any rate, there was no changing one's past, so one might as well move forward. That's what she had always done.

When the waiter came with the wide cup full of coffee on a saucer, Millie's eyes widened with anticipation. It smelled so *good.* Coffee in Italy was so much better than coffee in London. "*Grazie,*" she said with a nod, then lifted the steaming cup to her lips, inhaling deeply. There was so much to enjoy about being in Venice again, so much to see and smell and taste and experience, that had nothing to do with her past or with the men who were trying to find her. She knew her feelings for Jack were not what she had expected, but she also knew she was perfectly capable of keeping her hands off him and that there was a friendship beneath all those messy feelings that she valued, no matter what else happened between them. There were many worse things in the world than exploring one of the world's most beautiful cities with someone one cared for and whose company one enjoyed, she thought with a wry smile. She took another sip of the coffee and watched as the seabirds flew along the canal, occasionally dipping down to try for a fish or simply take a little bath. They were so free, and she was free, too, wasn't she? Wasn't it what she had always wanted? Just to be comfortable, safe, and in charge of her own destiny? There was nothing she valued more in this world than that freedom. She had enjoyed it as a lady's maid in Annelise's home, and she enjoyed it now as the mistress of her house. The thing she had hated so bitterly as a child was that lack of control, being always subject to the whims of her mother's illness and addictions.

It was clear Jack felt the same way. It was part of why they had been drawn to each other, wasn't it? And it was also why they could never be together. They'd each have to give up their most cherished, core values, and she wasn't sure any man would ever be worth that, not even Jack, who was turning out to be one of the finest men she'd ever known. Nonetheless, he was a man. He was a person she'd be beholden to, someone whose thoughts and feelings she'd have to consider. She wouldn't be able to just pick up and do what she liked if Jack were there. She wouldn't be able to just meet with anyone, make love to anyone, or go where she wanted to go. How steep a price that would be. And what if he decided to resume the Viscountcy? That was a wrinkle she hadn't even anticipated. The man was not only noble, but heir to one of the most substantial estates in England. He wouldn't be able to run from his life forever, she thought. Eventually he would go back, and what kind of life would that be for her? Could he even marry someone like her? No title, and a less than pristine background? How chained down would she be as a Viscountess, to the whims and gossip of the *ton*, the endless balls and parties and meaningless intrigues? Just imagining it felt like a vise on her heart. It made her nauseous.

She took a deep breath and looked up into the clear, crisp, coldness of the sky. It was a deep blue this morning, with a bright sunshine and a still chill hanging in the air. The blue was almost the color of Jack's eyes, she realized. She shook her head and took another sip of the coffee. She needed to get up and clear her head, so she downed the last bit, dabbed at her mouth with a napkin, and dropped some coins on the table. She stood up, took a deep breath, and started walking.

She made her way back up the street toward their hotel, and passed the Rialto bridge, looming large and gleaming white in the morning sunshine. It was still early, and relatively quiet in this usually bustling area. Only a few street vendors were there, setting up their stalls, and she could hear the distant shouts of gondoliers on the canal, making their way to deliver cargo or people. The most vibrant and gritty parts of the city would be fast asleep now, having spent their energy in the nighttime hours. She could hear the distant tolling of church bells, and as she walked, she passed several groups of penitents walking together and saying the rosary. It was a calming sight, and she started to remember some of the Latin prayers in her mind, Anne's mother insisting on attending mass every so often growing up, and the cadence soothed her as she walked. She found her steps carrying her to the tenements and *pensiones* where she had grown up, a little city unto itself, with its own routines, its own rules, and its own little fiercely protective community. Sure, they might be whores, thieves, charlatans, artists, and beggars, but they were, in a strange way, a family. Millie did have many fond memories of the streets at night, when a neighborhood considered dangerous, dark, and dirty, came alive with the most wonderful images and people. There was danger, it was true, but for a little street urchin, running in and out of alleys chasing cats, it was never a terribly threatening place. There was always some neighbor or other picking her up by the back of her dress and bringing her back to her mother. People who had been pushed to the margins of society had to stay together, she knew, or they'd starve.

Of course, she wasn't the only little bastard child being raised in the Rialto. Venice was famous for its courtesans, of both high and low class, and the streets were teeming with children who lived in that half-light between the streets and the palazzos. Millie's own mother had, given her opera talent, often moved among the higher classes of Venetians. She had been in and out of those grand palazzos on the canal. Of course, in her worse years, in the midst of her disease and her addictions, she had also walked the streets. But Millie had seen plenty of the nobility there, too, of course. In fact, she wasn't surprised at all to see men slinking out of alleys at this time of the morning, some carrying their disheveled waistcoats in their hands, looking this way and that to avoid being seen. Not by her, naturally, but by someone who *mattered*. Millie smiled. Men were the same everywhere, she thought.

She continued her stroll, just enjoying the sights and sounds, until she came to the block where she'd spent most of her time as a child. To her surprise, the run-down *pensione* looked exactly the same as it had when she was small. It did seem a bit less imposing, she supposed, but its pale pink stucco was falling off in exactly the same places, revealing the brown stone beneath. The *loggias* above the street still had broken railings and sported half-dead plants and fruit trees. Millie shaded her eyes and looked up to the third floor. That was where she and her mother had lived. She shook her head almost in disbelief that she was standing here again. Just then, a child ran out of the building, chasing a small dog that was barking ferociously. The little girl had a head full of dark curls, and when she looked up Millie felt a shock of nostalgia. She must have looked very like this child when she was young. Like so many of the children in the streets here, she was a little dirty, but her eyes sparkled with joy when she caught the dog and held it to her chest.

"*Mi Bella,*" the little girl crooned, rubbing the soft fur of the animal. Millie couldn't help but smile. It was like a scene from a painting.

Millie continued walking until she'd made it all the way south to the *piazzo San Marco*. It was as beautiful as she remembered it. The sun glinted off the domes of the basilica, and the square was full of seagulls basking in the warmth of the day and eating the scraps of food that had been dropped at night. Millie watched as a line of Franciscans walked two abreast down the street on one side of the square, under the arches that framed it, chanting. Millie felt a sense of serenity wash over her. The bell tower loomed tall and brown above all the white stone and marble. As she stood there staring up at it, it began to toll the hour, and she realized it was already nearly noon. The grumble in her stomach confirmed the bell's announcement, and she knew she needed to get back and collect Jack so they could find a midday meal.

Walking back to the hotel, she felt a sense of warmth and anticipation when she thought of being with Jack again. It was really ridiculous, she told herself, this way she got giddy even thinking of being with him. But he was turning out to be a true friend, so why should it be ridiculous? Then she remembered that she had no such thoughts about taking tea with Anne or having the Duke and Duchess over for a meal. She looked forward to their arrival, and enjoyed their time together, but she didn't get dizzy thinking about it. She sighed. Her footsteps echoed on the cobbles in the narrow winding street where she walked, and the sun was so high and bright that she had to shade her eyes as she turned the corner. When the Rialto bridge finally loomed in her sight, she turned right down the street to their hotel and laughed at what she saw.

Jack was standing outside, holding up a large, gilded mask, made of paste-work and papier-mache, its visage a huge golden lion with a mane around its head, and Jack watching her through the two eye-holes. "What do you think?" he asked, pulling it down and smiling.

"I think," she said, "you flatter yourself by choosing the lion."

Jack put his hand to his chest in mock offense. "The lion is the protector of this city," he said. "I can fancy myself a protector, can't I?"

She smiled. "You're *my* protector," she said, "but the lion is regal. If I'm not mistaken, you gave up that life."

He smiled at her and motioned to the street, holding the mask at his side and offering her his arm. "Shall we find lunch?" he asked, "I'm famished."

She tried to hold his arm as lightly as possible, hoping to avoid any of the heat that usually arose between them when they touched, but it was no good. She felt almost like a lightning bolt had struck her where his hand met hers.

They made their way to a cafe along the canal, very similar to the one where she'd taken coffee that morning, and made themselves comfortable. It wasn't long before a waiter came over to offer their daily special, and Millie was very excited.

"Have you had polenta?" she asked Jack.

"I've never even heard the word polenta," Jack said, laughing.

"It's delicious. It's like a porridge, but also the furthest thing from a porridge."

"Sounds wonderful," Jack said, "but then again, I'm so hungry I would eat literally anything."

Millie felt a warmth climbing the back of her neck as she imagined all the things he could eat. She closed her eyes to try to clear her head, then smiled. "Shall we order wine?"

"You can have a glass," Jack gestured to the table, "But water is fine for me."

"I forgot you don't drink," Millie said. She felt like an ass. This was such a fundamental fact about him, and she'd been so wrapped up in how badly she wanted him that she hadn't even given a thought to it. How could she be a good friend when the things that would make her a good friend were so easily buried under this magnetic attraction she felt.

"Have some," he said in a bright tone, evidently unaware of her inner turmoil. "It's a beautiful day to sit on the Grand Canal in Venice and have a glass of wine."

She laughed but shook her head. "No, we have work to do

today, remember?"

He lifted one eyebrow. "I started last night," he said, his voice just a little teasing.

She threw her napkin down on her lap when she saw the waiter coming with their food. "Jack Covert, you've been keeping secrets from me."

"We both needed our rest," he said, looking up to the waiter and nodding his thanks. "I met a few ladies of the night at the Rialto last night, and one," he said, leaning forward, "could be a good contact for us."

Millie raised her eyebrows in question and took a bite of the polenta. It was heavenly.

"A woman named Francesca," he said, "She's been working the Rialto for years. Maybe decades."

Millie frowned. "I don't remember a Francesca," she said, chewing thoughtfully. "But I didn't know every whore in Venice."

Jack smiled. "Of course not," he said, "but she may have known your mother, and even if she didn't, she may be able to point us in the right direction."

"Sounds promising."

"Yes, but I'm sure our Fanny won't be out until much later," Jack smiled, "So we have time for a little exploration."

"Speak for yourself," Millie said, her voice tart. "I've already walked to Saint Mark's and back this morning."

Jack put his hand to his heart, pretending to be wounded. "Without me?"

She smiled. "Don't worry, I'm already pining to go back," she said. "We may even be able to take in mass at the basilica."

They ate their food with gusto, and Millie couldn't get over how such a simple dish could be so delicious. When they'd finished, Millie wiped her lips with a few prim presses of her napkin, and they stood to go.

~*~

When Jack held his arm out for Millie to take, he wasn't sure she would. They didn't have to go everywhere arm in arm, of course. It was just a courtesy. But when she did, he felt a thrill of pleasure. Now that their deal from the ship was over, he wasn't sure what the limitations would be in terms of physically touching one another, but he'd be lying if he said he didn't want to be as near her as possible. He cursed himself even as he thought it but tried to push the conflict out of his mind. There was no resolving it, and therefore no reason to dwell on it. He just enjoyed the feeling of her hand around his bicep and her face turned up to his, smiling in the cool sunshine of the February day. He looked down at her and smiled back, able to be genuine in the way he felt and the way he responded to her. Here, in this beautiful city, on this beautiful day, next to this beautiful woman, he could not help but be happy, no matter the fraught tension between them.

They walked away from St. Mark's toward the palazzos of the Cannaregio, their brightly colored stuccos and arched windows and loggias gleaming in the sunshine. They passed street vendors, and men playing violins in the street, their caps tilted on their dark heads, their cases open for coins from passersby. Millie gleefully threw a ha'penny in each one from a seemingly endless supply in her reticule. Jack was glad they hadn't needed to change currency. After Napoleon's fall, currency from all over Europe was used again in every city, especially the ports.

They made their way to another side street that took them closer to the Grand Canal, and here Millie hailed a gondola for them. As they glided out into the middle of the water, Jack was able to see what he had not from the street—the imposing white columns and intricate marble work of a grand, beautiful palazzo.

Millie nodded and smiled a wide grin, evidently taking pleasure in his appreciation for the structure. "The *Ca D'Oro*," she said. "Isn't it beautiful?"

Jack could barely speak. Beautiful didn't begin to cover it. "Yes," he said, whispering. "It's incredible."

The gondola took them back toward the Rialto, and soon they were sliding under the bridge, a much more plain and simple structure from below than from above, he had to note, but as they emerged on the other side, it really was a sight to look back upon it and watch it recede from view as they made their way around the natural curvature of the canal. It wasn't long before they were nearing the open water, and Millie smiled again.

"Ready for your lion?" she asked, raising her eyebrows in excitement.

He grinned back at her. "Absolutely."

They reached the end of the canal and pulled out into the bay, turned left, and then there was, St. Mark's square, with its two imposing pillars at the waterfront. The lion and the protector of Venice—San Marco and San Todaro. In some ways, they were smaller than he'd imagined, but then again, they were also breathtaking. Just knowing the history of the proud Venetian Republic, and thinking of the many men and women who'd sailed under them and walked those streets, was humbling and awe-inspiring.

"Jack Covert, I don't believe I've seen you awe-stricken," Millie said. "I quite like it."

Jack laughed. He blushed a little, too. He *had* been awe-stricken. By her. Several times in the last week. But he wasn't about to say that out loud. Instead, he cleared his throat.

"It's amazing," he said. "Thank you for showing it to me this way."

"You have to see St. Mark's for the first time from the water," she shrugged. "I still wish I could have seen it that way the first time as an adult. But watching you is almost as good." She winked.

The gondolier pulled them into the dock near the plaza, and Millie paid him as they climbed out. Stretching out in front of them was the wide white plaza, framed by the arches of the Doge's palace, the domes of the basilica, and the great brown clock tower, standing up straight, tall, and out of place in the piazza full of white marble. The entire square was full of seagulls, flying up in great flocks when pedestrians walked in their path.

They walked around, taking in the sights, with Jack imparting his knowledge of the architecture that he'd read in books, and Millie listening to him, rapt. He couldn't be sure if she was pretending to be interested in what he was saying, or if she genuinely was, but either way it was because she enjoyed being with him, he knew, and that gave him a thrill unlike anything he'd experienced. They went into the basilica, and Jack was taken by the trappings of Catholicism, so similar, yet so utterly different, from the Anglican church he'd been raised in. The air was thick with incense, and the choir sang in Latin in the upper loft. Candles were lit, and there was a soft hush everywhere in the building, even the sound of the choir was somehow hushed by the giant space they found themselves in.

Millie went to the bank of candles and put a coin in the box. She used a long wooden stick to light a new candle, then knelt and started speaking in Latin. Jack stood in amazement watching her. She stood and saw him, then shrugged, and came close to whisper, "It seemed right to say a prayer for my mother."

Jack felt the sting of tears in his eyes. "Do you think I could light a candle for my father?" he asked, his voice soft.

Millie nodded and took him by the hand. She showed him how to light the stick, then they knelt together. She twined her fingers with his in a tight grip between them, and she said the words of the prayer. Jack only bent his head, but he knew if there was a God, he could hear his thoughts as well as the prayer. They stood.

"What about your mother?" Millie asked.

"My mother's still alive," he said, his mouth tight.

"She could probably use even more prayer," Millie said.

"What about your father?" he asked, and it came out more clipped than he'd intended.

She bowed her head. "Touché," she said.

"I didn't mean it that way," he said, bringing her hand up to his lips. "I didn't. Maybe they both need our prayers as much as the parents we loved and lost."

Millie's eyes were shining with tears as she looked up at him. "You're right."

They lit two more candles, knelt again, and again he listened to Millie speaking the Latin, mesmerized by the sound of her voice.

When they stood, they each squeezed the other's hand more tightly, not letting go. They made their way to a pew and listened to the choir sing. He had no way of knowing how much time had passed when they finally got up. He felt as if he were in a trance, as if there was no one else in the world but the two of them. He knew then, and admitted to himself for the first time, that he loved this woman. He knew it had been happening against his will for several days, but this was the moment when he knew that she had made her way into his heart. Now his soul, even. She was more than just a beautiful woman to experiment with in bed. She was more than a friend to read romance books with. She was a woman who'd helped him see the hidden, important parts of himself, who was helping him face things about his past that he'd been utterly unable to fathom two weeks ago.

When they walked back out onto the plaza, the light was blinding. The sun was just about to drop below the marbled buildings on the West side of the plaza, and was blazing across in front of them, the shaft of light almost divine. Jack sighed with the beauty of it all.

"Shall we find dinner here, then take a gondola back to the Rialto?" Millie asked.

"That sounds wonderful."

As they sat across from each other in the candlelight, Jack felt content. He knew he would face heartbreak when it was finally time to say goodbye to this woman he loved, but he knew it was worth it. He'd allowed himself one love, one time to experience this feeling, and it would have to sustain him for the rest of his life. They could say their goodbyes before either had a chance to hurt the other, and he'd remain solitary, with the memories of her to help him through. It wasn't ideal, but it was perhaps better than the life of loneliness he'd originally envisioned for himself, and also better than the life his father had lived, a slave to love, with no control over himself. Yes, Jack thought. This was the better option.

He even allowed himself a half glass of wine after the waiter recommended it to complement their risotto, and they toasted to Venice over their meal. The sun had set, but the sky was still a dark orange, blending into the deep blue of dusk. They talked about the history of Venice, the Napoleonic wars, and the handover of the city to Austria. Millie told him about her friend, the Duke of Sutcliffe, who'd been at Waterloo but had temporarily lost his memory in the battle. Jack knew the story, of course; everyone did. But to hear Millie's version of it, and her obvious affection for the Duke and Duchess, was something else entirely. He could almost picture Jonathan's experience at the battle, and then the courtship of the two when he'd returned. It was highly romantic, but it was something else, too. He realized Millie had a real family, though it wasn't a biological one. Jack had never experienced something like that. He'd always been so isolated. First by his childhood, and then by choice as an adult. He'd never felt particularly lonely, but maybe it was because he hadn't allowed himself to. Now he found himself longing for that kind of friendship, for people to have over for dinner, for little babies to coddle and spoil. It was not something he'd ever given thought to, but Millie was obviously so fond of little Maggie. She made it sound utterly charming.

They walked back across the square after their dinner, arm

in arm again, the moonlight casting an almost ethereal glow to the already magical evening. When they hailed a gondola and climbed down, Millie sat next to him on the narrow bench, and he could feel the heat from her body all the way from shoulder to foot. It was almost unbearable, being this close to her and remembering their time together, but it was also wonderful. He knew he was in dangerous territory, but he was determined to enjoy this time, regardless of the consequences to his heart.

When they arrived back at the Rialto, Jack squeezed Millie's hand. "Ready to look for Fanny?" he asked.

She nodded and squeezed back. "Very ready."

They walked across the bridge, Jack looking for the same group he'd seen the night before, but the fire barrel was unlit and there were no stools around it tonight. They walked the narrow streets and enjoyed the buildup of the revelry for the Carnevale atmosphere. There were vendors selling wine and the stronger anise-flavored liquor popular in the Mediterranean. There were also desserts of all varieties, and when Millie stopped at a vendor and bought them two little hand-held pastries filled with cream, Jack thought he'd died and gone to heaven.

"*Cannoli*," Millie said, eating with gusto. When she'd finished, he reached out to wipe a small dab of cream from the corner of her lip, and she sighed with pleasure, rubbing her cheek against his hand. He closed his eyes and just stayed there for a moment before dropping his hand back to his side.

"Come," he said, his voice gruff as he looked the other way. They walked down alleys and across small bridges over even smaller canals. They stopped to play with street children, and twice Millie bought food for them, telling the children to make sure they gave the scraps to the cats.

As the night wore later, the scene became more raucous, with masked people spilling out of private parties and pubs.

"Too bad you left your lion mask back at the hotel," Millie teased.

"We'll have to get you one and wear them both tomorrow night," he said.

"Deal."

"*Mamma mia*," they heard from across the street, "My Englishman!" Fanny was walking across to them, her face fully made up, and her large bosom barely contained by the tight bodice and corset she wore.

She leaned her face up, and Jack's eyes widened. She couldn't expect him to kiss her, could she?

Millie's laughter tinkled through the night. "You give one kiss on each cheek, Jack. We're on the continent, remember?"

He smiled in embarrassment but bent down to place his two dutiful kisses, and Fanny picked up a decorative fan she carried and made a big show out of cooling herself off before she turned to Millie with narrowed eyes.

"And who is this?" she asked, looking the younger woman up and down.

"Millie," Millie said, holding her hand out in the English way. "Millie diRossi."

"diRossi," Fanny said, taking her hand and shaking it. "An Italian?"

"I was born here, yes," Millie said. "Here in Venice." She paused, looking at the cobbles where she stood. "Here in the Rialto, in fact."

Fanny's eyes blinked, and Jack could almost see her wheels turning. Her voice was quiet when she asked, "Was your mother a working girl?"

Millie smiled. "How did you know?"

"I watched you helping the little ones," Fanny said, her voice gentle. "There was a look about you I recognized. You know your own."

Millie laughed a little. "I suppose I do," she said. "How about you, Miss Francesca?"

"I grew up right here, as well," she said, her kohl-rimmed eyes crinkling at the corners. "But I have enjoyed my life."

Millie nodded. Jack was watching her closely. He knew she wasn't ashamed of her sexuality, but he also knew she had no fond memories of her mother's time as a courtesan. He wondered what she was feeling. She was always so open with her emotions, but he had been unsure what she'd been feeling all day. He knew she cared for him, even if she did not love him. He knew she was conflicted about what had happened between them and their deal to cut it off. But he also knew she'd enjoyed their day just as much as he had. He wished he knew what she was thinking, but then again, he was glad he didn't.

"Who was your mother?" Fanny asked, breaking the silence.

"Her name was Sofia. I don't know her family name. She took on the name diRossi, after the *Magic Flute*, when she went on the stage, and she never told me the real one. I don't even know what part of Italy she was from," Millie said.

"She was a singer, or actress?"

"Opera singer mostly, but she did some theatre, too."

Fanny was thoughtful, putting her finger on her chin. "I don't remember her," she said, her voice careful, "But I may know someone who does."

Millie and Jack exchanged looks. Dare they be hopeful? Millie swallowed. "We would," she started, "That is, I would, I mean, we would be so grateful if you'd point us in the right direction."

Fanny took Millie's hands in her own and stared into her eyes. They looked like two dark goddesses there in the moonlight, the sound of the revelers in the distance. "It would be my pleasure," Fanny said. "Come to the bridge tomorrow around noon. This lady doesn't quite keep the same hours I do," she finished with a wink.

Jack watched as Millie squeezed the woman's hands in return and thanked her. Then he was surprised to see Fanny lean down and touch her forehead to Millie's. "*Fino a domani, allora.*"

"*Fino a domani,*" Millie whispered back, then turned to

Jack with tears in her eyes, but a smile on her lips.

They waved goodbye to Fanny and walked back to their hotel in a pensive silence. Jack wanted to talk, but he also wanted to respect Millie's silence and let her sit with the knowledge that they might speak to someone tomorrow who knew her mother. It was what they had come here for, but Jack nonetheless felt shocked that it was happening so quickly.

As they neared their hotel, Jack realized he was exhausted, though he'd slept so late. On the street, bustling now with people celebrating in the Carnevale night, he turned to Millie. "Shall we go in together? I believe I can sleep tonight."

Millie nodded. "I was thinking the same thing," she said. "We'll both need to be sharp and fresh for our meeting tomorrow." She surprised him by taking his hand. "I think we can handle this like grownups, don't you?"

He nodded, but his body was reacting to her already, just from the touch of her fingertips on his. He made a weak smile. "Shall we?" he motioned to the doorway, and she led the way in. He watched as she walked through the lobby, her hips gently swaying, and the fabric of her dress brushing the floor. He loved this woman, he knew, and because of that, he'd never be able to touch her again.

Chapter 11

Millie woke to bright sunshine flowing through the window. They'd neglected to close the blinds last night, and the room was flooded with light. Millie was surprised she'd slept so well. After the amount of walking they'd done, and the emotional energy it had taken not to imagine Jack's lips on hers, she wasn't surprised by how tired she'd been, though. She supposed that explained it. There was something soothing about the sound of Jack's breathing across the room, as well. It was just as well they were getting used to being together, but not *being together*. It would make everything that much easier. Nonetheless, Millie thoroughly enjoyed lying in bed, propping her head on her elbow, watching Jack go about his morning ablutions. He'd slept in his breeches and shirt, but when he sat up to get dressed, she could see the muscles rippling across his back beneath it as it stretched taut across his shoulders. He stood and turned to grab his waistcoat and cravat, and she averted her eyes, pretending not to look, but she took a sly sideward glance to take in as much in as she could.

The dark hair of his chest peeked out through the deep V of his shirt and her mouth almost watered at the sight of it. She realized no good could come of this, so she turned to her other side and sat up as well. She had slept in her chemise, but her dress was right next to the bed, so she pulled it on and did up the few low buttons in the back, glad she had chosen to bring simple gowns she could don without much fuss. She stood and pulled on her pelisse against the chill, then turned and began dealing with her hair. She could feel Jack's gaze on her but chose to ignore it. She was absolutely certain that if their eyes met, they would be in terrible danger of losing all their clothes even more quickly than they'd pulled them on. She was hasty in pushing pins in her unruly hair, not caring much at all what it looked like, since she'd be wearing a bonnet anyway. She took a deep breath and finally turned around, and she was right. Jack was standing in the corner against the window frame, strong arms crossed at his chest, fully dressed, with the most infuriating smirk on his face. He pushed himself off the wall with one foot and raised his eyebrows.

"Shall we?" he asked, the corners of his lips twitching.

She burst into laughter. It was contagious, and she couldn't help it. "We shall," she said, glad the tension was broken. "It's much later than I expected."

"It is," Jack said. "I'm glad we both slept so well, though. Now," he motioned to the door. "We have an appointment to keep."

It was a short walk to the bridge, but they stopped for a couple of pastries and coffee to tide them over. When they got to the bridge, it was bustling with midday activity, and they had to walk back and forth across it a few times before they finally spotted Fanny.

She stood from the bench where she'd been sitting and waved her hand at them. They made their way through the throng and stopped in front of her. The fire bowl had already been lit, and Millie noticed that clouds were moving in. Without the bright sunshine pouring down on them, it was getting much colder.

Fanny must have noticed Millie shiver because she laughed and said, "*Si*, it smells like snow."

Jack and Millie looked at each other. Millie knew

immediately what Jack was thinking because she was thinking the same thing: how incredibly lucky were they to be in Venice during Carnevale and a rare snowfall? They both smiled just a bit.

"Ah, *si*," Fanny said, "*Che romantico*, eh?" Millie frowned and looked sidelong at Jack, whose eyes were just the tiniest bit crinkled at the corners as he tried not to smile.

"Don't be meddlesome, Francesca," he said, offering his arm to her. "Will you take us to your friend now?"

"*Ovviamente, ovviamente*," Fanny muttered, taking his arm. "So impatient you are."

Millie followed the two of them as they walked across the bridge back toward the neighborhood they'd explored just the day before. It wasn't long before they stopped in front of a tall building, stuccoed in a deep orange, fresh and bright and not at all falling apart like so many of the houses here. They stepped up under the portico just as the first few flakes of snow began to fall. Millie felt as if she were in a dream. How was it that she was experiencing a snowfall in Venice, possibly about to learn something new about her mother, with a man she had never expected to have feelings for? She watched Jack help Fanny to navigate the steps. She was once again struck by how powerful his compact frame was, and how gentle he was in helping the older woman. Her body was drawn to his animal magnetism, even while her heart warmed at this secret, nurturing side. It was natural he and Fanny had been drawn to each other that first night, she supposed. They each seemed to have the instinct to care for people.

Inside the *pensione*, it was warm and cozy. A fireplace blazed in the corner of a little sitting area, where velvet sofas and chairs sat snugly close together. Two women were seated there, their heads close together in conversation, but the whole scene had the air of comfort about it. It was clean and well-kept, and Millie noticed how different it was from the run-down buildings she'd seen the children running in and out of, or the *pensione* where she'd lived with her mother. This was clearly a respectable boarding-house.

Fanny went to the counter where the attendant stood. She murmured a name and he nodded, then called over his shoulder. A young woman dressed in the gray dress and apron of a housemaid came out, bobbing in her little white cap.

"*Ciao,*" she said to Fanny.

Fanny put her arm around the maid's shoulders. "*Ciao bella,*" she said, lovingly, and with a start, Millie realized this maid was probably one of Fanny's girls from the street. It was difficult to tell if she were a current or former companion, but the easy friendship was clear between them. The maid motioned to the stairs, and Fanny led the way, on Jack's proffered arm, while Millie and the maid followed behind.

When they approached the third landing, they traveled down a short hallway and stopped in front of a door. Millie was surprised to hear voices coming from behind the door. She'd assumed that they were going to visit an old woman who lived alone.

The maid came forward and knocked softly on the wood paneling. They heard movement behind the door, and then it opened, and Millie came face to face with the blonde version of herself.

It was so shocking it was like looking in a mirror. The same tight curls, the same pointy chin, the same deep brown eyes. They were even about the same age. Millie drew back, recoiling in disbelief.

Jack gasped behind her, and Fanny and the maid just looked at them, back and forth.

The blonde woman stood only for a moment, staring, before she recovered herself and rushed at Millie, enveloping her in a tight hug.

Millie just stood there at first, unsure what to do, until finally she returned the embrace, rubbing the small of the other woman's back in a kind of perfunctory way.

"Mildred," the woman said, pulling back, then frowning. "You don't know who I am."

Millie shook her head. "I'm sad to say I don't," she said, her voice deliberate and questioning.

"Maybe you should come in," the blonde woman said, gesturing into the room. Millie just stood in the hall, unsure what to do until she felt Jack's hand. His fingers twined with hers and squeezed.

"Let's go," he whispered. "Courage."

They all went in except the maid, who curtsied at the door and pulled it closed behind her.

The room they entered was small, but comfortable. It was a little parlor, decorated in much the same manner as the sitting room downstairs. Red velvet couches sat on an oriental carpet, arranged neatly around a fireplace, where a cheerful fire leaped in the grate. Out the arched windows, Millie could see a small *loggia* off the room, and through the columns the snow falling in the air outside. Seated on one small couch was an older woman wearing a rather outdated, large dress, with ruffles at her chin and a big, powdered wig, holding the top of a cane in her two hands. Next to her was a much smaller, much younger woman, very clearly the sister of the blonde woman who'd answered the door.

"Mildred," the blonde said, clearing her throat, "Allow me to introduce you to Miss Isabella diRossi," she cleared her throat as Millie's head flew up in surprise, "and Miss Jane Elton. And I'm," the woman reached her hand out in greeting. "Miss Louisa Elton. We're your cousins."

Millie felt herself swaying. She hadn't realized Jack was still holding her hand, but he squeezed it now and led her to another couch, where Millie dropped her bottom down rather gracelessly in her shock. Jack helped Fanny sit next to her, but she was barely registering anything else in the room. She just stared at the two blonde women.

"Cousins?" she whispered. "I don't understand."

"Of course you wouldn't," the old woman rumbled from beneath her large coiffure. "Your mother was a damned fool not to tell you the truth."

Millie realized Isabella diRossi was an Englishwoman. She stared intently into the old lady's eyes, which were shrewd and piercing beneath their layers of wrinkles and powder. "You knew my mother?"

"I did," the lady said, rapping a cane on the floor. "And your father, too."

"My—" Millie paused, unable to comprehend what she was hearing. "My *father*?"

"Yes," the woman named Louisa said, sitting in a chair opposite them and crossing her legs beneath her skirts. She leaned forward on her knee, clasping her hands. "His name was Sir Walter Edgecombe, and he was my uncle. The very best of men. A baronet with a small holding in Hampshire."

Millie just stared, wide-eyed.

"We've been looking for you for so long," Jane said from the couch. "We didn't have a clue how to find you, until—"

"Until our bloody brother—" Louisa cleared her throat. "I'm so sorry, excuse my lapse."

Millie actually laughed at that. "Aren't we sitting here with two old whores and the daughter of one? It's bloody fascinating, isn't it?"

The tension in the room eased considerably at that. Old Isabella rapped her cane on the floor again in approval.

Jack took this opportunity to cut in. "You're the women who went to see Yvette." It wasn't a question.

Jane and Louisa nodded. "A fat lot of good that did us," Jane said. "She wasn't about to give up any information about you."

Millie smiled. "She's very loyal, it's true," she said. Millie wondered how much she should tell these women now, in fact. Had Yvette been right to remain tight-lipped with them? Were they connected to the men who had tried to kill her? Was she in danger now?

"You can trust us," Louisa said, evidently watching these thoughts move across Millie's face. "It's our brother, Thomas, who's trying to find you."

"Kill me," Millie corrected.

The two sisters looked at each other, their eyes wide in horror. "No, he wouldn't," Louisa said but Millie could see the doubt on both their faces.

Jack broke in again. "I assure you he would, and he tried," he said, his voice like steel.

"But why?" Millie asked. She felt like the only person in the room who didn't understand what everyone was talking about.

"You're an heiress, Millie," Jane said, her voice gentle and soft. "Our Uncle tried to find you after your mother's death, but he had no way of knowing you'd come to England." She shook her head in sadness. "The irony."

"How did they find me now?" Millie asked.

"We're not sure, but after he died, he left a portion of his fortune to you, and specified to the solicitors that they must put in the effort to find you," Louisa said.

Jane cut in. "But the estate was entailed to our brother, since your father never had any legitimate heirs."

Louisa continued. "And, though the estate without your portion is still large enough for him to be perfectly happy—"

"He's never been perfectly happy with any amount of money," Jane shook her head. "And he was furious that an illegitimate child would receive anything at all."

Millie nodded, starting to understand. "But that's easy enough. I don't need his money."

Jack coughed and leaned in close to Millie. "It rightfully belongs to you," he said, under his breath. "Don't be so quick to let it go."

Millie nodded at him but turned back to the cousins. "Truly, I don't need the money. I was left a nice and tidy sum and a neat little house in Bloomsbury by my employer, and that's all I've ever required."

Louisa and Jane both smiled. "That's wonderful," Louisa said, "But it doesn't change the fact that Thomas feels you are a threat. Once he confirmed you were real and still alive, he insisted you be removed from the equation."

"We didn't think he truly meant to kill you," Jane said.

Jack's face was grim. "You thought wrong," he said, and Millie felt a swell of emotion at the anger in his voice.

She turned back to the women. "How did you find me?" she asked. "And what do we do now?"

"That," Louisa said, and then Jane finished her sentence, "is going to take a little longer to tell."

Soon a tea service arrived, and their odd group fell into a homey sense of conversation, all asking questions and talking over each other as they ate and learned each side of the story from the others. It turned out that the sisters had unearthed some of the baronet's letters to his old flame while she'd still been alive. Evidently Sofia had corresponded with Millie's father all through her childhood. She kept him apprised of Millie's well-being but had mostly asked for money. They were gentle when they told her this, but Millie's lips formed a stoic line, unsurprised. Sofia had given Millie the locket with her father's hair in it to prove her identity should it ever be necessary but had died too suddenly to tell Annelise Heatherington about him. Millie found it infuriating, but perfectly in keeping with her mother's personality that Sofia had never told her own daughter the truth about her father. It wasn't like it was an unusual story. There were by-blows in every city in Europe from young men who'd gone on Grand Tours. Millie's story wasn't special or unique. Why had her mother kept it from her?

Isabella jumped in, almost as if she could read Millie's thoughts. "Your mother was fiercely independent," she said. "I knew her well. We quarreled constantly about you and what was best for you."

Millie met the old woman's gaze. Try as she might, she could not remember her. She didn't even look the slightest bit familiar. "I'm so sorry you didn't win the quarrels," she said, her voice calm.

"As am I," Isabella said. "But I was away a lot. I had men in London and Paris who kept me for months at a time, not to mention the opera."

Millie nodded. That, too, was an incredibly familiar story. And it explained why Millie had no memory of this woman. Not that she'd spent much time with her mother during "working" hours in the first place. She'd visited the theatre as often as it was possible, but aside from that, she'd stayed in their little set of rooms, reading or nursing her mother, or out in the streets, making mischief and enjoying herself.

There wasn't much left to the story. Sofia had died, Annelise had taken Millie to England, and that was the end of it. Until Thomas Elton learned about his lost bastard cousin. His uncle had detailed what he knew about Millie's possible whereabouts, including the locket, for his solicitors, and Thomas had hired VanHinkel to find her, prove her identity, and kill her. In the meantime, Jane and Louisa had launched a parallel hunt for their missing cousin.

"And we found you first," Louisa said, smiling. "Thank God."

"Well," Millie said, looking at Jack and trying to read the emotion in his face, "Jack found me first, and saved my life."

"He sounds like a wonderful man," Jane said, and her eyes appraised Jack in a way that made Millie's stomach roil with jealousy.

"He is," she said, and tried to keep her face passive.

The new group of friends spent the afternoon reminiscing about Venice before Napoleon while the snow fell softly outside. When it was drawing dark, Isabella leaned heavily on her cane, then stood and went to the doors that led to the *loggia*. She pulled open the glass, and stuck her head out, listening. They heard the strains of violin music floating up to them.

"*Carnevale* in the snow," Isabella said, smiling and staring into the distance. "There is nothing like it."

Louisa clapped her hands. "Tonight we must revel," she said, looking at Jane.

One side of Jane's mouth lowered slightly, but she nodded nonetheless. "I feel we must, indeed," she said. "Though it's highly improper without a chaperone."

"*Senza senso*," Fanny said, standing. "Nonsense utterly. We have two old women here to watch you, and a man to protect us all. He's proven himself capable, after all."

Millie smiled at them all. A night of joy would be just the thing, she thought. "Yes, we must join. I promised Jack we could join the Carnevale one night, and the night seems to have chosen us. We have much to celebrate." She smiled at her newfound cousins. "Now," she said, rising and going to stand by Fanny, "We must prepare. Jack has a mask, but I'm afraid I have nothing at all to wear."

Fanny took her hand. "Let me take you and the young English shopping," she said. "Then we shall meet back here and go out for dinner."

Isabella rapped her cane on the floor in approval. Then she looked up at Jack, her eyes crinkling with her humor. "And this young man will keep me company. I'm too old to flirt," she said, "but not too old to look."

Millie laughed. "Indeed, Miss Isabella." Her eyes locked with Jack's, and she tried to wish him luck, but he just smiled and shooed her out.

Jack watched the four women make their way out of the little parlor and listened to their laughter as they disappeared down the hallway. He settled back into the sofa and poured himself another cup of tea. The fire was lovely, and he couldn't believe they had solved the mystery of Millie's locket and assassins. Of course, they weren't entirely safe yet, but if he could get in touch with Thomas and offer him Millie's portion of the inheritance, he was sure he could cut a deal. It was true that the money belonged to Millie, but it was also clear that Millie cared far more about the value of finding her lost family than she did about any money. She hadn't been lying when she said she was perfectly comfortable. He'd seen that with his own eyes. Now she could keep her lifestyle, her independence, her visits to salons, her lovers. His chest tightened at the thought, but yes, her lovers. She could go back to her old life, and wasn't that what they'd both wanted?

Isabella was watching him, her eyes narrowed and shrewd as she sipped her tea in silence.

Jack cleared his throat. "I believe I can make a deal with Sir Elton," he said, trying to break the silence.

Isabella just nodded.

"Millie and I will leave soon and return to our old lives," he continued.

Again, the old woman simply nodded, taking another sip of tea.

"I can probably resume my profession once I clear things up with Sir Thomas. I can repair any mistrust potential clients might have had as a result of all this," he gestured around.

Isabella moved her lips into a thin line, but still said nothing.

Jack shifted in his seat. He was growing uncomfortable under the silent woman's gaze.

"It will be nice to have this behind us and get back to normal," he said.

The woman still said nothing, but he heard her "harumph" under her breath and she shook her head just the slightest bit.

"Spit it out, woman," he said, growing impatient. "What do you have to say?"

"Oh, me?" she said, feigning innocence with one hand at her chest. "Absolutely nothing." She picked up the cup and saucer and took another sip of tea. "It sounds like you have it all figured out."

Jack narrowed his eyes. What game was she playing at? He didn't want to take the bait. "Yes, I do," he bit off. He leaned forward and grabbed a corncake pastry and chewed it with gusto, never breaking eye contact with her.

She laughed out loud, and it angered him so much he almost leaped out of the chair to leave. But he had to stay here for the ladies' return. He took a deep breath and tried to calm himself.

Isabella leaned forward and grabbed a pastry herself, then smiled, much more gentle and less mocking now. "Bloody bothersome business it is, isn't it?"

Jack did stand up then, turning around and pacing behind the little couch. "I don't know what you mean," he said.

"Being in love," the old woman said, her voice soft.

Jack narrowed his eyes. "You're presumptuous."

"It's as plain as day," the old lady said with a dismissive wave as her hand. "Don't be so offended."

Jack sighed. "I'm not offended," he said, standing behind the couch and leaning forward on it. "Just exhausted."

"I can see that. I know that feeling. I know that look."

Jack's question must have been plain on his face because she continued without waiting for him to speak. "Yes, I've been in love. And with someone I shouldn't have given my heart to. Against my better judgment and indeed my own wishes." She chuckled but there was a sadness in the sound of it.

Jack came back around, threw another log on the fire, and perched himself on the edge of the sofa. "What happened?"

"I chose my head over my heart," she said, "and I never saw him again."

"Who was he?"

She smiled and looked at a spot on the wall over his head. Her eyes had a dreamy, faraway look. "He was the vicar's son," she said, her voice emphasizing *vicar* to play up the drama and the scandal, he supposed. "We were best friends all through childhood. My widowed mother was companion to the lady of the estate. He and I both traveled that narrow path between the gentry and the commoners."

"I had always wanted to sing," Isabella said, looking back at Jack's face now, a sadness in her eyes. "When my mother died, I knew it was my chance to get away. I did not want to stay in that little village and be a vicar's son's wife."

Jack leaned forward, listening.

"I knew he was about to propose to me, and so I ran," she said. "I ran and never looked back, and I haven't set foot in that town since."

Jack wanted to ask her if it was worth it, but he was not sure he wanted to know the answer. He reclined back into the cushion and watched the older woman, expectant.

"I had a good life. I have no regrets," she said. "Except that one." Her eyes were somehow both sad and happy at the same time. "I made my choice, and I think it was the right one for me at the time, but I wish I had tried harder to have both. He might have come with me. I never asked. I never even told him about my dream."

Jack swallowed, trying to clear the lump in his throat.

Isabella continued. "I became very successful," she said. "I sang, I learned, I was part of the political machinations of Venice. I had a wonderful life. But I will always wonder what happened to him."

Jack nodded, understanding completely. He had already resigned himself to having only memories of Millie. It would be hard, but he could do it. And it was not like Isabella could be sure it could have worked out any other way. She had made a hard decision, and she had lived with it She had done more than live—she had thrived. He should listen to her wisdom. But something told him she was trying to push him in the opposite direction. He sighed.

What if he were willing to try a compromise, though? What if there were some way for he and Millie to have their independence, but have each other, too? Was it so far-fetched?

Look what had happened with Jonathan and Anne, he thought. They'd overcome almost insurmountable odds, differences in class, Anne's desire to be a doctor. They'd done all that and ended up in a happy, fulfilling marriage. Of course, Jonathan was a Duke. He could do what he liked. Jack frowned. But he was a Viscount, however unwilling he was to admit it. And wasn't that an obstacle in this case? Millie loved her life in Bloomsbury. Would she be able to continue any part of her independence as the Viscountess Danbury? He shook his head and leaned forward to grab another pastry.

"I don't know if it could have worked," Isabella said, her voice very soft as if she didn't want to intrude on his thoughts. "But I do wish I had at least considered it."

Jack set his lips in a grim line. "Believe me," he said, his tone more biting than he wished. "I have done nothing for the past two weeks but consider it. It is torture being near her."

Isabella leaned forward and covered his hand with her own. "I can see it," she said, "She feels the same, you know."

Jack's eyes focused on the wrinkled hand atop his. Her palm was soft and papery, but warm. He felt unaccountably soothed by it. It wasn't as if her words were news to him. He would be an idiot not to sense how Millie felt about him. That wasn't a question. The question was how serious they both were about keeping their walls up, what this feeling might be worth in terms of the change in their lives it would bring. He couldn't answer that for himself, and he wasn't sure Millie was even considering it. So far they'd both slept easier in the same room, had enjoyed each other's company without physical touch, and Jack could see a companionship between them that went far beyond their desire for each other. And that was almost worse, more painful. He'd eschewed both physical and emotional entanglements for a good reason, and he'd always thought the emotional would be easier to guard against. He was a man made of flesh and blood, of course, and he'd fantasized and imagined sexual encounters enough. He knew he could fall prey to that if he found himself in the right situation. But he'd just assumed that his experiences with his mother and father had kept him safe from ever falling into *that* trap. Now he knew he'd been wrong.

He pulled his hand from under Isabella's and patted hers before leaning back into the cushion again. He stared at the ceiling in silence, but it wasn't long before he could hear the light sounds of snoring from Isabella's chair. She'd nodded off and sat there, head lolling, dozing. He took a small pillow and propped it beside her head and sat back down to doze himself. When he dreamt, it was of dark curls and darker eyes.

He wasn't sure how much time had passed when the door opened and the ladies came in, bustling and talking, bringing a blast of cold air from the hallway in with him, and shaking out their coats and bonnets with the snow that had fallen on them.

"You are all a vision," he said, standing. And he was telling the truth. All four of them had rosy cheeks, Fanny's artificially augmented, but still charming, and their hair was falling out of pins after removing their bonnets. They looked as fresh and warm as a spring day, and their smiles were what really set it off. It was clear they'd enjoyed each other's company.

Fanny made a little mock bow. "Thank you, sir," she said, nudging Isabella, who was still dozing, contented, on the little pillow. "I can see you lay-abouts did nothing while we were gone."

Jack smiled. "Not quite true. We finished the pastries."

Fanny cackled at that.

Millie, Jane, and Louisa all had big packages with them, and Millie smiled when she saw Jack's look of curiosity.

"For you to find out," she said, eyes twinkling. "Tonight we revel!"

They all enjoyed another warming cup of tea, then Jack and Millie bundled up to return to their hotel to get ready for the evening. They bid fond goodbyes to the other ladies and made their way back to the Rialto and to their room. Millie told Jack to get ready first, and she went down to walk along the canal while she waited. It didn't take Jack long to don his black breeches, black shirt, waistcoat, and coat. He even had a black silk cravat—formerly a scarf used as a mask. He donned his greatcoat and strapped the lion mask around his head, and the effect was quite dramatic. He made his way downstairs and enjoyed Millie's slow appraisal as she eyed him up and down before she smiled and went up to dress herself. While he waited, he wandered under the porticoes along the canal, watching the snow fall and melt into the salt water, accumulating on the little crenellations of the stone fencing, reflected golden in the lanterns being lit at sundown. It was truly a magical night.

When Millie came down, his breath caught in his throat. She wore a black velvet cloak, tied at the high waist under her breasts, and with a large bow at her neck. Her curls were wild about her head, and her eyes shone dark and deep behind the mask she'd donned—a purple face with stylized lips and eyes, and pink blushing cheeks. She looked exotic and elegant, but also so *Millie*. He whistled.

"You look incredible," he said, taking her hand.

"So do you," she said, wrapping her hand around his bicep and walking toward the bridge where they would meet the other women. "Quite dashing. I will have to keep my eye on you tonight."

Jack stopped and Millie stumbled a bit, tightening her grip on his arm. He turned to look at her, trying to read her gaze behind the mask. He knew she couldn't see his face and it gave him a little freedom to be more honest. "Millie," he said, clearing his throat. "You must know you are the only woman I'd end up with tonight, if that were an option."

He could not be sure, but he thought he saw a smile at the corners of her eyes. She didn't respond, though. She only nodded and turned back to pull them toward the bridge. He felt a little thrill knowing his honesty had pleased her. He knew the idea of her with another man made his stomach hurt. It was gratifying to think perhaps she felt at least a little the same about him.

When they got to the bridge, Fanny and Isabella stood out with bright orange and yellow capes, each adorned with elaborate beading and embroidery. Isabella wore the yellow, with a mask of the same stylized face Millie wore, but it was golden, with delicate tendrils of metal coming off all around, to look like the rays of the sun. The face wasn't a full mask, and Isabella's rouged lips were wide in a welcoming smile. Fanny wore her orange, with a half mask sporting the orange and black stripes of a tiger, with little pointed ears of porcelain rising from the top.

"You two look incredible," Millie said, leaving Jack's arm to greet them with the traditional two kisses. Jack watched as she squeezed each woman's shoulders, wondering again at her openness and ease with new people.

Jane and Louisa came forward for their similar greetings, each dressed in a similar costume to Millie's—a simple black velvet cape with one of those stylized face masks. Where Millie's was purple, Jane's was pink, and Louisa's was blue.

Louisa leaned over to Jack. "Isn't this exciting?" she whispered. "The snow just adds an air of magic to the whole thing."

Jack agreed. "I am a lucky man to be out tonight with the five most beautiful ladies in Venice."

Fanny batted at his arm. "Please, three of the most beautiful, and two of the most experienced."

Jack laughed and offered Fanny his arm. She took it and they all strolled together to the bistro where they would take their dinner. When they arrived, the place was warm and crowded with revelers, masks propped up against the legs of their chairs so they could enjoy their food and drink. There were two large fireplaces, one at each end of the big room, and the place smelled heavenly, of spices and baking and the heavy redolent odor of stewing meat. They were seated at a large round table, and they all took their fill of the meal, with much wine being passed around. Jack had one glass, and it complemented the food perfectly. He had always been concerned he might develop a liking for drink the way his mother had, but he realized it was easy for him to have one glass, enjoy it as an experience, and then let it go. That was something he'd never allowed himself to do but being with Millie had shown him that some of his old ideas had been mistaken, born of fear and trauma, and not reality. He wondered which others were as false as that one, but he shook the thought out of his head before he got to territory too dangerous.

When the desserts came out, Jack was almost embarrassed by the extravagance of it. There were those delightful *cannoli* Millie had introduced him to but elevated for the dining area. There were the cornmeal pastries he had learned to covet since arriving. There were French things as well—petit fours and macarons, and there was a very English figgy pudding. They all drank that excellent Italian coffee, and the conversation flowed as easily as the wine had. The din in the dining room was loud as people neared the end of their meals, and diners started to spill out into the street, the big wooden doors leading to the portico letting in gushes of refreshing cold air with each party's departure. Each time the door opened they could hear the strains of music from the *Carnevale* atmosphere outside. The anticipation was delightful.

When they finally pulled on their cloaks and masks and made their way back to the street, it was like a city transformed. The usual lanterns were lit, but now there were revelers carrying them on long poles, with frosted glass of various colors that threw a moving kaleidoscope across the fresh white snow. Wherever there were musicians set up on a corner, there was a crowd of dancers, doing traditional Italian dances, but the waltz as well. Each new street, each new little bridge across a tiny canal, was its own new party, complete with musicians and ballroom, and tables set up with wine, cider, stronger drink, and food of all kinds, both savory and sweet.

At each new spot, they all enjoyed a round of drinks and a toast, and Jack cycled through dances with all of them, though often Isabella and Fanny sat to the side with other older women and matrons. Jack stuck to water after dinner, but it was fun to watch Millie enjoying her wine without lapsing into the drunkenness that filled his memories of his mother. Though they had shared a few dances together, it was clear Millie was trying to share him with the other ladies so no one would lack for partners, but when they arrived at another bridge, covered with snow and shining in the lantern light, the quartet of strings struck up a waltz and he took her in his arms. He couldn't resist.

Her eyes were lifted into half-moons behind the mask, and he could hear her gasp with joy when he lifted her up to take a turn in the steps. She threw her head back and laughed, and he could see the barest expanse of skin at her neck as her mask lifted just a little. He put a possessive hand at the small of her back and pulled her against him. He was a little worried she would resist, but she melted in his arms, her hand gripping his through both their gloves, and her other hand, which had rested on his shoulder, snaked around behind his neck.

The waltz was not a fast one, but Jack felt his head reel as if he were running at a breakneck pace. The feeling of Millie's body against his was like an intoxicant, much more powerful than any wine, and he felt himself losing control of his grip on reality. The snow was like a veil between the seen and unseen worlds, and every turn they made through the misty multicolored light felt like a turn toward himself, his real self, and what he really wanted, and away from all the rules he had set for himself.

He closed his eyes, listened to the music, and let the feeling of Millie against him pull him through the steps of the dance. He could have this night.

Chapter 12

Millie looked up through her mask to see Jack's eyes close behind his, and she moved closer into him. She could have this night, couldn't she? So much had happened since she'd discovered the truth about her father. She'd spent a delightful afternoon with her newfound cousins, who were as down to earth, sweet, and kind as anybody she'd known, despite their being part of the minor aristocracy. They'd fallen in love with Fanny and Isabella already and had no misgivings whatsoever about those two ladies' life work. In fact, they seemed to rather enjoy being scandalized, Millie thought. And who wouldn't? For women who'd been raised in the confining prison of "proper" English life, seeing other women who'd taken life by the reins and mastered it on their own terms was empowering. Millie had grown up around such women, so she had learned that lesson young, but she was glad Louisa and Jane were seeing it now. One didn't have to run off and become an opera singer to take charge of her life.

Now, though, Millie was again thinking of Jack. The ladies had all asked rather impertinent questions about their relationship during their afternoon, but Millie had evaded as much as possible. She didn't want to bare her heart in that way, and not only that, but her feelings for Jack were like a secret room she could visit, and she didn't want anyone else intruding there. She knew by now that she was in love with him, and she'd made her peace with it. He was a lovely man, a loveable man, and it hadn't taken much for her to see it. Their time in bed on the ship was one thing, but their time here in Venice had shown her quite clearly how she felt about this man.

Now, she was determined to enjoy this one last night. Soon enough they'd be able to find her cousin and make the deal that would protect her and allow them to return to their lives in London. She'd already discussed it with Louisa and Jane, who would accompany them back home. There would be no more shared cabin or nights of passion for Millie and Jack. This night, this incredible dreamy night in the snow of a Venice *Carnevale* might be the last night she'd ever spend with him. She had no intention of seeing him once they returned to London. She hoped the trip had encouraged him to reconcile with his own mother. She'd seen the idea form in their conversation in the church, and again over lunch. She felt Jack needed to approach his mother as an adult rather than the child he'd been when he ran away. His mother might never be able to overcome her drinking, but Jack could set boundaries and forgive what he could. And, more importantly, he could become the Viscount he was clearly meant to be. Jack was a talented, sensitive, and perceptive man. He'd make an excellent member of Parliament. She could only imagine the good works he could help support with his knowledge of the streets.

All these thoughts ran through Millie's mind in the barest of seconds. They rushed through because she'd been thinking them constantly for days. Now, though, she could see Jack losing himself in the rapture of the moment, and she could do nothing but fight with all her might against losing herself right along with him. The feeling of his warm arms around her, the sound of his breathing at her ear, the soft coolness of the snow falling—it was all too much. She could feel herself slipping. The waltz was ending, and Millie pulled the mask up over her face to rest on top of her head, looking up at Jack as he did the same. She gave the barest of smiles and he pulled her all the way against him, their bodies warm and pliant in the magical cold. He bent down and covered her lips with his, and she was lost. Her knees weakened, and his strong arms tightened around her back, holding her upright and pulling her tighter against him. He did not deepen the kiss—they were in public, after all—but his lips stayed on hers for long moments, and she just stood, melting against him, feeling the gentle press and the soft flakes of snow melting on her face.

He pulled away and brought his mouth to her ear. "This place is magic," he said, wonder in his voice, and all she could do was nod. The waltz ended, and she stepped back, clapping with the rest of the dancers. But her head was a whirl of sensation and emotion. She tried to steady her breathing, but there was nothing she could do about the pace of her heart as she looked at him. Handsome as the devil, his eyes grayish blue and deep in the lantern light, sparkling with the reflection of the snow, were trained directly on her, as if an invisible force held his gaze. She looked down, trying to be demure, trying to gather herself, but it was to no avail. His gaze had a magnetic pull, and she was helpless in the face of it. She looked back up and his face was full of wonder. She blushed but didn't look back down. She could only smile.

"You two dance beautifully," Jane said, out of breath from her own round about the bridge with a tall stranger in a mask. He nodded to them and bowed to her before disappearing into the crowd. "Isn't this the most fun you've ever had?" she asked.

Millie smiled. "It really might be," she said, "and I've had a *lot* of fun before."

Jack elbowed her but bowed over Jane's hand and motioned to the improvised dance floor. They both smiled back at Millie, and Jack took Jane off into the snow. Millie smiled. Her heart was so full, she wasn't sure what to do with herself. She went over to sit with Isabella and Fanny and drink a cup of warm cider.

"That was some kiss," Fanny said, nudging her.

Millie took a sip of her cider and frowned, lifting one eyebrow. "I don't know how to do it any other way," she said, her voice prim.

Fanny laughed heartily and lifted her glass in a toast. Millie lifted her own, and they clanked them together before drinking deeply.

Isabella leaned forward. "What secrets are you sharing over here?" she asked, above the din of the musicians. "Is it about that young Jack?"

Fanny nodded. "Of course it is."

Millie shook her head. "You two are incorrigible."

"We just know love when we see it," Fanny said, her voice softening.

"This isn't not a novel, Fanny," Millie said. "There's no happily ever after waiting for us."

"Why not a happily-for-now?" Fanny asked.

Isabella nodded sagely. "That's all any of us are guaranteed anyway."

"I'm not so sure we're even guaranteed that much," Millie said, staring up at the falling snow.

"Oh posh," Isabella said, leaning forward and swatting Millie's leg, "We're not guaranteed anything, but we can certainly take it when we know we want it."

Millie was starting to tire of the meddlesome old women, as well-meaning as they were. She sighed and looked at the lantern, wondering what time it was. "I think you both know it's not that easy," she said, trying to add an edge of finality in her voice. To no avail, of course.

"Isn't it, though?" Isabella said, taking another sip of wine. "The choices we make for ourselves are rarely so difficult as we make them seem at first. Haven't you ever decided something and suddenly felt completely free, knowing that even if it was wrong, at least you were moving forward?"

Millie swallowed. Everyone knew that feeling, of course. She felt a flush starting in her shoulders and creeping up to her face. She had to get away. She stood and nodded at the ladies, lifting her empty glass. "Would anyone like another?"

They both shook their heads and then shared a knowing look with each other. Millie frowned and turned, muttering a curse under her breath.

"I heard that," Isabella said, snickering.

Millie took a deep breath and pushed forward, pulling her mask back down over her face and walking to the vendor to refill her glass. She stopped at the musicians to drop a few coins in their cases, and then turned to watch the dancers whirling about. Could those meddling old fools have a point? Would it be as easy as simply making the decision to love Jack and then just doing it? Her brain still thought it was impossible, but her heart felt any other option was impossible. Jack was becoming more important to her than just a friend or a lover. She was starting to feel like he was an extension of her own life, like going back to Bloomsbury and living the rest of her life without him would be like having a limb cut off. But that wasn't even right. She knew lots of people, especially after the war, lived perfectly happy lives with missing limbs. She had trouble imagining a perfectly happy life without Jack.

She stood against the stone balustrade lining the bridge where they danced and watched Jack and Louisa twirling. Millie laughed a bit, wondering how often they'd changed partners. Jack had pulled his lion mask to rest up on top of his head, and his face was flushed with merriment. His midnight hair fell down on his forehead in damp locks from the snow and the heat of the dancing. His blue eyes were so light in the glow of the lanterns that they almost appeared to shine from inside. Louisa kept throwing her head back in laughter and she looked just as pink and happy as he did. He made people so happy, with such little effort. It seemed like such a tragedy that he had been so alone for so long. Millie's heart filled with sadness thinking about it. He owed it to the world to rejoin society. He owed it to England to take his place in Parliament—to live a normal life. She didn't want to stand in the way of that. But what if she could help him navigate it? What if she could be there, by his side? Millie shook her head. Marrying a former Bloomsbury housemaid was not the kind of gossip a new Viscount needed, especially one who wanted to shake things up a bit. And Millie had no desire to be Jack's mistress. She scoffed at propriety, but she didn't want to have to hide their relationship. The more she thought about it, the more impossible it became to imagine a life after all this with Jack, and the more heartbreaking it became to imagine a life without him.

The sound of the church bells tolling the hour shook her out of her reverie, and she waited to hear more. She was shocked to hear just one. She'd had no idea it was after midnight already. The revelers on the bridge had a similar reaction and the party started to disperse, some headed home to sleep, and others stumbling toward the next impromptu street party. Jack, Louisa, and Jane appeared by her side, laughing and holding their arms around each other.

"I've never had so much fun in my life," Louisa said.

Jane nodded. "Nor have I. This is an experience I'll never forget."

Millie smiled at them. "It's magical," she agreed, but she saw the lines of worry forming around Jack's eyes when their gazes met. They all pulled their masks back down and made their way back to Isabella and Fanny, who were just rising with yawns.

"This is a bit more excitement than we're used to," Fanny said, patting Millie on the arm. "You'll excuse us if we make our way back home."

Jack stepped forward. "I'll escort you."

Isabella laughed. "No need, my boy," she said. "It might as well be daylight during Carnevale time. We'll find our own way, won't we girls?" She looked around, and all three of the other women nodded.

"We're exhausted, too," Jane said, nodding her head a little too emphatically for Millie's taste. She frowned, seeing that everyone was conspiring to leave her and Jack alone together. Something had shifted for both of them tonight, she could tell. She wasn't sure what would happen when they got back to that cramped little room, and she thought she might go crazy waiting.

The two younger women offered their arms to the two older, and they all set off down the street, waving and shouting their goodbyes over their shoulders. Jack held his elbow out for Millie to take, but instead she put one arm around his waist and leaned her head in toward him. He hesitated for just a moment before he wrapped his own arm around her shoulders and pulled her even closer. She sighed and he squeezed her in, their steps starting to synchronize in the soft snow. Millie pulled her mask off and let it dangle from her free hand, the glow of the lanterns reflecting off it and sending little glittering lights across the white street. It had begun to snow even harder, and Millie stuck her tongue out, laughing.

"What on earth are you doing?" Jack asked.

"You never caught snowflakes on your tongue?" Millie said, alarmed.

Jack threw his head back and laughed, a big hearty sound that filled the air. "I do believe I did, but I'd forgotten it until just now." He stepped back and lifted his chin again, sticking his tongue out and darting around to catch snow.

"You look ridiculous," Millie said, giggling. But it looked like too much fun, so she joined him. They both lurched around, and they saw other couples and revelers walk by them, first laughing at their antics, but then furtively darting their own tongues out.

They wandered around, enjoying the fun, until they bumped into one another, and Millie nearly fell on her bottom. "Watch out!" she teased, and Jack caught her, their foreheads nearly banging as well. They were both breathless with laughing, but as Jack held her shoulders in the warmth of his fingers, Millie looked up into his face and she found no breath available at all. Their eyes locked, and she could see little flakes of snow in the dark lock of hair falling on his forehead. As if by instinct, she reached up and brushed it out of his face.

"I think you missed one," Jack said, touching her nose with one gloved finger.

"Here it is," he said, then laid a soft light kiss where his finger had been. "I think I got it."

Millie's knees felt like they were turning to liquid. She swayed a little in his arms and he pulled her to him.

"Here's another one," he said against her skin as he kissed her forehead. "And another one," he whispered as he laid a small kiss on her cheek. She sighed. She knew she had given herself to this man, heart and soul, but she could never tell him with words. Instead, she'd have to live in this moment, enjoying this, and not thinking about the future.

"Did you catch any?" she asked, looking up at him through her lashes, dotted with little drops of melting snow.

He bent his head down and whispered, "Just a few," so close his lips were brushing against hers as he spoke. That was all she could take. She lifted her face fully, tilted her head, and kissed him like her very life depended on it.

Jack closed his eyes at the feeling of Millie's mouth on his as she deepened their kiss. He felt like the snow was swirling around them and trapping them in their own small world, where nothing outside mattered and he could admit to her how he really felt, even if not with words. He pulled her closer to him, and barely noticed as both their masks fell into the snow at their sides. Her hand went up behind his head, and her fingers tangled with the hair at the nape of his neck. His hands roamed her back, trying to pull her closer, closer, until the entire length of her body was pressed against his. He moaned a little in the back of his throat, and she shifted slightly against his arousal, showing him that she felt it. Her hand came around to caress his cheek as her tongue darted around his mouth, tasting and teasing. Jack pulled back, panting. "Shall we go upstairs?"

Millie nodded, and Jack reached down to scoop up both their masks in his left hand as Millie took his right into her own, tangling their fingers together and tugging him toward their hotel. They made their way, half running, half tripping, up the narrow flight of stairs before they crashed through the door of their room between kisses. Jack threw the masks safely over to his bed and pulled Millie toward hers. He had never felt such a loss of control in his life, and he loved it. There was no way this woman wasn't going to be his. At least for tonight. He would make her his, and he would make sure neither would ever forget it.

They stood next to the bed, and Jack reached down to pull his boots off, but Millie wouldn't let his lips leave hers. She was grasping at him, pulling at his waistcoat, pulling him back for a kiss whenever possible. Jack stumbled trying to pull his boot off with the heel of his other foot, and they both tumbled down to the bed, laughing. Jack lifted both feet in the air and pulled the boots off, wincing at the noise as they clattered to the floor. Millie stepped aside for the flying boots, but then straddled him, and he felt the room whirling around him. He held her hips in his hands and squeezed, looking up at her, her face just visible in the glow from the lanterns outside.

"You're magnificent," he said, running his hands up her sides and grasping for the buttons of her dress. She reached up and pulled the pins out of her hair, then shook the wild curls around. His hips bucked upward, his arousal straining against her bottom where she sat.

She smiled, a little half-smile that was both sweet and wicked, then she shifted her weight just a little, first to one side and then the other, teasing him. He groaned and grabbed the bodice of the beautiful gown she'd just bought and ripped it down in one motion, freeing her breasts. He could hear the little clatter of the buttons as they fell to the floor, and Millie's gasp as her nipples were exposed to the cold air. Jack lifted his hands to cup her breasts in his palms and ran his thumbs over the tightened buds, delighting in the sounds she made. She leaned forward and kissed him, and Jack felt as if her heat was surrounding both of them, protecting them from the outside world, creating that special place where only the two of them existed. He kissed her back with an almost aching slowness, trying to savor her, to savor this moment. Something shifted between them then, and Millie became less frenzied, too, slowing down to nibble and lick at his lips, pulling her hands to the sides of his face and holding him there in a gentle embrace.

She pulled back just a bit and asked, "Shall I pleasure you, My Lord?" her eyes twinkling in fun at the honorific.

"Tonight we'll pleasure each other," Jack said.

"Of course," she said, raising an eyebrow. "But—"

"At the same time," Jack said, pressing a finger to her lips, his breathing heavy and his heart pounding out of his chest. "I want you, Millie. All of you."

Millie smiled but shook her head. "No," she said, "You don't have to—"

Jack sat up, holding his one arm around Millie's back and moving his other to pull her legs around him. "Of course I don't *have* to. But I've never *wanted* anything more in my life."

He kissed her nose, then her forehead, then back down to her lips again. "I want *you*, Millie. You've changed something in me. You've—"

She pressed a light kiss to his lips to stop him and nodded. Then she put both her hands on his face again and rubbed the pads of her fingers over his cheeks and chin, leaning her forehead against his. "You don't have to say it," she said. "Show me."

Jack purred in the back of his throat, overcome with

emotion and need. He held Millie's back and laid her down on the bed, maneuvering to stretch out beside her, running his hand over her stomach and her breasts, up and down her arms. He propped himself on his elbow and looked down at her, marveling at all the curvy shapes and hollows her body made in the soft snowy lantern glow.

"You are so beautiful," he said, his voice full of reverence. He leaned down to kiss her again, this time soft and gentle, just his lips on hers, over and over, pulling back and then kissing her again. She snaked her hand around to the back of his neck to keep him close, and Jack thought he could stay in this moment for the rest of his life, just holding her and kissing her like this. But there was something else urging them both on, a primal need for each other that they couldn't deny. Millie wriggled herself out of her dress and chemise without her lips ever leaving his, and Jack could feel her hands at the ties of his breeches. He pulled back and put his finger to her lips, shaking his head.

"Not yet," he said. "Let me love you first."

Millie lay her head back against the pillow, her eyes closed, and Jack brushed her hair back from her forehead with his fingertips, trailing them down the skin of her nose and her cheekbones, then her lips and her chin. He bent his lips to follow, leaving gentle kisses on her forehead and the tip of her nose while his fingertips moved lower, caressing the side of her neck and then her shoulder. He kissed her mouth, and her lips parted for him. He darted his tongue in to taste her sweetness as his fingertips brushed lightly against the bottom curve of her breast. He deepened the kiss as he ran his thumb over her nipple, which was taut and tight from his feathery touches. She moaned against his mouth and his entire body caught fire. But he restrained himself to continue his tender teasing. He was going to make this last. He was going to worship every inch of her before he took her.

He trailed kisses down the side of her neck, licking here and nipping with his teeth there, until his hand found its way to the curve of her belly, where he lay his palm flat against it and wondered at her softness. His fingers played their way over her skin to her hip where he squeezed just as his mouth hovered over her nipple. He licked it to make it wet, then blew on it, and Millie's hips bucked in his hold. His fingertips moved between the sheet and her bottom, and he cupped her with his hand, kneading and moving while his lips curved around the tight peak and he suckled her, feeling like nothing had ever tasted so sweet. His hand came back to her belly, and he moved it down to rest gently against the soft hair of her mound. He pressed the heel of his hand against her, and her hips rotated slightly to rub him, the friction making Millie pant with her need.

Jack kept suckling Millie's breasts, moving between them, licking and nibbling, circling his tongue around her nipples, before he brought his fingers to part her. He moved his fingers into her slit, wiggling each of them just a bit as he played up and down from the nub of her pleasure to her opening. Millie's hands came to his head, and she pulled his hair, moaning and writhing.

"Please, Jack," she said, breathless. "Please."

Jack pressed his tongue flat against one nipple and licked as he slid one finger inside her. She was so slick and wet with her need, Jack wasn't sure he could control himself. He pulled his finger out and then entered her with two fingers, driving up into the heart of her while his thumb flicked across her.

"Jack," she said, pulling his hair harder, "I want it. I want your cock inside me."

Jack growled and pulled away from her just long enough to divest himself of his breeches, then settled himself between her legs. Millie reached down and grabbed him, squeezing and stroking before she placed him right at her opening.

"Now, Jack," she said, "You're so hard. Please. Now."

He pushed forward just the smallest bit, knowing he would not last. He felt like he was primed to explode now. He put his hand between them and stroked her at the top of her slit while he guided himself in further. He looked down at her, and her eyes were pools of midnight, open wide and meeting his gaze while she brought her hands up to her breasts to squeeze her nipples.

"God, what are you doing to me?" he said, before he lost all control and pushed himself into her, burying himself into her deepest places, kissing her like a prayer and a curse all at once. He drove his tongue into her mouth while he stilled his hips, just feeling himself enveloped in this woman, this woman he knew he loved and would always love.

She kissed him back with all the fervor and heat he was feeling, and their bodies began to move almost against their will. Jack felt like a man possessed. He tried to go slow, to be gentle, but his body betrayed him in its need, his movements becoming more frenetic, more urgent. Millie's pace matched his, her hips bucking in the rhythm and her tongue reaching deep into his mouth. Jack knew he couldn't last much longer. He whispered Millie's name against her lips in apology, then his whole body went rigid as he spilled himself into her. Her eyes met his, and she brought her hands to his cheeks again, pulling him down for another kiss.

He started to pull away, but she grabbed his buttocks and held him. "No," she said, "I want to come with you inside me."

She reached between them and rubbed herself just for a few moments before he felt her spasming around him, her head falling back on the pillow. Jack felt himself melt against her as he rested his head on her shoulder before he finally pulled out and stretched beside her. He played his fingers across her chest and belly again, wondering at her.

"You're a miracle," he said. "I have never seen such a perfect body."

She laughed. "You've never seen *any* body," she teased.

He frowned. "I don't need to," he said, "Yours is perfect."

Millie ran her hands along his shoulder, then down his bicep and back up. "Yours is pretty wonderful, too," she said. Millie lay back against the pillow again, her arm above her head, and stared at him. Her eyes were piercing in the darkness. "How do you feel?" she asked, her voice flat and serious.

Jack smiled, smoothing his palm against the side of her face. "Happy," he said. "What about you?"

"Happy," she said, smiling and turning to kiss his palm. "Very happy." Jack pulled her in close, nestling her back against him and wrapping his arm around her torso. He breathed in the smell of her hair, a mix of the woodsmoke from the night air and the floral soap she used. He had never felt so content in his life.

Chapter 13

Millie woke up on her side with her face on Jack's chest, his arm wrapped around her, their legs tangled in the blankets of the bed. There was a chill in the room since the fire had died down. A shaft of light was coming through the windows, and Millie realized it must be fairly late in the morning. She hopped out of the bed to throw another log on the dying embers of the fire and grabbed the blanket off Jack's bed to make a cozier nest over them as she snuggled back in close to him.

She closed her eyes and sighed as she allowed herself to lie back down on his chest, the soft hair that grew there tickling her face. She breathed in the scent of him and turned her face to place a gentle kiss on his skin, tasting the salt of his sweat and the sweetness of *him*. He stirred just a little but did not awaken. He just tightened his hold on her and sighed. Millie lay perfectly still, trying to hold on to this moment as long as possible. She knew their night together had been a stolen moment from time, a result of the magic of the snow and the *Carnevale* and the relief of learning the truth about her would-be assassins. They'd reached a turning point now. Millie knew there was no going back, but she also still didn't see a way forward. That was why she was trying to lie as still as possible and keep Jack from waking up. When they were both awake, it would be the end of the night, the end of the magic, and they'd have to face themselves and what had happened between them.

Millie did not regret what had happened. She had wanted to feel Jack Redstone inside her almost from the moment she'd met him. But she couldn't lie and tell herself that he was just another lover like others she'd bedded. She'd fallen in love with this man. Not just his body, not just in friendship. She had lost her heart to him. What had happened last night had been special, not just because she loved him, but because she had been his first. He had given that gift to her, and that must mean he felt something for her, too, something more than what they'd agreed on. But how could they ever say it, knowing as they did that a life together was impossible? She just wished that she could stay here in this moment—that time would stop, that they'd never have to get up, put on real clothes, pin her hair, and walk back out into the cold, crisp, clear light of day to a new reality. A reality where they had fallen in love but could never build a life with each other. She felt tears prick the corners of her eyes. She wondered if it might be best to make an escape now, to spare both of them that torture.

A plan started to form. What if she went to Jane and Louisa, and made the plan to find her cousin and offer him the inheritance? She could resolve the situation, escape Jack, and protect him all in one fell swoop. Once she had the deal with Sir Thomas worked out, she was sure it would be safe for her to travel back to England with Jane and Louisa and resume her life in Bloomsbury. The sooner she could get herself away from Jack, the sooner he could clear his head, face his own issues with his mother, and assume the Viscountcy. It would be what was best for him and would give him the best chance at a real, fulfilling life. One where he wasn't always hiding from his problems. She was sure he would make friends and maybe even find love. She winced at the thought, but she also knew he needed it. If there was anyone in the world who deserved to be loved, it was this man, and he deserved to be loved by someone who could be everything he needed—a Viscountess, a friend, a lover, and a mother to his children. Millie knew she loved him, but she also knew in the depth of her heart that she could never be those things for him, not without considerable risk and sacrifice on his part. It was up to her to be the brave one, she realized. She had to make a clean break before it was too late.

She raised herself on her elbow and looked down at him, tracing the line of his jaw with her fingertip. She bent forward and laid the smallest kiss on his cheek. He smiled in his sleep but once again did not wake. When she backed out of the bed and tucked him under the blankets, he stirred only a little to readjust himself, and his breathing slowed and steadied. Quick and silent, Millie dressed and pinned her hair, pulled on her thick woolen overcoat, and donned her bonnet and scarf. She tiptoed to the door in her socks, carrying her boots with her, and she slipped them on in the carpeted hallway after pulling the door to with the softest click.

As she made her way down the stairs, she gained speed and stopped trying to be silent. When she came out of the door onto the Grand Canal, her eyes were strained by the blazing brightness of the sun reflecting off the snow. She imagined most of it would be melted away by evening. The air was still but smelled of the snow and the canal, a salty fresh smell, but not as bracing as it had been. Millie took a deep breath and closed her eyes, just taking a moment to enjoy such a morning, then she trudged toward the hotel where Jane and Louisa were staying. She only hoped they were also awake, and they could put her plan into action as soon as possible. If she had to spend another night in that room with Jack, she didn't think she'd have the strength to resist him, and she knew she would never be able to leave him. She sighed and set her chin. She was determined not to let that happen. For his sake.

She passed the Rialto bridge and saw the vendors in their stalls, and she could smell the sweet corn fritters frying, the nuts roasting, and the pleasant acrid smell of fish being brought in from the docks to the markets. She turned down a side street toward the hotel and here the streets became narrower and darker, with the low morning sun blocked from all the taller buildings around the Grand Canal. It became markedly colder, and she adjusted her scarf around her neck, pulling it up to cover her ears. She could still hear the bustle and voices from the awakening city behind her, but here there was an eerie silence. No children were out running around yet, and even the cats seemed to be hiding, having probably found shelter from the snow the night before. For the first time Millie stopped to wonder if she was arriving too early to the lodgings. She didn't want to wake the older women and certainly didn't want to intrude on the rest of Louisa and Jane. Millie smiled to herself. Those two were probably going to wake with a hell of a hangover. She didn't imagine they were used to the kind of evening they'd all had the night before. Millie decided to turn toward St. Mark's and take a longer stroll before she awakened anyone else.

Her thoughts raced through everything she'd learned and done in the past twenty-four hours. It was mind-boggling that she'd learned about her real family, that she'd discovered inside herself the depth of love she felt for Jack, and that she was on the verge of completely changing her life based on these new revelations. As she wandered the square, scaring up pigeons as she walked, the city began to bustle to life once more. The sun rose higher, and as she suspected, the snow began to melt under its influence. The stalls were all bustling now, and Millie stopped at a café to enjoy a coffee. It would be a perfect morning if it weren't for the tumult in her mind, she thought as she sipped the piping hot liquid. But no use dwelling on all that. She had a plan and she must put it into action.

The sun was much higher and the city much more alive and awake when she finally returned to the hotel where Jane and Louisa were staying with Isabella. She was pleased to find them all up and partaking of their breakfast, only the slightest bit worse for wear. They were happy to see her and recount the joys of the night before. It had been a magical night, they all agreed, but Jane, Louisa, and Isabella all had a mischievous look about them as they grilled Millie on her feelings for Jack. Millie tried hard to be evasive, but she knew it was fruitless. Everyone could see how they felt for each other, but no one seemed to want to acknowledge the insurmountable facts surrounding that attraction. Millie changed the subject.

"Do you suppose we'll be able to find Sir Thomas here?" she asked, taking a bite of the scone that had been offered to her.

"He must be around," Jane said, frowning. "Or arriving soon. He always appears to be one step ahead of us."

"I, for one, can't wait to get hold of his grubby little fingers and rap them heartily for what he's done," Louisa said, slathering butter with gusto on a helpless piece of toast.

"You've both known him a lifetime," Millie said, "Did he ever strike you as capable of murder before?"

"Never," Louisa answered, her face coloring. "He's become an embarrassment to us all. It all started with gambling," she sighed and paused here. "I wish he'd never stepped foot in one of those London hells!"

Jane patted her sister's hand to calm her. "It's true," she said in a more restrained voice than her sister's. "It was the gambling that really changed him. I think he got in over his head and just didn't know how to get out. He pawned our mother's jewelry without telling us, and that was when I knew it had gotten serious. But I still don't believe him truly capable of murder. He only wants the money."

Louisa stood and began to pace. "But as soon as he gets more, he'll only want more after that. It's the gambling we must fix."

Jane's lips formed a flat line as she leaned back into the cushion of the settee. "I'm afraid that's not in our power," she said in a soft voice. "The gambling has a hold on him."

Millie immediately thought of her own mother, and Jack's mother, too. She began to feel more sorrow for her cousin than anger. She shook her head. "I know too well what it's like to watch a loved one go down a dark path."

Isabella hadn't spoken much, but now she leaned forward and placed her hand on Millie's, her skin papery with age, but soothing in its gentleness. "I watched your mother go through it all," she said in a low voice, her grasp tightening on Millie's hand. "She never wanted to leave you like that."

Millie brushed a quick tear from her eye with her free hand, then placed it atop the old woman's. "I spent a long time believing I just wasn't important enough for her to change for."

Isabella squeezed Millie's hand again before letting it go and leaning back against the cushion with a deep sigh. "I know how that feels, too." She didn't say more, but wouldn't meet Millie's gaze, her face seeming to age with the memories. "But," the old woman said, shaking her head as if to clear those shadows away, "it's not the truth. It's only a feeling. The truth is much more complicated. It's not about how much she loved you, but how well she could believe in herself."

"By the end, I don't think she believed in much of anything," Millie said, staring at the carpet.

"She believed in you," Isabella said, her voice so soft Millie had to lean forward to hear it. "She believed you'd find a life with Annelise. And look," here Isabella straightened and gesticulated with both hands, "You did."

Millie couldn't help but smile and acknowledge the old woman's point. She had found a life. But what kind of a life would it be without Jack?

Almost as if Louisa could read her mind, her cousin exclaimed, "Shall we go get Mr. Covert and find ourselves some amusement?"

Millie cleared her throat. "I think Mr. Covert is resting," she said. "Let's leave him and do a little shopping?"

The other women were all too happy with this plan, so they began clearing the breakfast things and took turns readying their bonnets in the mirror. Soon enough they were young

Englishwomen about town again, strolling arm in arm and peering into little shop windows at the famous Venetian glass or little ribbons of silk. Millie could almost feel content with a life like this, she thought. Almost.

Jack woke to a chill in the room. He was covered with both blankets, but his cheeks felt nigh frozen where they'd lain on the crisp linen of the pillow. He peered through the half-light from the closed curtains to see that the fire had burned down to just embers. Still groggy, he felt around the bed to be sure Millie wasn't there. He whispered her name but there was no answer. The other bed lay empty. He jumped out to throw a log on the fire, then blew a quick blast with the bellows to get a flame going before he burrowed back down into the blankets. The warmth from the fire soon spread through the room and he felt almost contented. Almost. Where had that little vixen gone? Last night had been transformative, in more ways than one, Jack thought to himself. He knew now he'd never be able to leave this woman behind. She'd come back to London with him, become his Viscountess, and he'd take her to bed every night and discover what new ways he could make her squeal with delight. There was simply no alternative.

And, since Jack had realized what he wanted to do with the rest of his life, and whom he wanted to do it with, he wanted to waste no time starting. He groaned again at Millie's absence, but he figured she'd probably just gone to get some breakfast or coffee or take a stroll. She'd be back soon. It was still the first day after they'd found the truth, and he felt he could let his guard down. He was determined to fall back asleep and enjoy his dreams of his beautiful curly-haired lady, but every time he closed his eyes, he only saw visions of the night before replaying across his mind. He felt himself start to get hard again at the memory and reluctantly rose from the bed to wash and dress. He paced the room, wearing a path on the carpet from the bed and back to the window, where he kept peering out to look for Millie.

After making up the two beds and piling all the pillows on one, he leaned back and tried to read, but after having scanned the same paragraph three times without comprehending a word, he threw the book down on the bedside table in disgust. He pulled on his boots and greatcoat, checked his hair in the mirror and smoothed it down with a brush, then grabbed his hat and made his way downstairs. Perhaps a bracing walk was just what he needed after all.

The sun was dazzling and most of the night's snow had already melted. It was back to being a usual day in Venice, but that had its own magic. Jack realized he was a little stiff and sore from the night's activities, so he lengthened his strides to warm himself up. Without knowing where he was going, he found himself back at the Rialto, now bustling at midday with vendors, tourists, and tradespeople. In all the commotion, he couldn't stop himself from looking for a head of dark, familiar curls, but it was to no avail. He recognized no one there today. His steps took him down the side streets toward the hotel where the Elton sisters were staying with Isabella. He wondered if Millie had come this way also, hoping for a visit with her newfound family. He didn't want to intrude on their time together, but his impatience to find Millie was starting to wear on him. He began to wonder if something had happened to her. He didn't think it was like her to leave him like that, without a note or telling him where she'd gone. Did she regret their night together? He didn't want his mind to travel in that direction, but it seemed he could not help himself. What if he hadn't lived up to her expectations? What if she had realized she no longer cared for him after all? He sighed to himself. He would do himself no good thinking this way.

At the next street, Jack turned the corner away from the hotel. He wasn't going to stalk Millie around Venice. She was a grown woman and deserved her space. He decided to walk to St.

Mark's and try to enjoy the city. After all, now that they'd accomplished their goal of discovering Millie's past and the truth about her would-be assassins, he assumed they'd be leaving posthaste. He wondered if he'd ever have the chance to come back here. For a moment, he turned his face up to the sun, feeling its warmth spread through him, and allowed himself to imagine bringing Millie back here as his wife, on their honeymoon, or with a gaggle of little children. The thought warmed him even more than the sunshine. He knew in his bones that this was what he wanted. But how would he convince Millie? And would she even want the same thing?

Jack spent the rest of the afternoon walking and wandering and trying to stay away from their hotel so it wouldn't appear that he'd been so eager to find her. He knew she valued her independence, and he was determined to give it to her. When the sun began to set, he made his way back, hoping against hope that she would be there when he arrived. He wanted to take her out for dinner, to tell her how much he loved her, to enjoy the magic of this city with her again. As he made his way through the deepening twilight, the sounds of revelry again began to peal through the streets. Laughter, music, the clinking of glasses. *Carnevale* was still in full swing. Just as it had the night before, the excitement ignited him. He found himself smiling in spite of himself. When he got to their hotel, he was in such a state of anticipation that he bounded up the stairs two at a time, throwing open the door of their room with a bang.

"Millie," he shouted. "Let's—"

Jack stopped and looked around. The room was dark, the fire had gone out, and everything on both beds was exactly as he had left it. His heart began to race. Where was she? He ran back down the stairs and out into the evening. His first thought was to find the Elton sisters. Perhaps Millie had gone to them and spent the day there. He clung to that hope against all else, his breathing ragged as he raced through the night. He passed revelers on every corner, and though it was warmer tonight and the magic of the snowfall was gone, every sound and smell reminded him of Millie and last night. His chest was tight as he imagined her in danger, picturing her having fallen victim to robbers, or being found by her cousin. He focused on his mission, repeating to himself over and over that she was safe, that he would find her cozy by the fire in the Eltons' hotel room. He clung to it as he sidled his way past masked men and women in long dominoes, waiting with crossed arms and tapping toes at cross-streets while crowds passed.

When he finally arrived at the hotel, he could barely breathe or even think, so high was his anxiety and hope. When he knocked on the door of the hotel room, he felt so lightheaded and nauseous he was worried he wouldn't be able to stand. He'd spent a life steeling himself against this rush of panic, learning to quell it, learning to stay calm in the thorniest situations. His experience with his mother had taught him not to avoid uncertain situations, but to stay steady in the face of them. It was no surprise he'd chosen the vocation he had; he was singularly prepared for it by his childhood. Now, though, he was experiencing a panic he hadn't felt in years. So this was what it was to love, he thought, balancing himself against the door frame while he waited for a response to his knock. When it took longer than he expected, he leaned forward, his hands on his knees, trying to breathe deeply and keep from throwing up. After long moments like that, though, he heard footsteps on the other side of the door. He stood, trying to clear his face of its emotion, and when Louisa Elton opened the door, her face had no such blankness. She was clearly concerned.

"Mr. Covert," she said, her forehead wrinkled with worry. "I'm glad you've come. I was getting ready to send a messenger to you so you wouldn't worry."

Jack tried to restrain himself, but even still he pushed past her into the room. "Where's Millie?"

Louisa closed the door behind him and came forward, her hand resting on his arm. "She's...indisposed." Louisa's eyes darted from Jack to the closed bedroom door. Jack paused to take stock of his surroundings. Jane was seated on the couch, perched on the edge like a bird about to take flight. Sophia and Isabella were nowhere to be seen.

"Is she safe?" he asked, still looking around the room, trying to get his bearings.

Louisa and Jane both smiled, and their lips were almost identical in wan, thin lines. "She's safe," Jane said, but the smile did not reach her eyes.

"Will someone tell me what's going on?" Jack burst out, unable to contain himself. "I've been looking for her all day. I've been beside myself with worry. I've imagined every possible outcome, but the one I didn't picture is you two casting furtive glances to each other and evading my questions."

Louisa put her hand on Jack's arm again and he shrugged it off. "Just tell me what's going on," he said, his voice dropping to a plaintive whisper.

"She's—" Louisa began, trailing off.

"For heaven's sake," Jane said, standing, "She's drunk as a monkey."

Louisa laughed a small laugh, one of surprise more than humor. She covered her mouth with her hand and looked out the window.

Jane motioned to the couch next to her and sat back down. Jack followed her direction and perched on the velvet settee, unable to make himself comfortable. He felt an uneasiness creeping up the back of his neck.

"She came here this morning," Louisa began. "She was obviously upset, but we took her out shopping, hoping to cheer her up."

"We had a lovely day," Jane added, taking over the story from her sister, "But at dinner, she drank a little too much wine."

"We brought her home," Louisa continued, "And proposed some tea."

"But she had purchased a bottle of brandy on the way, and she just would not stop drinking it," Jane said, looking back into the fire. "We got worried and tried to stop her, but she grew—"

"Belligerent," Louisa finished her sister's thought. "She wouldn't listen to reason."

Jack felt his lips tighten into a grim line. "I know that behavior all too well," he said.

Louisa and Jane both snapped their heads up to look at him. "She's done this before?" Louisa asked, shocked.

"No, no," Jack said. "I've seen her enjoy her wine, but never to excess." He paused, squinting into the fire. "No, I've seen this before with my mother," he said. It was amazing how easily he could talk about this now that Millie had opened those doors for him. "My mother drank to excess."

Louisa and Jane nodded in unison with sympathy. Jane cleared her throat. "It's like our brother and his gambling," she said. "You watch them lose themselves to it."

Jack closed his eyes and swallowed. "Yes," he said. "I suppose it's like that." He looked toward the closed bedroom door. "Is she in there?"

"Yes," Louisa said, her voice low, "But I don't think it's a good idea for you to go in there until the morning."

Jack ground his teeth. "I need to see her," he said. "I've been through hell imagining her falling into the canal or being stabbed by robbers. I need to see her and make sure she's safe."

Jane covered his hand with hers. "She's safe," she said, "We promise."

Louisa stood and went to the fire, poking it to bank the coals. "It's obvious you two love each other," she said, not turning to face him. "Why do you play this game?"

Jack was startled by the frankness of her question, but he found it easy to answer. "I'm done playing it," he said, his voice flat but strong. "That's why I've been looking for her all day. When you find out you want to spend the rest of your life with someone, you want it to start as soon as possible."

Jack watched as the two women shared a look. He frowned. "You have to let me see her."

Jane's dark eyes widened in sympathy, her forehead crinkling just the slightest bit. "I don't think it's a good idea," she said, her voice low and kind.

Jack could take it no more. "You both know something, and you won't tell me," He said, standing and striding to the window. The lanterns and streetlamps cast a warm glow on the revelers who still crowded the streets below. He propped his forearm against the window and rested his head on it. His voice was quiet again when he spoke. "Just tell me," He said.

Jane came to stand at the window next to him. She was silent for a few moments while they both stood there, looking down on the happy scene below. "That's not how she spent her day," she finally said.

Jack understood, with a sudden piercing pain in his heart. Millie didn't love him. Something had happened last night between them, all right, but it wasn't the same for both of them. For him, it had only pulled his love for her into sharp, clear focus. For her it had been the final deciding factor in her fully pulling away from him. It was all so clear now. He was a fool. An idiot. He was a man who had so carefully guarded his heart and even his true identity, had cultivated his loneliness for years, and it had only taken one brazen, curly-haired minx to ruin everything he'd worked for. He understood now, and he'd take his leave and be done with it.

He looked back at Jane, but only shook his head as he made his way toward the closed bedroom door. Neither woman made a move to stop him. It was as if they understood what he needed.

It was dark and quiet in the room as he pushed open the door. He had no interest in coddling her drunkenness, though. "Millie," he said, his voice loud and harsh even to his own ears. "I need to speak to you."

There was a muffled groan from the bed and Jack moved

toward it. "You don't have to get up," he said, disgust clear in his voice. "I know why you ran from me."

"No you don't," Millie's voice came from somewhere in the covers, a little slurred, but clear.

He laughed, but there was no mirth in it. "I do," he said, "I just never thought you'd go and run to a bottle instead of telling me the truth." His voice was full of bitterness. "I don't know what I was thinking imagining that you were different. I should have known. But I won't bother you again." He tried to see her face in the dim light from the parlor, but he could only see a few of those curls peeking out beneath the blankets. He heard what could have been a sob catching in her throat, but he knew better. She was probably laughing at him. No matter. He'd said what needed to be said. *"Arrivederce,"* he said, his voice dripping with sarcasm. And with that, he turned on his heel and fled, waving only the briefest goodbye to the Elton sisters, still standing with mouths agape in the parlor.

Chapter 14

Millie woke with what felt like cotton in her mouth and a hammer in her head. She opened one eye, afraid of the light, but it was pitch black in the room. She shook her head to try to get her bearings, but that only made the pounding more intense, so she settled back into the pillow and closed her eyes. It took only moments for the last thing she remembered to come rushing back at her: Jack's cruel voice as he had taken his leave. She felt the tears welling in her eyes again, but she shut them tight against the unwanted moisture. It was all for the best. Better he believed the worst and let it be rather than trying to convince her they could somehow make it work. If he knew how she really felt about him, she knew he'd stop at nothing to try to be with her, even though it would be the worst decision for him. It was better this way. A clean break. She could travel back to London with the Eltons, and she could stay in Bloomsbury, far out of the Viscount Redstone's way.

She swung her legs over the side of the bed and sat up, holding her head to try to keep it from pounding straight off her neck. She made her way to the washbasin and splashed some cold water on her face before going to the curtains to pull them back and try to ascertain the time. It was still dark and the streets were quiet. It must be close to dawn. She couldn't remember when Jane and Louisa had put her to bed exactly, but it had been sometime in the afternoon. She likewise had no idea what time it had been when Jack had visited, but she knew she'd slept away almost the whole night. Thank God for sobriety. She vowed never to go on a bender like that one again. She wasn't the type to try to run away from her problems, but she hoped she could be forgiven for letting herself go just this once. She'd only ever felt a pain this acute once before, and when she'd lost her mother she'd been too young for strong drink, she thought to herself with a wry smile.

She crept into the parlor where the fire hadn't quite died down. She threw another log on it, wrapping her dressing gown tighter as she sat on the settee near the fire, folding one leg beneath her and staring into the flames. She wasn't quite ready for coffee, but it was comforting to just be alone in the silent warmth, calming her stomach and her emotions before anyone else woke up and the bustle of breakfast began. With a sigh, she picked up the nearest book, hoping to lose herself in another world for a little while, but when she opened it, her mind was flooded with memories of Jack reading to her on the ship, of Jack standing at the rail with the wind whipping his hair, of Jack snuggled against her in that small bunk, of Jack's kisses. She shook her head to try and rid herself of the thoughts, but that only made her temples ache again. She leaned back against the cushion and stared at the scrollwork on the high ceiling. She'd almost dozed back off again when she heard a thud in the hallway. She sat up and listened, and within moments she could hear a jostling of the doorknob. She stood and crept toward the door, wondering if it was the maid arriving early with breakfast. It would be just like the Elton sisters to have ordered early the night before, knowing she'd need it. But why would the maid be jostling the knob rather than just knocking?

Millie stood before the door, her forehead wrinkling then the door flew open and two masked men entered, one coming behind her and holding his gloved palm over her mouth and the other pushing a knife to her throat. Millie couldn't even think.

She blinked in confusion, her eyes darting from the arm of the man behind her to the dark, dull eyes of the man in front of her, visible through the black mask.

He brought his face close to hers and hissed, "Don't make a sound, Miss, or—" he tightened his hold on the knife and Millie could feel it just piercing her skin. She winced in pain but remained still. She wasn't about to do anything foolish now and jeopardize her chance to escape later. Not to mention she wasn't at her physical best this morning. She allowed the men to coax her back out the door, then watched as the one with the knife closed it silently behind them. He motioned to the partner that held her and they made their way down the stairs.

Once they got out to the deserted street, the men pulled Millie along the dark stone and stucco of the buildings, staying out of sight of the windows above. They turned down a side alley and made it to a small connecting canal where a gondola with a third man was waiting for them. They coaxed her down into it, then pushed her into the floor, finally releasing her as they untied from the slip and pushed off into the pale light.

Millie thought it might be safe to speak, though she kept her voice very low. "Are you sure you have the right person?" she asked, rubbing her mouth where the gloved hand had bruised her.

The two men laughed. "We're sure," the one with the knife said. "Been chasing you all over Europe, we 'ave," he said, a cockney accent coming through though he was trying to hide it.

"Do you also know I have no interest in Mr. Elton's inheritance?" she hissed.

The men looked at each other, then at the third man holding the long pole and steering the gondola out toward the main canal. They looked back down at her, but remained silent.

"Where is your Mr. Elton?" she asked, "Are you taking me to him?"

Another look passed between the men and the one with the knife went to the back of the boat to speak to their gondolier.

They whispered fiercely, but not loud enough for Millie to hear them. She lay her head back against the bottom of the boat and tried to orient herself by looking up at the buildings going past. She didn't recognize any of them and realized she was not on the Grand Canal as she'd originally thought. Her head still pounded from her overindulgence the night before, but her mind was clear and calm as she took deep breaths and tried to conserve her energy.

The man with the knife came back toward her, rocking the boat just a little as he closed the short distance to where she lay. He knelt down and soon she felt that blade against her neck again.

"Where did you hear that name," he whispered, his mouth so close to her ear that she could feel the sharp stubble of his whiskers against her cheek.

"Elton?" Millie asked, confused, but keeping her voice low. "That's my cousin, the one who's trying to steal my inheritance. I want him to know I don't need the inheritance. He can have it."

The man relaxed his hold on her a bit, but did not move the knife. Millie knew if they hit even a small wake or wave, it would break her skin, and she made her breath shallow and closed her eyes tight with concentration. The men made no sound, and the gondola slit the water with only the slightest splash. Millie could feel the warmth of the coming sunrise before she could see it. The air was heavy and humid with the mist and she willed her heart to slow its beating lest the men hear it and kill her right in the boat.

The ride felt interminable, but it couldn't have been more than ten minutes before the man holding her relaxed the knife from her throat just before the gondola bumped against the mooring in a dark canal alley. The man moved to Millie's back and pushed the knife under her shoulder blade as he moved her forward. "Don't get any ideas," he said against the back of her head, and she nodded just a little to show she understood and proceeded to walk where he indicated. She dared not look around her, but she didn't recognize where they were or which direction they'd gone. They went only a few steps over darkened cobbled streets before they knocked a rhythm at a door under an unassuming pergola. Soon the door opened and she was pushed inside, where, again, all she saw was darkness.

Jack heard the bells peal each hour from the time he got back to the hotel until long after the sun had risen. As the number of peals increased, so did his inability to sleep. Around four, he finally took off his boots and lay in bed. At five, he got up and ran water through his hair and over his face, hoping the cool fresh feeling would wash away some of his...he didn't know what to call the emotion he was feeling. There was some anger in it, and some sadness. There was some frustration and some despair. But most of all, Jack felt empty. He felt like a part of his body had been amputated., something vital. The room was dark, Millie's bed was empty, and Jack still had the sensation of her skin against his burned in his memory. He thought about a future without her and all he could see was a long stretch of dark emptiness, curving around the corner of his life and into infinity. He sat in the chair by the window and listened to the distant sound of revelers, watching the small waves lap against the stone edges of the canal in front of the hotel in the dim gas light and the mist.

At six bells, he threw a log on the fire and closed the heavy drapes. The only light in the room was the crackling, echoing flame, now rising and now guttering in the grate. He carefully undressed and folded his garments on Millie's empty bed. Each time he removed one, he remembered the feeling of her hands on his body and the way she'd so lovingly caressed each part of him as they'd made love. Left only in his nightshirt, he hurried under the covers on his own bed and pulled them up to his chin while he waited for the fire to warm the room.

At seven bells, Jack could see the light of dawn showing dimly in the cracks between the drapes, and he turned over to his side and pulled a pillow over his head.

At eight bells, Jack turned back to his other side and watched the sliver of light coming through brighten on the floor.

At nine bells, Jack let out a loud curse and stood up, running a hand through his unkempt hair and pacing the room. He went to the window and threw the drapes open, wincing at the brightness of the light. He put a hand to his forehead and peered out to the canal, where cargo barges were beginning to crowd the lane, making deliveries in the *Carnevale* morning all throughout the city. There were not many pedestrians or tourists yet, but Jack could not imagine going back to the bed and tossing and turning any more. Though he was bone tired, more tired than he'd ever felt, sleep would not come, and he knew it. He went to the chamber pot and relieved himself, washed his face and teeth at the washstand, and tried to comb his hair down in the cloudy mirror that hung above it.

What he saw there shocked him, even though he could feel it before he saw it. His hair, even after running the comb through it, seemed to stand up on all ends. His eyes were bloodshot and wild, with dark circles beneath them. His whiskers were all wire and stubble, and his mouth was set in a grim, straight line. The blankness of the stare was familiar to him, but he hadn't seen it in weeks. Not since he'd met Millie. Now, it seemed to have deepened in its intensity, a man he almost didn't recognize stared back at him. A broken man.

Jack turned away and dressed with haste. He grit his teeth and settled into motions both deliberate and restrained as he pulled on his breeches and knotted his cravat. He wanted to scream. He wanted to throw things. He wanted to punch the wall until he could feel a hint of the pain in his heart in his bloody knuckles. But he had a lifetime of practice in hiding his emotions, even from himself, and it served him well now. He chose a simple dark waistcoat from the press, and his fingers found each button without trying. He wanted to shave, but getting out of Venice was even more important to him now. He pulled on his boots and his coat, then found his big greatcoat and bundled himself up before donning his hat. He stood at the door and looked around. Millie's things were all still here. He knew she'd be back to get them at some point, and he wanted to be gone when that happened. He closed the door behind him with a deliberate softness and made his way down to the street.

The Venice morning was still quiet and subdued after the night's revelry. Jack hurried through the streets with a long, bold stride. Having made his decision, he wanted to be over and done with it now. Once he approached the London shipper's office, he set his hat slightly askew and ducked inside.

"Mornin' sir," a voice behind the desk said in English. A short, balding man with a ring of white fuzz above his ears stood and pulled a ledger up to the counter. "Can I help you?"

"Yes," Jack said, "I need to book passage back to London."

The man let out a long, low whistle. "Not many berths to be had these days," he said. "Everyone be leavin' after *Carnevale* season, you see."

Jack took a deep breath and set his mouth in a frown, pinching the bridge of his nose. "I understand," he said, keeping his tone even, "but I need to get out of this city."

The man tilted his head and smiled in sympathy. "We do get that often here, sir," he said. "The city of masks does lose its romance when the masks come off."

"You can say that again," Jack said, looking around the dingy office while the man flipped through a big ledger.

"Looks like we got somethin' on the packet sailing Tuesday," the man said, his finger stopping its run down the ledger at a blank space.

Jack leaned forward over the counter. He knew he could be intimidating, but he preferred to intimidate those who deserved it. This poor old clerk was trying his best. He took a deep breath.

"I would pay handsomely to anyone who could get me out of

Venice sooner," he said, his voice soft but edged in steel.

The man leaned forward with a conspiratorial air, looking first left, then right, then whispering, "I would *take* your money quite handsomely, were I able to get you out any sooner." He stood up and closed the ledger. "Come back if you want that Tuesday packet," he said, and his eyes had a kind crinkle at their corners. "If you want my advice—"

"I don't," Jack bit off as he turned on his heel and stalked out of the office, slamming the thin door shut behind him, and taking some comfort in the rattle it made.

He couldn't go back to the hotel, nor could he go to any of the few friends he had made in Venice, for fear he would see Millie. He wandered the city, stalking about like a ghost in the mist that still enveloped every canal after the snow melt. He knew he shouldn't be alone now, his thoughts echoing around his brain like shouts in a cave. He also knew only one way to turn those thoughts off, at least temporarily.

Jack stopped at the edge of St. Mark's square and looked out on the island of San Giorgio Maggiore, the tower and dome rising from the mist and lit by the sun, now much higher in the sky and spreading its warmth over the city. It was growing late in the morning, but the streets were still quiet, the banging of pans and the rattling of wheels over cobblestones were faint, as was the smell of the street vendors' stalls, fish and oil and sweet baked breads, wafting over everything as the mist receded. Jack stared out at the water and the church and thought of his mother, of all people.

A moment ago, he had felt a thirst for strong drink such as he had never experienced. Having abstained for so long, he had never really had the urge to drink. He had thought he had known what that craving felt like. He had craved many things in his life: women, certain foods, privacy. He had always been able to overcome cravings with willpower. It seemed so simple. His mother had to have been weak, a woman with appetites she couldn't control, and that had always disgusted him—that she had seen him and his father and decided that they weren't worth putting down the claret, even when he had begged her.

Now, though, he felt a tingle at the back of his neck. A feeling he didn't like to admit to himself. What if he had been wrong? What if his mother hadn't made the choice at all, but the drink had made it for her? Jack felt like he'd spent his whole life running from the emotional pain of his childhood, but nothing he'd experienced had prepared him for the feeling in the pit of his stomach when he'd realized that Millie didn't care for him. The day before he had experienced the highest joy he'd ever felt and the lowest despair, too. This morning, when he felt nothing but dead inside, when he couldn't turn off the memories and the voices in his head, it had occurred to him that one easy way to escape would be to turn around, find the nearest cafe, and drown his sorrows in a bottle of madeira.

Was that what his mother had felt? Jack felt memories tumbling down, as if he'd pulled a rope and let loose a whole cargo net on top of his head. He saw his mother's tears as she hugged him and apologized. He saw her in a heap on the floor, crying and begging his father to leave so she couldn't hurt him, so he wouldn't have to deal with her. Jack saw his mother as an adult for the first time. All his life he'd only viewed her as a distant parent, not a woman of flesh and blood with hopes and dreams of her own. She'd been about the age he was now when he was born, he thought. She had tried to be a good mother, but something had happened to her, something had driven her to drink, whether it was an event or just something deep inside her that had always been there. But it hadn't been a failure of her will. Somehow, he could see that now.

Millie's mother, Jack's mother, Louisa and Jane's brother— they were all victims of this terrible unseen hand pushing them, driving them toward the thing they knew would destroy them. Jack had never felt pity for his mother, but now it all came rushing in at once, an overwhelming sense of sadness at the waste of his mother's life, the waste of his own relationship with her. Just like Thomas Elton had been driven nearly to murder in the pursuit of his gambling.

Jack gripped the railing on the seawall and felt the wind pick up and ruffle his hair. He closed his eyes and turned his face toward that breeze, bracing and cold. He would take that Tuesday packet, and as soon as the ship docked, he would ride for Redstone.

Chapter 15

Millie woke in darkness. After arriving at the mysterious door, she'd been led into a dark room, then down a set of damp, and even darker, stone steps. She'd been left alone in what appeared to be a cellar for what felt like hours, but she had dozed on and off and could not be certain of anything. She sat up and rubbed her arms against the chill. She was still dressed in her shift and dressing gown, and she was thankful for the dressing gown. The damp and the darkness made the cold feel somehow more intense. The stone beneath her made the bones of her hips ache, and her head pounded from lack of water. At least she'd been able to get some sleep, she thought to herself with a wry smile. She opened her eyes and tried to get a sense of the room. Having spent so long in total darkness, she could see the outlines of the stone a little now, could see the "room," such as it was, was really just a small storage cellar, not more than two yards in either direction. She could lie down, but barely. There was a wooden door at one end, and she pulled on it, knowing before she did so that it would be locked from the outside. She paced the small room, trying to get some feeling back in her aching legs.

She looked up and pondered the situation. She knew the men had been sent to kill her. Jack had heard the original command back in London. That's what had started all this. If that were the case, why wasn't she dead already? Had the men taken her message about the inheritance back to her cousin Thomas? Was Thomas even here? She allowed herself to hope based on the fact that she was still alive pacing this room. The fact that she had not been fed or brought any water was a mark against that hope, though. She forced herself to stop and take a deep breath. Panicking would be no help.

Millie felt her way along the wall, starting as high as she could reach and making her way around the small room. She pushed and tugged on ragged edges of stone, hoping one might be loose enough to dislodge. Her fingers started to chafe against the rough surface, but she kept breathing and pushed the pain away. She had made perhaps five circuits of the room this way, with no luck, when she heard voices as she neared the wooden door. They were very faint, and she wondered how long they had been talking before she noticed. Was it possible they'd been there all along and it was only after she calmed herself that she could hear?

She pushed her ear against the hard, cold wood of the door. The voices were distant, up at least one floor, more likely two. She could only hear the vague murmuring that indicated voices, and could not make out any words, or even what language was being spoken. Every so often the voices would rise in anger, but even so the subject of the conversation was lost to her through the thick stone and wood of the centuries-old building.

Millie pulled back, then rested her forehead on the door, her hands clenched in fists at the sides of her head, every ounce of her being tempted to bang on that door and demand that they set her free. But she breathed deeply and forced her body to calm. There was nothing she could do about the loud rumbling of her stomach, though. How many hours had it been since she'd eaten? And not only that, but she was nursing the dehydration that came along with that hell of a hangover she'd been battling all day. Her mouth tasted like cotton and she knew she must smell like wine, even now. She wasn't sure how long she stood there against the door, trying to focus on her breathing and thinking of the possibilities, before she finally heard the voices coming closer.

"She'd be dead already if it weren't for that gutter rat, Jack Covert," one man said in what was very clearly an English accent, before spitting in disgust at the name.

Millie put her ear back against the door. The footsteps had stopped, so they weren't coming down to her, but now they must be on the floor above and she could hear them clearly once she tuned out the beating of her own heart.

"He made a right mess of the 'ole thing, he did," a lower cockney voice said. It was unmistakably one of her kidnappers.

"A reputation for discretion, my arse," the first man said. "I've never had a job so muddled up by someone who came so highly recommended."

"Aye," the cockney responded, with a low cackle, "but what do you expect from a man named Covert, eh?"

Millie heard a smack and assumed the cockney had been reprimanded for his smart mouth. She couldn't say she was sorry about it.

"Ow," the man shouted, "there ain't no need for that, now."

There was a pause and some shuffling about. Millie could hear the clink of flatware and took it to mean the men were sitting down to a meal. Her stomach rumbled again, this time so loud she was afraid they'd hear it upstairs. But the meal appeared to continue unabated until one of them spoke again.

"So, VanHinkel, what are ye goin' to do now?" the cockney said, his mouth full, "Yer Mr. Elton—"

"That's *Sir* Elton now, don't forget," VanHinkel said, laughing.

"Aye, *Sir* Elton. 'E ain't like to look real kind on you killing 'is cousin, is 'e?"

"He isn't in a position to look kindly or unkindly on what I do," VanHinkel said, his voice edged in iron.

Millie stepped back from the door. Of course. It made sense

now that Louisa and Jane had been so adamant that Thomas wouldn't hurt her. Thomas wasn't the one who wanted her dead. This VanHinkel was. But why?

~*~

Louisa Elton yawned and stretched, pulling the blanket over her head as she turned away from the light shining through the crack in the drapes. She'd loved having East-facing windows when they arrived in this magical city, but after the few nights she'd had, she wished they'd all fall into the canal, or stay closed at the very least.

"Louisa? Is that you awake in there?" her sister Jane called from the adjoining room. "It's about time you're up. Millie's evidently been out and about already." The door opened without so much as a knock and Jane came bustling into the room, pulling her gloves on. She went to the window and threw both curtains open. Louisa groaned and sank lower in the nest she'd made herself in the big bed. But it was no use.

"I didn't know you were still *abed*," Jane said, pulling the covers off and exposing Louisa to the chill of the winter morning, Venetian mild though it was.

Louisa sighed and sat up, blowing an errant hair out of her face. "I'm up," she said, swinging her legs to the side. "I'm up." She pulled on her dressing gown and stood, yawning again before registering what Jane had said. "Did you say Millie isn't here?"

Jane nodded, going to the window. "She must have gotten up early and gone down to get coffee. I was hoping to get you to come out with me and meet her."

"Coffee wouldn't go amiss," Louisa said as she went to the clothes press to choose a walking dress. "I have enjoyed every bit of Venice so far, but I believe last night was my last hoorah with strong drink."

"I couldn't agree more," her sister said, sidling up next to her and looking over the dresses laid out. "Choose the green," she said, "it brings out your eyes."

Strangers were always getting Louisa and Jane mixed up, but anyone who knew them could tell them apart in an instant. They looked alike, certainly, but Jane was a doer, a chooser, an organizer. And Louisa was happy to let Jane do, choose, and organize to her heart's content, if it meant more time abed, reading, or wandering the moors back home for herself. Here in Venice, and ever since they'd embarked upon the trying ordeal of attempting to right their brother's wrongs, she'd been especially happy to let Jane lead the way. And she had, to great success. Now all they needed to do was find Thomas, sort the bit about the money out, and book passage home.

Louisa went about her ablutions and dressed quickly in the morning chill. She held her hair up while Jane did up her buttons in back, then pulled it up in a rough knot on the back of her head with the pins she'd left on the nightstand.

She was pulling her gloves on as they walked out into the sitting room of the small apartment they'd taken and immediately felt the hairs on the back of her neck prickle.

"Jane," she began, looking around, "Do you notice anything different about the sitting room?"

Jane was busying herself with the fire, but turned around with her hands on her hips. "I didn't, no," she said, but then did a survey of the room. "But now that you mention it..."

Louisa walked to the settee, where Millie had spent the earliest part of her drunken breakdown before they'd sent her off to bed. Now it was empty, of course, but the glass of water they'd set out for her had been knocked over. She bent over and saw a small wet spot on the carpet, though it had been there long enough to no longer be a puddle.

Louisa stood up straight again, and she and Jane looked around them, trying to place what else seemed different about the room. Now that she thought of it, the fire had already been tended and new logs thrown on. She hadn't been surprised because she'd assumed Millie had gotten up early and gone out to get coffee or take a brisk walk to clear her mind. But if that were the case, why would she have tended the fire first?

Louisa walked to the door and pulled it open to look out in the hall. She realized when she turned back around that it was unlocked. Millie wouldn't have left the door unlocked if she had gone out, would she?

Jane came to join her as they looked around the door. Louisa squatted and gathered her skirts around her to get a closer look at the keyhole. She felt queasy.

"Jane," she said, pointing, "The lock has been tampered with."

Their heads came together to look at the little metal plate around the keyhole. There were scrapes all around it.

"Someone has picked the lock," Jane said, her voice almost a whisper of shock.

They both looked at each other. "Thomas," they said at the same time, in disbelief. Was it possible that their brother had come and actually kidnapped Millie? The thought made Louisa's stomach drop, not for the first time. Her mind buzzed with thoughts. She still hadn't truly believed Jack's story about men wanting to kill Millie. Thomas's lust for gambling had changed him, but she simply could not imagine her brother a murderer.

"Louisa," Jane began, pulling her back inside the room and closing the door. "We cannot believe it of him."

Louisa sat on the settee with Jane, both defeated. "I agree, and somewhere inside of me, I still do not."

"I feel a 'but' coming," Jane said, and her wan smile did not reach her eyes.

"But," Louisa said, swallowing, "What else could it be?"

"There may be an explanation," Jane said, standing and pacing. She brought one hand to her mouth and began to chip away at a fingernail with her teeth.

Louisa leaned back on the cushion and stared at the ceiling. "If there is one, we must find it," she said. "For Millie's sake, but also for Thomas's."

She looked over at her sister, to find Jane's piercing gray eyes on her, her mouth set in a grim line. "We need to find Jack," she said.

Louisa sat up, shaking her head. "I don't think that's a good idea," she began, but Jane had anticipated this answer and cut her off.

"I know," she said, "I don't either, but it might be our only option."

"What would Millie want?" Louisa asked, her voice quiet.

"To be alive, I'm sure," her sister said, an edge of steel in her voice. Louisa had to agree. But after what had happened between them, she felt like she'd be betraying Millie to run to Jack first thing. She hesitated.

Jane stood and began to pace again. "You know as well as I do that Jack Covert is the only person we know in this city with the skills and the motivation to help us. If there is something sinister, if Millie really has been taken, two wide-eyed innocents from Shropshire and two whores who can't walk without assistance aren't going to be the ones to save her on their own."

Louisa gasped a little at Jane's harsh language, but she knew her sister was right.

Chapter 16

Jack sat on the bed in his hotel room, staring at Millie's clothing, which still lay in the press where she'd left it. He'd hoped when he returned, they'd be gone, that she would have come and gotten her things quietly and been off without his having to see her. But since they were still there, he assumed she'd been sleeping off the overindulgence of the night before. Jack shook his head and tried to turn his eyes back to the book on his lap. He had almost gone back out to avoid seeing her, but he didn't have anywhere to go in this dratted city, every step of which reminded him of Millie and the time they'd spent here. Not only the time they'd spent in the hotel room, loving and exploring each other, but the time they'd spent as friends, exploring each other's histories and ideas. In fact, even the book reminded him of her, having shared their love of the author and so much of the story together on the ship.

He turned his attention back to the plate of cold food he'd had brought up. He hadn't eaten since last night and he still had no appetite. He knew he must eat *something*, though. His heart was breaking, but underneath that, he also felt a sense of determination. He wanted to get back to his mother, to stop running from his life, and to try and live as fully as he could from now on. Millie had taught him that much. He'd imagined he'd be doing it with her, but even without her it was still worth the effort. He could see that now.

Sighing, he picked up the drumstick of the chicken lying on the plate and took a resolute bite. It was greasy and cold, but it tasted good. He closed his eyes and savored it, realizing that he was ravenously hungry after all. He approached the rest of the plate with a renewed vigor and was almost done and ready to wash up when he heard a timid knock at the door. His heart sank. Was it Millie? Would he finally have to face her?

But the knock was soon accompanied by a stronger one, and he heard voices in the hall. Two female voices. He strode to the door and threw it open.

"Jane and Louisa?" he exclaimed. "What on earth—"

They pushed their way past him into the room, and both sat on one corner of Millie's bed, their hands in their respective laps, as if part of a choreographed dance. He just stood there, his mouth agape, the door still wide open.

Jane cleared her throat and nodded her head toward the door, eyebrows raised. "If you would, Jack," she said.

Dazed, Jack closed the door behind him and leaned back against the jamb. There was only a moment of silence before both sisters began speaking almost at once. He could make out only snippets of what they were saying. *Millie–disappeared– water spilled–lock broken–we fear our brother–need your help.*

"*Stop*," Jack shouted, as loudly as he dared in a genteel hotel room. "Stop. Start over from the beginning. One at a time."

He listened to their story and felt his stomach drop again. This time, it wasn't out of fear he might see Millie, it was out of fear he might never have the chance again. He stood as they finished, and each one of them came forward and took one of his hands.

"We know you love her," Louisa said. "She loves you, too."

Jack shook his head. "No, she doesn't," he said quietly. "You didn't hear her last night."

Jane squeezed his hand then backed up. "For the best thief

in London, you certainly aren't very good at seeing what's right in front of you."

Jack closed his eyes and took a deep breath, counting to three before exhaling. "We don't have time to discuss this now," he said, "Let's go."

It took only moments for him to dress for the chill afternoon. The sun was already beginning to set as they made their way up the Grand Canal and back toward the Rialto. The same revelers were out, but as this was finally Shrove Tuesday, the endless *Carnevale* would be over tonight at midnight. An anxious tension infused the city, like a climax and its aftermath occurring at the same time. The snow having passed, there was a humid chill in the air, not really of winter, but not of spring either. Jack wondered if this was all in his head. He couldn't trust his emotional state, and he knew the Elton sisters were watching him, waiting for him to say something. He had nothing to offer them. He knew what had happened between Millie and him. They only thought they knew. But none of that mattered right now. What mattered was getting Millie safe. He realized that he could live with knowing she didn't love him, but he couldn't imagine living in a world where she was gone. At least if she lived, she could go on to live a happy life. And regardless of what had happened between them, she had changed him. She'd gifted him with perspective, something he'd been sorely lacking his whole life.

His strides became more purposeful when they reached the bridge and the bustle of vendors and revelers just coming out in the evening gloom. Once they were there at the entrance to the bridge, he stopped, both Elton sisters bumping into him from behind.

"Jack," Jane began, her voice timid, "What exactly are we looking for?"

He looked around, surveying the scene. There were the usual street vendors, hawking both food and wares. Some of the women of the night were already out, their garish makeup even more ridiculous in the fading sunlight. Everything looked the same as it had since he'd arrived in Venice. But everything *felt* different.

"It's eerie, isn't it?" Louisa asked, echoing his thoughts.

He could only nod.

"I suppose we should start back at your rooms," Jack said. "Maybe there are some clues you missed in your haste to find me."

Louisa and Jane agreed, so they navigated the crowding streets toward their hotel. Jack grilled them on details along the way. One thing he hadn't put together was where the older women had been. Neither of the sisters knew. They'd assumed Isabella and Fanny had returned to one of their own *pensiones*, but they weren't sure. Everyone had simply parted and fallen into exhausted sleep. A chill ran up Jack's spine. He had grown quite attached to Isabella. "I sincerely hope nothing has happened to either of them," he said as the sisters rushed to keep up with his quickening pace.

When they got to the rooms, everything was exactly as they'd found it. Jack knelt and ran his hand over the soft carpet in the hall. There were still impressions of several footprints, but that really told them nothing since this was a busy hotel in the middle of *Carnevale* season. The lock had definitely been picked, though, and not by a professional. Sloppy scuff marks and gouges marred the bronzed metal in several places. When they went in, there was little sign of a scuffle, except that one fallen glass of water.

Jane and Louisa explained the evidence that there had been another log thrown on the fire, and not by them, and that it had since burned down in the interval. They made their way to the room where Millie had slept, only to find, true to the sisters' memory, that the dress Millie had worn the night before was still there, meaning if she had gone out of her own volition, it would have been in her nightclothes, which was highly unlikely in the colder weather.

Jack had hoped against hope that when they made a thorough search of the rooms, they'd find something that gave them an easy explanation. Better yet, when they threw the bedroom door open they'd see Millie lying there, her dark curls splayed against the white of the pillowcase, and they could all laugh and know it had been one huge misunderstanding. But now, standing in the evening chill of the room where she'd last been seen, Jack's blood ran cold. Something nefarious had happened, he knew that with certainty now. There was no other explanation. And precious few clues as to where they would have taken her.

Jane plopped herself in the chair in Millie's room and stared straight ahead. Louisa came to stand beside her, wringing her hands, then putting one palm on Jane's shoulder as if to steady both of them. "How could we have let this happen?" she cried.

Jack walked over and grabbed Louisa by the tops of her arms. "Listen to me," he said. "It wasn't your fault. You've traveled half the continent to try and protect your cousin, and even I thought the danger was over."

He backed up. Had he truly thought the danger was over, though? Or had he relied on the illusion to help make it easier for him to leave last night? Shouldn't he have known that until they found Thomas Elton and cleared things up, that there was still danger? He felt the familiar nausea rising up, but used all his training to push it back down. Now was the time for action.

"Let's find Fanny and Isabella," he said, holding his hand out to help Jane out of the chair. "We must be sure they are safe, and hope they might have seen or heard something."

Both sisters agreed, and they made their way to the less fashionable alleys and smaller canals where the courtesans and ladies of the night lived. Jack couldn't help but remember the day Millie had told him with fondness about visiting the *pensione* where she'd grown up. The same dark children haunted the streets now, the same kittens clattering in the empty bottles and crates of the alleyways. But when this had appeared picturesque those first few days in Venice, today they were menacing, haunting. He thought of the child Millie had once been, suffering here in this city, not knowing she was to have a new chance at life in London. He couldn't let her live her last hours the way she'd lived those first years. He wouldn't.

When they reached Fanny's bordello, they were all instantly relieved to see her sitting on the front portico, where the lanterns had all been lit in the eerie half-light of the gloaming. When she saw them, Fanny stood with a cheerful smile on her rouged lips, but her face fell as she took in their anxious countenances.

"What is it, *miei cari*?" she asked, coming forward and taking Louisa's hands in her own.

Jack tilted his head toward the door. "Can we talk inside?" he asked.

Fanny took a deep breath and sighed, closing her eyes. She clucked her tongue and gathered her skirts, leading them into a large, clean room with only a few furnishings scattered here and there. "The *salotto* will do, I hope?" she asked, gesturing for them to sit down in one of the intimate conversational groupings. Jack looked around him and tried to absorb the surroundings. They had an air of quiet gentility, but everything was just a few years out of date, threadbare and worn, but spotless. He realized this was a room that would normally only be seen in the dark. The waiting room for the gentlemen callers. There was nothing welcoming about it. A fire burned in the grate, but it was low and the room was high-ceilinged and chilly.

He turned to Fanny where she sat, waiting for them to explain themselves. He started to speak, but Louisa began first. "We're so happy to see you safe," she said, putting her hand on Fanny's knee.

One of Fanny's eyebrows rose. "Why wouldn't I be safe?" she asked.

"Have you seen Millie?" Jack said, keeping his voice quiet.

"Not since last night," the older woman replied, then one

eyebrow rose and she lowered her voice, "Why? What has happened?"

"We think she may have been taken" Jane said, voice cracking.

Fanny stood. "Good God," she exclaimed, gathering up her skirts. "Then what the deuces are we doing sitting here, *talking*?" She went to a bell pull and rang a servant. From somewhere in the bowels of the brothel, the small tinkle of the bell could be heard, and it was only moments before a girl no older than twelve came running in, a little white cap on her head bobbing as she curtsied.

Fanny said something in rapid Italian to the young girl by the door, who dashed into the bordello. The large space felt small as Fanny paced around it, talking a mile a minute, half in English, and half in Italian.

"We must to the Rialto, *subito*, we'll gather the girls and *mandali fuori*."

Jack took her arm and held her still. "Fanny, be calm and slow. What do you plan?"

She stopped and looked into Jack's eyes, her own brown ones holding depths of emotion. "We'll rally the girls," she said. "The ladies of the night. They have eyes and ears all over the city. Men talk in front of us like we are nothing. Tonight, they'll know we are not nothing."

Louisa and Jane each took one of Fanny's arms and led her to a chair so she could put on her walking boots when Giulia came back. They helped her on with her boots while Jack stood behind her and eased her into her big knit blanket of a wrapper. With her bonnet and gloves on, and that big red shawl draped around her, she looked even more like the Italian grandmother he felt she had almost become to them all. As she hugged Giulia to her and whispered something in the girl's ear before sending her back to the kitchen, Jack realized Fanny played this role all throughout the district. He smiled as Fanny grabbed her cane and took his arm. She pointed the elaborately carved instrument in the direction of the bridge and they all made their way there through the throngs of revelers who were flooding the streets now that night had fallen.

"Tonight the *Carnevale* ends at midnight," Fanny said as they went single file across a narrow little bridge. "It will liven up earlier but be more subdued than many other nights."

When they came to the plaza that opened up to the bridge, the fire was blazing just as it had been the night he'd met Fanny. Several women sat around it, dark kohl lining their eyes and their hair piled on their heads. When they approached and their faces were illuminated by the lantern light, one of the women stood and offered the little velvet cushioned stool to Fanny, who sat with a smile of gratitude.

"*Signore*," she said in a low voice that drew them all closer. Jack could hear them all speaking in rapid-fire Italian.

They all started agreeing without hesitation, but Fanny held her hand up to silence them. She said something else in Italian, and the women stopped nodding.

There was silence for a long moment as Fanny looked each one of the women in the eyes. Jack had time to take in their faces. They ranged in age from late teens to possibly late forties. Each one of them had the steely glint of hard-won experience in their eyes, and now all their mouths were set in similarly grim lines, despite the varying colors they had used to make themselves up before leaving their rooms tonight. They all looked at each other after Fanny had surveyed them, and one of the women, a small figure with fire-red hair and an emerald green domino over her gown, finally spoke in Italian. Jack couldn't make out the words themselves, but the sentiment was easy enough to understand when the rest of the women nodded their agreement and leaned in to hear their instructions. Fanny explained, translated for Jane and Louisa so they could describe their brother, then sent the women off like a small army.

Jack felt doubly helpless when they left. He paced back and

forth in the little piazza, looking at the rising moon and listening to the revelers. Though the snow was gone, and that strange humid chill in the air lingered, much of the atmosphere was the same as that magical night they'd all spent together...could it have been only the day before yesterday? He sighed with the pain that constricted his heart.

He was startled out of his reverie by Fanny calling his name. She'd pulled up another one of those little velvet covered stools and now she patted it, indicating for him to join her. He lifted his hat and ran a hand through his hair before he sighed and sat down.

"You look terrible," Fanny said, pulling a flask from her voluminous skirts.

He frowned. "Thank you."

She handed the flask to him but he waved it away. "You know what I mean, boy," she said.

He nodded and leaned forward, elbows on his knees. He tented his hands, then released them, repeating the movement out of some instinct.

"We'll find her," Fanny said, patting his shoulder. "You know we will."

"I don't," he sat up, then leaned his head back to look at the stars. "I don't know that, Fanny. When I left her last night..."

"She said what she thought she needed to, not what she felt."

"You don't know that either, Fanny," he said, his voice cold.

Fanny laughed, but there was no joy in it. "I'm sorry, my boy," she said, her voice soft. "I may not know for sure we'll find her. You're right about that. But I do know she loves you."

Jack's heart constricted. He'd always heard of heartbreak, but he'd never known that it physically hurt like this. It was hard to catch a breath, and there was a shooting pain that came and went in his chest.

He looked up to see Fanny watching him. The crows' feet at the corners of her eyes deepened a little as she narrowed them.

"She's a strong woman," Fanny said. "You know that."

"I do."

"She won't go down without a fight."

"I know that, too."

"So you shouldn't, either."

Jack took a deep breath and stood to pace again, but he bent down to kiss Fanny's cheek. "I don't plan to," he said in her ear.

Chapter 17

After Millie heard the men's conversation, all had gone quiet, and she had lain down on the cold stone floor and fallen in and out of a fitful sleep. She still had no concept of the time or how long she had been here, but she did know it was long enough to be very thirsty. She was still hungry, despite the queasiness she still felt. Her stomach's rumbling noises woke her twice, in fact. She was uncomfortable, and so anxious that her heart would not stop pounding, but the only way to try and pass the time was to sleep, so she lay there and tried to focus on her breathing. No matter how hard she tried, her mind went back to Jack. She frowned to herself and shut her eyes tight against her tears as she thought of the absolute waste of dying in here, the waste of a life she had committed herself to when she'd sent him away. How could she not have seen that? Now that the prospect of losing that life was so close, she realized that she'd been utterly wrong. There was no obstacle she couldn't overcome for one more minute with Jack. Now that she faced the idea of never seeing him again, she realized that all the things she'd thought were so important could be worked through if she'd thought to discuss them with him.

In her fitful dreams, she imagined that she would die here, that she would starve to death, and that in her last moments she'd feel her own flesh being devoured by rats. In fact, their scratching was so real and so loud that she woke with a start. When she sat up, she rubbed her eyes and realized the scratching was still audible, but this was no rat. It was coming from high up on the wall, maybe from outside? She stood and felt her way along the stone, listening and moving toward the sound. When she got to the corner of the room the sound was the loudest, and it was coming from up near the ceiling. She could not reach the beams there, but she reached as high as she could and scratched back, biting back pain as her nails ground down on the rough rock and her fingertips stung. She stopped to listen. The scratching resumed, but this time in a rhythm. *Scritch...scritch-scritch...scritch.* She copied the sound. Another rhythm came. Again, she copied it. She swallowed the hope she felt, trying to keep herself calm, but soon all the noises stopped, and she couldn't contain her grief. She sank to the floor and screamed before bringing her fist to her mouth.

Only minutes could have passed, though, before she heard another sound from the same place. It was different this time, more of a scrape than a scratch. It sounded almost like—

She jumped up. Someone was removing one of the stones in the top of the wall. She could see the crack of light around it growing larger as the stone slid out. Though it was already dark out again, her eyes still squinted against the lamplight that shone through the small opening. A face, backlit and blurry, peered in at her. She could see from the wild mass of hair that gleamed in the lamplight that it was a woman.

"*Ti chiami Millie?*" the woman hissed in a whisper.

Millie stood on her tiptoes to whisper back in her halting Italian, "I am. How do you know me?"

The woman looked over her shoulder to be sure she wasn't seen and whispered in Italian so rapid Millie could only make out bits and pieces, but she knew she heard "keep heart and rescue."

Millie started to answer, but she could hear footsteps on the stairs. The girl heard them, too, and quickly replaced the stone.

Millie lay down on the floor and tried to look asleep. She had no idea how she would hide the sound of her beating heart; it was so loud.

When the heavy wooden door slid open, the room filled with light from a candle that the man held in front of him. She held her hand up to shield her eyes. When her vision adjusted, she knew it was the man who'd held the knife to her throat this morning. He was carrying a basket in the other hand, and he set it down with a thud on the stone floor. It was covered with a rough cloth, and the man pointed at it. "Food an' water," he said with a nod. "Eat it slow. You might not get any more for a while." He held the candle up and looked around and Millie trained her eyes on the basket, too scared to look at the stone in the wall and give it away. The man grunted and pulled the heavy door closed, lowering the bar in place on the outside and taking the candlelight with him.

Millie crawled to the basket and took the cloth off. She couldn't see, but she could feel the rough bread and the hunk of cheese, and her mouth watered just at the thought. There was also a clay jug full of water, and this she brought to her lips, spilling a little in her haste. She forced herself to drink slowly, but nothing had ever tasted more delicious.

Once she'd eaten some of the bread and cheese, she carefully wrapped it back up in the cloth to try to keep it fresh as long as possible, and she lay back down, curling up with her knees to her chest, and thinking of the mysterious young woman who'd found her. What had happened? Had Thomas found out what was going on? Were Jane and Louisa safe? Her head was still full of questions as she drifted back to sleep.

~*~

Jack held the meat pie in his hands resting on his legs, the grease congealing on the once-delicious pastry as he waited for word from Fanny's network of spies. She had given him the pie and entreated him to eat, but he had found it nigh impossible.

To appease her, he'd taken a few bites, but now it just hung there, something to hold on to and stare at while he lost himself in his worry again.

Jane and Louisa had taken a walk, hoping to hear some news or look for some sign of their brother, but they all knew it was really to have something to do, a way to clear their minds. Jack wouldn't leave Fanny's side, though, in case one of her girls came back. He wanted to be there to hear it first.

So deep in thought was he that he barely noticed when Fanny stood, but soon he could hear the footsteps and he looked up, dropping the meat pie to the cobblestones as he stood. A girl of about twenty was running toward them, her slippers clicking on the street as she held her skirts in both hands. She ran right past him and directly into Fanny's arms, breathless.

The girl started spilling out words in Italian and by her excited movements and smile, it was clear to Jack that she'd found Millie.

Fanny and Jack locked eyes over the girl's head.

"*Sedere*, Gianna," Fanny said, moving the girl to Jack's now vacated seat.

Jack could barely get the words out, but he forced himself to ask, "Is she alive?"

The girl galnced at him and turned to Fanny for translation. Fanny obliged, and the girl nodded. Gianna said something else in Italian, shaking her head, her nose wrinkling like a foul smell had wafted their way.

"*Chi?*" Fanny asked, her eyebrows coming together.

"*L'uomo oscuro,*" Gianna said, "*L'inglese.*"

Jack looked at Fanny. He recognized the word for Englishman. Fanny turned to him.

"She has said Millie is at the dark man's home. That he has a dungeon, and he thinks he is clever, but she checked there when she heard we were looking for a man from England." Fanny was serious, but her eyes were alight, and color was coming back into her face.

"You said dark man?" Jack asked. Louisa and Jane had described their brother Thomas as fair, with light blond hair and blue eyes.

Jack listened as Fanny asked Gianna more questions.

"No, *Signora* Fanny," Gianna said, looking up and squinting her eyes, trying to remember. "Von? Van?"

Jack's entire body went cold. "VanHinkel?" he asked.

The girl nodded and turned to Fanny to again. Fanny listened then spoke to Jack. "He came a couple weeks ago and he thinks it's funny to put working girls down in that chamber, scare them, and get them to beg him to let them out. The girls have been spreading the word about him."

Fanny rubbed Gianna's shoulder and listened to her continue her story. She translated for Jack.

"A few of the girls helped work one of the stones out of the outer wall," she said, "so they could call for help if they needed to."

"Smart," Jack said.

"Safe," Fanny corrected him. "She says so far he's been harmless, and he'll pay extra, so some of the girls will still go and play along, but they moved the bricks as a precaution."

Jack smiled. "Like I said—smart."

Fanny took Jack's hand and patted it. "I know you want to run over there now and save her, but we, too, need to be careful."

Jack nodded and sat, running his hand through his hair again. "You're right. We can't go barging in there, swords out, so to speak."

"I will ask Gianna to give us more information about this man and his lodging. Gianna," Fanny said, handing the girl a flask and addressing the girl in Italian once again.

Gianna took a long swig of the strong drink, then wiped her mouth with the back of her sleeve before looking between Jack and Fanny Fanny, translating again, told Jack that the girls didn't know much but that they did know where to find him.

Jack nodded and took the girl's hand, asking Fanny to translate for him. "You found Millie, and for that we'll be forever grateful," he said, covering her hand with his own. "Do you know if he's still alone there now?"

Fanny did as he asked, and the girl shook her head.

"*Millie stava bene*?" Fanny asked, leaning forward with narrowed eyes.

The girl nodded. Millie was unhurt.

Jack let out the breath he hadn't realized he'd been holding. "Thank you, Gianna," he said. "*Grazie.*"

Just then Jane and Louisa came strolling back up, clearly empty-handed, but perhaps more clear-headed. They took a look at Jack and at the young woman who'd arrived after they left, they rushed forward, guessing quickly that there was news. "Have you found Thomas?" Louisa asked, her voice high-pitched with worry.

"No, even better," Jack said, "Gianna here has found Millie, and Thomas was nowhere to be seen."

Louisa sighed and leaned back against her sister's shoulder. Jane spoke in a low tone. "Do you think Thomas was involved?"

"That's the second-best news, Miss Elton," Jack said, "I truly don't think he was. Or if he was, he is not aware of what's happening to Millie right now."

Louisa and Jane pulled some of the small stools closer around the fire to create a little circle where the five of them sat. Jack went on. "The person who originally hired me to steal the locket from Millie was a man named VanHinkel. He was also the person who hired the assassins to kill her. All this time I thought VanHinkel was working for your brother, but now I'm not so sure. He appears to be here in Venice of his own volition, which is surprising to me. There's a mystery here that I haven't quite worked out."

Louisa leaned forward. "That can wait. My brother's gotten himself into his own trouble, and he'll have to get himself out. Right now, we've got to save Millie before anything happens to her.”

“I agree,” Jack said, “but with all due respect to present company, I don’t see myself taking on VanHinkel and whatever henchmen he’s got in there with just you lot to back me up. I’m a skilled thief, but not much of a fighter on my own. I try to avoid other people in my line of work, not confront them.”

Fanny looked up, eyes narrowed. “You *are* a skilled thief.”

Jack was confused. Hadn’t he just said that? But he waited patiently for the older woman to explain.

“What if we break in and steal Millie back?” Fanny asked, her head cocked.

Louisa jumped up. “Yes. What if we can get one of us inside, posing as a working girl?”

Jane leaned forward, listening, her elbows on her knees and hands fisted under her chin.

Gianna held her arms across her chest against the chill and asked Fanny to tell her the plan

She argued back and forth with Fanny for a bit but finally Fanny sighed and lowered her shoulders, turning to Jack. “The girls insist on helping. It’s one thing to like it rough or play pretend. It’s another thing to murder. We girls take care of each other here.”

~*~

Louisa’s heart pounded as she raised a hand to pull the door knocker on the ancient wooden door set in the stucco facade of a respectable, but slightly shabby villa off the main canals. The streets were still full of revelers, but it was more subdued here. Still, the light from the lanterns on the busier streets flashed down the small, cobbled street as people walked by, and boats moved at different paces out on the bigger canals. Louisa paused, hand still raised. She took a deep breath to steady herself. She didn’t even recognize her own hand in the lace gloves she wore beneath the red velvet domino. She had a red *Carnevale* mask on her face, with so much powder, rouge and even kohl around her eyes, that she'd truly thought the mask to be unnecessary. But the girls had assured her she needed a mask for the ruse to get her in the door, and she needed the makeup underneath to carry it through.

She took another deep breath then finally pulled the knocker, hearing the loud booming inside reverberating through the hall. She pulled her hand back beneath the voluminous domino and felt at her waist for the tools on her belt. She reached further down her skirt to feel the knife strapped around her thigh. She smiled and sighed, bringing both hands to a mock-demure fold in front of her while she waited for the door to swing open.

It was only a few moments before she heard footsteps on the slate flagstones behind the door. When it opened, though, it only opened a crack. As soon as the man in the shadowy room saw her, he said, abruptly, "No, we didn't order none of that tonight."

Gianna had told her this would happen. VanHinkel wouldn't have planned to get a whore on the same night he already had a real prisoner in his little dungeon. The man tried to close the door, but Louisa's foot was already near the jamb, stopping it from closing.

"VanHinkel may not be expecting me," she said, trying to make her voice low and seductive, and speak with an Italian accent. "But I know he'll want to meet me." She looked down and batted her eyes, then looked back up at him through her lashes. She had no idea how well she was pulling this off, but she knew Millie's life may depend on her, so she forced herself to stay in character.

The man frowned at her with narrowed eyes. His eyes were watery and rimmed in red. He was either drunk, sleepy, or both. He rubbed the stubble on his chin as he thought. "All right, come in, but stay right 'ere while I find out what's goin' on."

Louisa only smiled and stepped in, keeping her eyes down. When the man left the entrance hall, she leaned back against the door, shaken. They had all hoped it would be this easy to get inside, but she also realized now that she was absolutely terrified to be here. She felt down for the knife again and closed her eyes, swallowing her fear and forcing herself to stand up straight. She knew her sister and Gianna were across the street watching her, and she hoped Jack was having success with his own entry.

~*~

The wood in the window frame groaned a little as Jack tried to leverage it open with a small chisel from his tool belt. The humidity in Venice did not make for easy burgling, he thought with a frown. He stepped back and reexamined the wall in the rear of the building. Unlike many of the ancient buildings in Venice, this one had been arranged such that the entry and hall was on the cobbled street, while the back entrance came straight up from the small alleyway canal. There was only a thin line of brick walk stretching out from the rear door, and this was where Jack stood in the darkness, assessing the best way to break into this mysterious house where his love was being held. At every noise and every soft line of lantern light that shone down the narrow canal, he flattened himself against the stucco and took deep breaths, willing his heart rate to slow and his stomach to settle. He was used to creeping around undetected, to entering homes silently, to padding on soft slippers throughout the halls of empty houses. But there had never been such high stakes. In fact, he'd lived the last several years almost in hope of being caught. He had no care for his own life, or for the Viscountcy. Now, though...he knew he wasn't about to live without Millie.

As he stood, back against the cold wall, he could hear muffled voices coming from inside, but there was still no light visible through the window next to him. From some of the girls who'd been in, they'd gotten a rough outline of the floor plan, and Jack knew this window led to a rear parlor that was unused.

Through the window he'd gotten confirmation of that when he'd seen the ghostly shapes of the white drapes on the furniture. He still didn't want to risk the noise of the window squeaking open. He'd need to complete this operation with delicacy. He took the chisel in hand and tried once again, this time with a quick, hard tap on the lever end he held out. He winced at the crack of noise, but as he'd suspected, that freed the pane and it moved up easily after that. He slid it all the way open, looked up and down the canal, then slid himself in like the end of a dark drape falling. He pulled the window back down behind him, but not all the way. He wanted to be sure of a quick escape if necessary. He stood and took stock of the room, a few groupings of furniture under the dust cloths, an unused fireplace full of brass andirons and fire tools thrown there haphazardly for storage. There was only one door in, and under it he could see a small sliver of light that must be coming from the entry hall. Jack moved toward the door and then flattened himself next to it, listening.

"Himself said he ain't got no time for ye right now, but he might later. He told me to bring y'upstairs."

Just as he'd instructed her, Louisa did not respond, but he could hear the swish of her domino as she followed the man who'd spoken past the door and then heard their footsteps moving up the stairs. Jack turned the knob on the door and was relieved to find it moved easily beneath his nimble fingers. He pulled the door open and crept into the hall, where one single candle burned. All was gloom in this house, and it matched his mood. Per Gianna's instructions, Jack turned to his left and looked for the open doorway that led down two steps to the kitchen. He stopped just next to the jamb and looked inside, relieved again to find it empty.

Again, there was light here, but not much. One oil lamp burned near the stove, and there was a small fire in the hearth with a kettle hanging over it. Jack looked at the little stair going down next to the hearth and his heart pounded. This was the way to the cellar room where they all assumed Millie was being kept. He made his way down the cold stone steps and found himself in front of a huge wooden door. There was no lock to pick, just a big iron bar settled into an equally massive iron bracket. Jack lifted it with light fingers and pulled the door open just a crack, hissing Millie's name into the darkness.

"Jack?" he heard her say, and his heart leaped. He dared not speak above a whisper, and he did not want to risk the door coming closed behind him. He leaned into the cavernous dark.

"Millie," he whispered, "It is me. I'm here. Come to the door, Millie."

When she fell into his arms, he felt a rapturous sense of relief and happiness he had never before known. Her nestled her curly head under his chin and his tears fell freely as he tightened his eyelids against them. He kissed into her hair, though she smelled of dirt and must, his arms tightening around her as her own came around his waist.

"Millie, Millie," he said against her curls. "I was so scared. I thought..."

"I know," Millie said, her voice muffled against his chest. "I know. Jack, you can't leave. I can't be without you. I know it's not what's best for you, but I can't—"

He cut her off with a kiss, not one of passion, but to convey the endless love he felt for her. Their lips just stayed like that, frozen in time, both of them drinking in the warmth of being reunited A noise in the hall startled them, and Jack moved Millie back into the room, pulling the door nearly closed, watching through the slit. He pushed Millie behind him and pulled out the blade he kept at his belt.

They could hear two voices, and one was unmistakably VanHinkel's. Jack's stomach filled with dread, but he held tight to Millie's hand behind his back and kept his grip light on the knife in front of him. The men were arguing, and he could only hope that meant that they wouldn't look down the stairs or notice the bar out of place on the door.

He and Millie just held their breath, listening. They couldn't yet make out the words at first, but as the men came closer, it was clear that Louisa's ruse had worked.

"She's upstairs, she won't hear anything," VanHinkel said.

"You said you wasn't gonna do any of that," the man with the cockney accent replied.

"We'll just leave her with our Mr. Elton for a while," there was a hint of darkness in VanHinkel's voice. "He hasn't had much fun here, I'm afraid."

Millie's hand tightened on Jack's and he squeezed back to let her know he'd heard. They waited for what seemed like ages as the kitchen echoed with the clinking of tankards. Jack closed his eyes and prayed, for one of the only times in his recent life that he could remember, that they didn't come to check on Millie.

His prayers must have been answered because soon enough the footsteps receded and he and Millie both let out a sigh of relief, turning to each other to embrace again, weak with the tension.

Jack took Millie by the shoulders and pulled her away from him so he could look down into her eyes. "Are you hurt?" he asked, trying to make a survey of her face.

"Not physically," she said. "A little sore, a little hungry, but nobody has mistreated me."

"Good. Let's get out of here." Jack started to pull her along, but she resisted.

"Jack," she said, letting go of his hand. "We can't go without Thomas. You know that."

"I know," he said, "And Louisa's up there with him."

"Louisa—*what*?" Millie exclaimed.

"There's no time to explain," Jack said, and he hugged Millie close to him again. "I want you to listen to me carefully. You need to head to the rear parlor and sneak out the window. I left it open. Jane and the others will see you and get you out of here."

"How will you rescue them alone?" Millie asked, stepping

back and crossing her arms in front of her. Jack saw the fire dancing in her narrowed eyes and knew this wouldn't be easy.

"Not sure yet," he said, "But you're not coming with me."

"I'm sorry, Jack Covert," Millie said, sounding an awful lot like his father, "But you are in no position to tell me what to do."

He sighed and leaned against the stone wall, enjoying the rough, cold feel on his back, grounding him in this moment. He closed his eyes and then opened them to see Millie standing just in front of him, the warmth of her breasts just touching his shirt front, the top of her escaped curls tickling his face. She turned her face up and met his gaze square on.

"Let's make a plan," she said. "We're wasting time."

Chapter 18

Once again, Millie found herself trying to still the beating of her heart as she crept up the back stair in the lonely stucco house. Neither she nor Jack knew what had become of VanHinkel and his associate, but there was no sound at all as they made their way up to where they assumed Thomas and Louisa were. Millie was feeling such a whirlwind of emotion she wasn't sure where her mind would go next, so she tried to focus on the here and now—each step, soft and careful, one foot to the next tread, then the other. She followed behind Jack, and she tried to avoid looking at his backside in the black breeches, no waistcoat or coat to hide the curved musculature of him. Her conscious mind told her that she was still right to have sent him away that night, but her heart told her that there was no way she'd ever be able to stay away from this man. He held her, body and soul. There was just no way around it.

Now, though, they were in terrible danger. Even more danger, perhaps, than she had been in down in that locked cellar room. And it wasn't only their own lives at stake, it was Thomas and Louisa's. So, she tried to focus. She tried not to think about Jack's scent, or the feel of his lips on hers, or the way his face had looked when she'd sent him away.

When they reached the top of the narrow stair, they found themselves in a small hallway with four rooms leading off it, all with old wooden double-hung doors. Two of the doorways were open, a third was closed with a simple knob, and a fourth was closed with a large old-fashioned padlock hanging from the two door handles.

"Bingo," Jack whispered, standing in front of the locked door. He knelt and inspected the padlock, and Millie stood, shifting her weight from one foot to the other, chewing her lip, and glancing toward the open rooms and the staircase. Jack pulled tools from his belt and got to work on the padlock, and Millie realized that, if someone were to surprise them here, she was utterly defenseless. She had no weapon, and barely any strength after her ordeal in that locked room. She was a little dizzy and disoriented as it was. She held her breath and listened to the little clicks and clangs of Jack's tools, but it wasn't long before the lock sprang open.

"Amateurs," Jack said, shaking his head as he pulled the lock free and pushed one of the doors open.

"Louisa?" he whispered, pushing the door wider, and motioning for Millie to enter.

She found herself in a sumptuously appointed room, thick velvet curtains hanging from a huge wooden bed that looked like it had sat here since the Middle Ages. There were equally thick draperies hanging in front of tall windows, and a small fire burned in the fireplace. It was here Louisa was huddled with a man so similar to her that he could only be her brother, and they both sprang to their feet while Jack closed the door behind him with a soft click.

"*Millie,*" Louisa said, her voice exuberant despite being barely above a whisper. "I'm so glad you're safe."

"Yes, but VanHinkel seems to have exchanged one prisoner for another," Millie said, hugging her cousin.

"Two prisoners," Thomas said, keeping his face down. "I am so ashamed, Millie, so ashamed of what's happened to you." She could see a tear glistening on his cheek.

"You should be," Jack said, leaning against the wall with his arms crossed. Millie shot him a frown.

She approached her cousin and laid a hand on his arm. "Thomas," she said, keeping her voice gentle, "Tell us."

Louisa led them both to the fireplace, and they all sat on the rough wooden chairs that were ringed around it. "He got himself in deep with VanHinkel, Millie," Louisa said. "It was VanHinkel who thought to recover the debts from your inheritance, not Thomas."

It all made so much sense now. Her cousins had been so kind and so certain that Thomas couldn't have been trying to harm her. And they had been right. VanHinkel had been his own client all along.

Jack still eyed them with suspicion. "Thomas isn't innocent, Louisa," he said. "He ruined your family and almost got Millie killed. Twice."

Thomas wept more openly now, wiping the tears from his eyes. "It's true, Louisa, don't make excuses for me."

Louisa's lips met in a grim line before she spoke. "No one is making excuses, believe me, Thomas," she said. "But pardon my relief in finally knowing you're not an outright murderer."

Millie took this time to really take in the appearance of her final long-lost cousin. There was a clear resemblance among all the Eltons, but Thomas was fairer than either sister. He was not very tall, but handsome in his own way, though he was gaunt and unshaven right now. Millie's eyes narrowed as she watched him.

"Thomas, have you been mistreated? How long has VanHinkel held you here?"

"He's kept me essentially a prisoner, albeit a gentlemanly one, since I discovered his plan to kill you."

"Since London?" Louisa asked, shocked.

"Yes. I tried to stop him when I found out what he planned." Thomas buried his face in his hands. "I even gave him the deed to the London house, Louisa."

Louisa rubbed her brother's back, even as she frowned. "Thomas," she said, leaning her head toward his, "I'm glad you're safe, but we can't allow that."

"I'm afraid it's too late," he said. "I've sold away our family's legacy, and for what?"

Jack stood and began pacing. "I know we all have things to say to each other," he looked directly at Millie, "but right now we've got to decide how to get out of here, and how to solve the VanHinkel problem once and for all."

Millie leaned back against the cushion and crossed her arms. "We could kill him," she said, not entirely joking. She was having trouble trying to see a way out of this that wouldn't keep VanHinkel after her for a long time to come.

Jack frowned at her. "No, of course," she said, her tone wry, "You're far too honorable."

Louisa stood. "I'm not."

Thomas pulled her back down next to him. "Yes, you are," he said, "And so am I, though don't think I haven't fantasized about it."

Millie chewed her lip. "If what he wants is my money, I can give it to him," she said.

"A man like VanHinkel isn't likely to stop at just that," Jack said. "He's likely to invent other debts or follow us for blackmail."

Thomas ran a hand through his hair, grown just enough too long in his captivity to make him look rakish. "He's already told me he plans to charge me for what it's cost him to find you and keep me in 'high style,'" he said. "But then again, something must be wrong now because he didn't kill you immediately when he found you."

Louisa rubbed her chin. "Yes, that is a wrinkle," she said, "I'm glad of it, but it is surprising given all else we know."

Jack paced in front of the fireplace. "No, it's not. He knows I'm Redstone. He knows I'm the Viscount, and he thinks he knows about me and Millie."

"You would be correct," a voice came from the doorway. In their eagerness to work out their dilemma, they hadn't heard VanHinkel come up the stairs.

He sauntered in and it was the first time that Millie had been able to get a real look at him. His hair was as dark as Jack's, but his eyes were a brutal black as well. He had an unkempt beard and his hair hung in greasy strands, pulled back in a queue with a black ribbon. He was in some ways so like Jack—both underworld figures who lived in the shadows and wore all black, but the contrast between them was still stark. Jack wore his usual Jack Covert uniform: black silk shirt, black breeches, his quiet slippers and the black scarf belt that concealed his tools. He wasn't wearing his mask, but he looked every inch the thief. VanHinkel also wore black, but he had on a leather waistcoat that strained at his rounded belly and he wore black boots, worn in places from long use. He wasn't trying to hide who he was or sneak around anywhere, and the ultimate proof of that was the pistol he held. Millie knew Jack was thinking the same thing she was. She was unarmed, and so were Thomas and Louisa. She had no idea what Jack might be hiding, but she knew it wasn't a pistol. There were four of them, but she didn't think they could overpower a big man like VanHinkel. She also knew he had accomplices, at least two, though they weren't with him right now.

VanHinkel laughed, and the sound was dark and sinister. "I had hoped to save young Mr. Elton," he said.

"*Sir* Elton," Louisa corrected, and Millie shot her a look. It wouldn't do for them to provoke the man.

"Yes, *Sir* Elton now," VanHinkel said. "All the more reason to keep him alive. He could be lucrative to me in the future." Jack and Thomas had been right—VanHinkel planned to keep extorting him.

"But now that you've all had a chance to conspire, I'm afraid it's a little more complicated," VanHinkel said.

"It is," Jack agreed, stepping forward. "But even you wouldn't risk killing a Viscount."

"A Viscount nobody knows is still alive," VanHinkel sneered. "Hardly my concern."

Millie felt her spine stiffen, but she forced herself to keep her face neutral. She wouldn't give this man the pleasure of seeing her fear.

"As for your little...trollop...here," VanHinkel continued, gesturing to Millie, "She may associate with a Duchess, but she's common trash."

"Come now, VanHinkel," Jack said, his voice steel covered with velvet. Millie had never heard this side of him before, this thief who belonged to the underworld. "Surely we can make a deal. This many murders would be impossible to pull off, even for you."

How could he stay so calm? How could he keep his voice steady like that? Millie realized again, not for the first or the last time, that the man she loved was a wonder.

And VanHinkel was taking the bait, too. For the first time, a note of uncertainty sounded in his voice. "Maybe," he said, "But I've done worse."

Jack chuckled, a low, dark sound. "I know," he said, and he motioned for VanHinkel to sit. Jack took one of the wooden chairs, turned it backwards, and straddled it, his elbows light on the back. He looked, for all the world, like he owned the room. And, Millie realized, in a way he did. The control had shifted.

VanHinkel sat, leaning forward on his knees, pistol held in one hand, the barrel resting on the palm of the other. He, too, was choosing his posture carefully. Not directly threatening, but not conciliatory either. "I'm listening," he said.

"You want these debts paid," Jack said. "Sir Thomas isn't the cash cow you think he is. One day the money will run out, even Millie's money. Sir Thomas has a disease, VanHinkel, and you know it. He's drawn to the gambling. He can't stop himself. You'd be better rid of him now when you can walk away with the money."

VanHinkel didn't speak, but his narrowed eyes showed he was hearing Jack's words.

"As for Millie, you're right. She's a common trollop," Jack said, not daring to look at Millie. She realized he was counting on her to play along.

"You didn't say that between my legs," she said, trying to sound as nonchalant as possible.

"No, but then again, we didn't talk about much else," he said. "She means nothing to me. You can do with her what you will."

VanHinkel looked over at Millie, and his gaze took her in from the top of her head to her the tips of her toes. The look on his face made her feel like she needed to jump in the nearest canal. "I could think of a lot of things to do with her," VanHinkel said. She swallowed the bile that rose in her throat.

"You can take the money, get rid of her, just like you wanted," Jack continued. "But you'll have to let the Eltons go. You'll have to evade a lot of investigating when a whole family goes missing. They're not high *ton*, but they're gentry."

VanHinkel nodded. "And I suppose I let you go, too?" he said. "It all works out rather well for the *Viscount*, don't it?"

"You don't know the half of it," Jack said, standing up and poking at the fire. "I think it could work out rather well for both of us."

"Explain."

"I propose we go into business together," Jack said. "I have no interest in taking the Viscountcy. I never did. I love my job, and I'm very good at it. You and I together could cut a fierce swath through the dirty work that needs to be done, in London and maybe even across the channel."

VanHinkel's eyes narrowed, and Millie held her breath. She dared not look at Thomas or Louisa. She dared not move a muscle for fear she'd give away Jack's ruse.

VanHinkel's greasy mouth cut itself into a grin. "Now you're talking sense, Jack Covert." He stood and slid the pistol into his belt. "Come with me. You lot will stay here until we've worked out some details," he said, with a pointed lascivious look at Millie.

When they had gone out and locked the door behind them, Louisa and Millie let out deep breaths, but Thomas stood in disbelief. "How can you two be so calm? That man just betrayed us all."

Louisa pulled him back down next to her. "You are so self-involved, you don't see anything that's happening around you," she said. "That man just saved all our lives, you dolt."

Millie and Louisa discussed Jack's plan. Neither were sure of the details, but they both knew he must have one. They just needed to be patient. Millie wondered how far Jack would let VanHinkel believe him. Most importantly, what would they all do about the two henchmen who were somewhere around the villa?

They were all silent after a while, and Thomas couldn't seem to sit still. He paced back and forth, stopping every once in a while and running a hand through his hair then resuming the pacing again.

Millie watched him through narrowed eyes, trying to learn more about this cousin who had caused so much horror for her and her friends. She could see he was tortured, but it was his sense of unease that piqued her interest. It reminded her so much of her mother. Memories that being in Venice had raised to the surface were becoming even clearer now that she was with Thomas. It was seeing him in the grip of his craving that was so eye-opening. Though he was clearly devastated by how low it had brought him, how he had endangered and impoverished his family, how he was a prisoner to it now, she could see he was going through the pains of being without it. She had seen her mother in this cycle many times, and had always assumed it was just the physical effects of being without the spirits or laudanum, but now with Thomas she could see it was not just physical. His wagering had never been physical, but the effects were the same.

She stood and went to him, putting a hand on his shoulder. "You are thinking of gambling even now, aren't you?" she said, her voice low so Louisa wouldn't hear.

Thomas's eyes snapped up to meet hers. "How could I?" he said, but the tone of his voice told her she'd been right.

She squeezed his arm. "How could you, indeed." she said. "It has ruined your life, and yet still you crave it."

She could see tears forming in his eyes. "How do you know?"

"I've seen it before," she said.

"If I could just have one big win," he said, "it would solve all this." He waved his hand around.

She shook her head and took his hand. "We both know that's not true," she said.

"My head knows it, but here," he put his other hand to his chest, "Here it still feels real, it feels possible. It feels like the only way."

She nodded. "What we feel isn't always what's true," she said. "That's the hard part, isn't it?"

He only turned to look at the fire, but he squeezed her hand before he dropped it and resumed his pacing.

Millie went back to Louisa, who'd been watching them in silence. "He was always a sensitive boy, you know," Louisa said, her eyes wet with unshed tears. "He was so protective of us."

"I think in some twisted way, every wager was a chance to try to make it right for him," Millie said. "He couldn't stop himself."

"I know," Louisa said. "It has happened like this time and again. Yet he always returns to it."

"My mother was the same way with the drink and the poppy," Millie said, sighing. "It took her in the end."

Louisa hugged her tight and Millie thought again how lucky

she'd been to find so many friends. First Anneliese Heatherington, then her daughter, then Jack, and now the Eltons. Life was better when you could count on someone, when you knew there was someone to turn to in a time of trouble. She took a deep breath and pulled away, wiping a tear with her sleeve.

Louisa smiled. "So, are we about to have a Viscountess in the family?" she asked.

"Louisa," Millie said, her voice resolute, "If we make it out of here, I will be whatever Jack wants me to be, as long as it is with him."

"That's more like it," Louisa said. "I was starting to worry you two would keep up your foolishness forever."

"The moment VanHinkel's men threw me in that cellar room, I knew I'd made a mistake," Millie said, "The idea of dying down there with Jack thinking I—" she trailed off, unable to say it out loud.

Louisa understood. "I know," she said. "But you didn't die, and you're not about to." She pulled her skirt up to reveal the knife she held there, and then flicked it back down. "No matter what happens, we're all getting out of here."

Thomas sat and buried his head in his hands. His fair hair splayed around his fingers as his back heaved with sobs. Millie could brook no more of this. She strode to him and grabbed him by the shoulders. "Snap out of it, Sir Elton," she said, her voice sharp but kind. "We've no time for this. You can make your amends later."

"How can I ever?" he said, lifting his tear-stained face to look up at her. "What could I do that could possibly fix this?"

"The job isn't to change the past," Millie said, "The job is to keep going, and make your future-self better one day at a time."

He nodded and wiped his eyes with his sleeves. "What do we do now?"

"Now we wait," Millie said, sitting down again. "But we also plan. I trust that Jack knows what he's doing and will get us out of here safely, but we should make our plans if he fails." They all leaned forward and got to work.

~*~

Jack sat at the dining room table, leaning back in his chair and swirling the brandy around in the glass, watching it reflect the gleam of the candlelight from the table. VanHinkel sat across from him, already on his third glass, his eyes becoming bloodshot and his words slowing. The two henchmen had been in and out, pouring themselves drinks and then returning to the kitchen to eat and carouse on their own.

The villa had no cook or maids to speak of, but evidently VanHinkel sent the men out to procure food from the stalls for meals. Jack gleaned from the conversation that VanHinkel often invited Thomas to the table, probably more out of loneliness than any sense of hospitality. The meal was simple, but delicious, as most of the street fare in Venice had been. The hour was growing late, and already the reveling seemed to be winding down. From what Fanny had told him, when the church bells tolled midnight, it would be Ash Wednesday, and the streets would empty entirely. Jack couldn't see a clock anywhere, but he knew it must be at least eleven. Time was running out if they wanted to escape under cover of *Carnevale*. But now that Jack had changed tactics slightly, he knew they may not need the same escape plan they'd originally made.

Jack narrowed his eyes and watched VanHinkel. The man was clever, clearly, but he was also overconfident, used to getting his way, and had been getting sloppy since arriving in Venice. He'd let all those working girls know where he was, he'd let Thomas out time and again, and here he was drinking to excess when he should be keeping himself alert to any signs of escape. He was ill equipped to deal with three prisoners upstairs, and even less equipped to deal with Jack Covert. Jack allowed the corner of one lip to turn up in a little smile at that.

"Listen, VanHinkel," he said, "we're wasting time. We need to get rid of Millie diRossi and we need to let the Eltons go. The sooner we do that, the sooner we can get back to London and find the real business to be had."

VanHinkel drained what was left in his glass and poured himself another before stabbing a piece of meat with his knife and chewing it with his mouth open. A small stream of bloody juice dripped out the corner of his mouth and he wiped it with the napkin before taking another swig of the brandy.

Jack forced himself to keep his face neutral, even while he sneered at the man in his mind. He realized this was going to be easier by the second. His task now was to keep VanHinkel in this room, drinking and talking, as long as possible. He only hoped the men in the kitchen were imbibing as much as their boss was.

"How do you propose we get rid of that little minx?" VanHinkel said, leaning back in his chair, his hands resting on his ample belly.

"She'll be easy enough," Jack said. "She fancies herself in love with me. She's probably upstairs crying about my betrayal right now." He forced his mouth into a sinister smile even while he prayed that Millie was smart enough to know what he was doing.

VanHinkel's belly shook with laughter and he leaned forward to raise his glass again. "You're even more devious than I thought," he said, toasting to Jack.

"More important," Jack continued, "Is how we let go of the Eltons without them running off to any pesky authorities."

VanHinkel's eyes narrowed. "You didn't seriously think I'd let them go, did you?"

The hairs on the back of Jack's neck stood on end. He leaned forward. "That's part of the deal, VanHinkel," he said, "Killing them will bring investigations."

"Everyone knows *Sir* Thomas is on the hook for gambling debts all over the East End," VanHinkel said, waving his glass about, "Nobody will bat an eye at his disappearance."

"Maybe not," Jack said, "But two missing sisters with

sterling reputations might raise a few eyebrows."

"Not if they were last seen dancing at Venice *Carnevale* like a couple of wantons," VanHinkel said, chuckling.

"And who do you think will spread that rumor around?" Jack asked, leaning back and pretending to sip his brandy. Apparently, VanHinkel hadn't noticed that Jack had yet to refill his own glass.

"We can insinuate it any number of ways," VanHinkel said. The man was so in his cups it sounded like he had no concept of what he was even saying. Jack could still hear the men in the kitchen, but they had grown quieter. He tried to keep all his senses alert. He had to choose the exact right time to pounce, and he needed to somehow signal upstairs for the rest of them to be ready as well.

They both sat and ate in silence for a time, until Jack saw VanHinkel starting to nod off into his polenta. He stood. "If you'll excuse me," he said, "Nature calls."

VanHinkel only grunted in response. Jack made his way back to the kitchen, pleased to find the two other men in a similar state. He made to go out the back into the alley, but instead crept silently up the rear stairs. He let Millie, Louisa, and Thomas out of the room they were in, and they all handed around chisels and knives to be sure they each had some way of defending themselves. They did not speak or take any time to plan, but instead ran as quickly and quietly as they could down the stairs, Jack in front, and Thomas bringing up the rear.

When Jack reached the bottom of the stairs in the front hall, though, Jack stopped short. VanHinkel stood there in the door to the dining room, and the two other men flanked the door to the kitchen. VanHinkel held the pistol, though unsteady, pointed right at Jack.

"So, you thought to double-cross me, eh, Covert?" he said.

The cockney man with the beard chuckled. "Ye won't be doin' that again, bruv."

VanHinkel's eyes narrowed in annoyance at the man. Jack

knew they had no time to waste. They must act while surprise was still on their side. He spared a quick glance at Millie, saw her nod, and leaped into action. He crossed the hall in one quick stride, knocking the pistol from VanHinkel's hand. The man was much larger than Jack, though, so a struggle ensued, with Jack unable to see anything as he tried to wrest the gun from VanHinkel. Until, that is, he heard a loud thump followed by VanHinkel falling to the floor. As Jack stood and dusted himself off, he was amused to see Sir Elton standing there with a heavy candlestick in his hand and a look of shock on his face.

"I didn't think it would be that easy," he said, going pale.

Jack clapped him on the shoulder. "The brandy did most of the work, lad," he said. There was a commotion by the kitchen door as the henchmen decided to try to flee now that their villainous boss was temporarily unconscious. But Millie and Louisa weren't letting that happen. No sooner had Jack seen the men turn, but then Millie was right next to the one with the beard, knife in hand. She held it to the man's neck and twisted one beefy arm around his back, whispering something to him that Jack couldn't hear.

Louisa went to the other man and mimicked Millie's actions, first pinning the other man's hand behind him, then prodding him forward to the middle of the hall.

Jack took a moment to smile at his love. She was more than capable of taking care of herself. He should have known that, but it was wonderful to see it in action. He watched as she held the knife close enough to the skin of the man's neck that a little trickle of blood appeared against his grizzled beard.

"Let's get these men tied up," he said. "Elton, find some rope. I'd check the kitchen."

Elton rushed off and Jack went to help Millie and Louisa. As he approached, the man Millie held pleaded with his eyes. "Can't you get 'er offa me?"

Jack smiled. "I was thinking she wasn't holding you tightly enough." He raised his eyebrows at Millie and the man squealed when Millie wrenched his arm harder.

"I thought you was joinin' up with VanHinkel, like," the other man said. "You played us false."

"VanHinkel played you all false," Jack said. "He was planning to kill you once you'd taken care of Millie."

The men's eyes narrowed. "I don't believe that," the one Louisa held said. "We been good to 'im."

"Yes, but he didn't need any pesky witnesses, you know," Jack replied, shrugging. Just then Thomas came back with some kitchen twine. Not ideal, but it would do. They quickly got to work tying the men up, VanHinkel last since he was still unconscious. Jack went to the door and beckoned to their companions who waited across the street.

Fanny knew an officer of the *carabinieri* who had always been kind, and she rushed off to find him with Gianna as her escort as Jack and Jane cared for Millie and Louisa, wrapping them in warm blankets and hugs.

It didn't take long for the police to arrive and question them all. Once they all sat down in the dining room, it became clear that VanHinkel had been busy in Venice on several little side projects, and that the *carabinieri* were very interested in taking him into custody. They need not even worry about taking him back to London. He'd done enough to be hanged in Venice even without the murder and extortion attempts from abroad.

Jack very much wanted to be there when VanHinkel woke up, but the *carabinieri* loaded all three of the men into a gondola and poled off into the silent canal toward the revelry.

Not long after they left, the motley crew of friends made their way down the cobblestones back toward Louisa and Jane's rented rooms. They were all exhausted, but there was so much to say, to catch up on, and to celebrate. Just as they arrived, he heard the church bells tolling all across the city. They all stood and counted, knowing it was midnight, but waiting to hear that twelfth bell pealing out and echoing up and down the canals, big and small. The uniformed *carabinieri* walked up and down the streets, clanging bells and herding the revelers back home. An eerie silence fell upon the city more quickly than Jack would have thought possible. He looked over at Millie, and she returned a shy smile, one curl falling into her eyes as she looked up at him. He wanted nothing more to kiss her, but it could wait. They had a lifetime of kisses to look forward to. She bit her lip almost as if she knew what he was thinking. And he was sure she did.

Chapter 19

Mildred diRossi, Viscountess of Redstone, stretched out and yawned, the cold of the room held away from her by the voluminous plush blankets and the warmth of the naked man next to her. She rolled over and snuggled her behind up to him to get warmer, pulling the covers up to her chin. His arm wrapped around her and traced a circle around her belly button.

"Good morning, wife," Jack said, nuzzling her shoulder.

"Viscount Redstone, you're awake," she said, twining his fingers in her own and pulling them up between her breasts. "I think all of you is awake," she said, nestling her bottom against him.

"I am always awake when you're near," he said. "But you know the Dowager expects us for breakfast."

Millie turned and ran a finger down the side of his cheek and across his chin before stretching up to kiss his forehead. "She does," Millie sighed, "And we can't keep her waiting." She jumped out of the bed in one fluid motion and ran to throw a log on the fire. The Redstone family seat was beautiful, but cavernous, empty and cold. She'd have to do something about that, she thought. But there would be time.

Jack pulled his dressing gown around him and ran to wrap her up in it too, both of them standing in front of the fireplace while the log caught and sent up a blaze that surrounded them in a warm glow.

He held her to him and bent down to nip her earlobe. "Things might not stay so easy with my mother," he said.

"Things rarely ever do," Millie sighed, hugging his arms tighter around her. "But we must try."

"When will Jonathan and Anne get here?"

"A few days' time," Millie replied, "It seems Maggie is to have a little brother or sister soon, and Jonathan's having a very hard time handling his brother David."

"Sounds serious," Jack said. "Have you heard from Thomas?"

"Yes. He and Louisa have written volumes of letters every day, but Jane remains somewhat silent."

"That's not surprising," Jack said. "I see a lot of me in her. I'm not sure she'll ever be able to trust Thomas again."

"And she would be just as right not to as Louisa is to hope," Millie shrugged. "There's nothing you can do but what feels right in your heart. The rest you have to let go."

"I have married a very wise woman," Jack said, resting his chin on the top of her head. "Let's go down to breakfast."

About the Author

Renee Wilde is a writer, teacher, mom, runner, quilter, and Girl Scout leader living in the suburban wilds of Western Connecticut with her family. As a lifelong lover of language, teaching high school English was always her calling, but as a lifelong lover of historical romance, writing was always her dream. She grew up in rural Missouri and has a BA in English from Yale University and an MS in English with teacher certification from Southern CT State. She considers Henry Thoreau her spiritual guide, Julia Quinn her writer hero, and her cat Ewok her comic foil.

www.ingramcontent.com/pod-product-compliance
Lightning Source LLC
Chambersburg PA
CBHW031441200726
48289CB00007BB/2067